SECOND CHANCE
Charmer

BRIGHTON WALSH

♡ Brighton
Walsh

Edited by Lisa Hollett of Silently Correcting Your Grammar, LLC

Cover Art © Brighton Walsh

Second Chance Charmer is a work of fiction. Names, characters, places, and
incidents are either products of the author's imagination or are used
fictitiously, and any resemblance to actual persons, living or dead, business
establishments, events, or locales is coincidental.

Digital ISBN: 978-0-9971258-5-6
Paperback ISBN: 978-0-9971258-6-3

To Christina who said, "You should totally set your series here."
Thanks for playing tour guide and letting me borrow your cute little town.

chapter one

W illow Haven didn't have bad days. It wasn't in her planner, so it just didn't happen, plain and simple. Her life was one of order and routine—she'd already gone off track once, and she didn't have even the slightest inclination to do it again. Which meant she woke up at the same time each day, whether or not she needed to go into work. She did a yoga sequence, sat down and enjoyed a cup of coffee and the morning paper, and then got ready for her day.

What she did *not* do was sleep through her alarm—thanks to a completely inappropriate dream she didn't want to think about, starring a completely inappropriate man she *definitely* didn't want to think about—and wake up too late to be able take a shower or even put on makeup. She glanced at the clock on the wall as the second hand ticked past the big twelve at the top. 9:04. Even if she could blink her way to her office and transport instantaneously, she'd still be late for her nine o'clock appointment. Which was absolutely unheard of. Willow had never missed an appointment—had never even been later than fifteen minutes *early* to one, if you wanted to get right down to it.

"*Dammit*," she hissed as she flew around the house, trying to ignore the knot in her stomach at the prospect of disappointing the people waiting for her. Not to mention, this was going to upend her whole day, send the line of dominoes tumbling over. She could feel it.

She grabbed her favorite black heels, hopping on one foot as she slipped each shoe on, plucked her travel mug full of liquid sanity from under the machine once the stream had cut off, and snatched her messenger bag off the hook by the front door. Town hall wasn't far—definitely close enough to walk. But not in Mississippi in late May. Mother Nature held all the beauty in the world, but she didn't have air conditioning. Willow's Prius did.

Thankfully, the path from her home to town hall was clear, so she made it there in record time without having to go more than five miles over the speed limit. Lord knew if any of her daddy's cop buddies had seen her speeding, they'd have thought she'd been body snatched.

Grabbing her bag and her coffee, she stepped from her car. It was already busy in the town square, though that was to be expected considering it was—

Willow froze with her travel mug halfway to her mouth, her eyes glued to the man across the street as he strolled into the coffee shop, casual as you please, leaving her to gape in his wake. She stared at the space he'd just been. Blinked. Stared some more. She'd only managed a brief glimpse of his face before he'd disappeared inside. But he'd looked so much like the man from her dream—so much like the man she'd once known better than herself—that a mountain range had formed in her stomach, its jagged edges cutting through her insides.

A truck pulled up to the single stoplight on Main Street, blocking Willow's view of the coffee shop and breaking her trance. She shook her head and muttered to herself under her breath, "Get your head on straight, girl."

She had to have seen incorrectly, no doubt a product of her dream playing tricks on her mind and her frazzled morning throwing her off. There was no other explanation. For one thing, Finn Thomas hadn't set foot in Havenbrook in ten long years, and she didn't anticipate he'd suddenly gotten a craving for the coffee at Higher Grounds. Second—and this one was harder to admit, even to herself—she hadn't felt that zing of awareness she'd always had while in Finn's presence. And despite the fact that he'd broken her heart and then hadn't even had the courtesy to stick around and watch while she'd attempted to get over him, she sort of hated the idea that maybe that spark was gone.

Her phone rang from inside her bag, tearing her from thoughts better left beneath the heaps of baggage she'd stuffed them under years ago. After a quick glance at her screen, she blew out a heavy sigh. Her father's name flashed, and she pushed aside the wave of exhaustion that swept over her just seeing it there. With her daddy at a conference and his assistant, Gloria, on maternity leave, making sure town hall ran smoothly fell solely on her shoulders. It'd been damn exhausting.

The kicker was it would've been a much easier job if only her daddy had faith she could actually do it.

Shuffling the items in her hands, she swiped across the face of her phone to accept the call. She plastered on a bright smile, hoping it would carry through the line. "Mornin', Daddy."

"Will," he snapped. He *always* snapped. And he always called her Will, never mind the fact that Willow wasn't the boy her daddy'd assumed she'd be, or that she didn't particularly like the nickname. At least, not coming from him. Not when she knew the story behind it.

Having four girls after a decades-long line of only boys had done nothing but piss off the old man. The Havens were known for producing virulent males, but it'd only taken one to break the streak. A false reading on an ultrasound meant Willow's older sister had come home in a blue outfit, to a blue nursery, and had worn only blue the first month of her life. And Rory James had morphed into Aurora Jane on her birth certificate.

When Willow had come along three years later, Momma and Daddy had decided not to find out the gender at all, considering the last time had been a complete shitshow— her words, not her momma's. But her momma had carried Willow low, had craved nothing but salty foods, and her heart rate had been slow. So, based solely on a bunch of old wives' tales, Willow's father had been certain she'd be a boy.

When she'd come out lacking one very important appendage, foresight on her momma's part meant she'd had an appropriate outfit in which to bring Willow home. Her nursery had still been painted blue, but this time, there'd been bits of pink everywhere. And Will Grant—her father's choice of name—had been changed to Willow Grace. But

Daddy had always insisted on calling her Will. To remind her she'd failed him even while taking her first breath? Maybe. Probably.

And thus began what she liked to think of as the biggest practical joke her father had ever been on the receiving end of, all courtesy of the big man upstairs. Her daddy was a good old boy and completely old-fashioned from his bull-head all the way down to his stubborn feet. He was a *man's man*—whatever the hell that meant. Thought a woman's place was barefoot and pregnant in the kitchen. Didn't think a woman could do a "man's job"—and certainly couldn't do it as well.

Which put him in quite a pickle, seeing as their town was their namesake, and at least one person from each generation of Havens had served as the mayor of Haven-brook. Being plagued with four daughters—each one more headstrong than the previous—for a man who was perpetu-ally stuck in 1950, thinking women belonged only to the men in their lives, was laughable.

Karma, if you asked Willow.

All she knew was it was exhausting having that man for a father. Having him for a boss? It was a wonder she'd managed to keep her sanity intact.

She blew away the stray hairs hanging in her eyes, working hard to keep the smile in place. "Yes, sir?"

"Why aren't you in the office yet? Correct me if I'm wrong, but I do believe the work day starts at nine o'clock, not whenever you get around to it."

Of course, he'd called on the solitary day out of the hundreds she'd worked for him when she hadn't been in the office early. It was like he had some sort of sixth sense to Willow's failures. And he took the opportunity to call her out on every single one of them any chance he got. But because she knew he was anxious being away from the town and his job, stuck at a conference he didn't want to go to, she bit her lip and forced herself to swallow any back talk. Buying herself some time so she didn't bite his head off, she glanced down and kicked a stray rock away, hating how the weight of his disapproval made her feel all of seven years old.

The sun shone bright in the sky, illuminating her favorite shoes far better than the lighting in her house did. Which was how she realized she wasn't wearing her pair of black heels, as she'd intended, but rather one black and one navy. That'd teach her for buying multiples of the same style of shoes.

"You've got to be kidding me," she mumbled.

"'Scuse me, young lady? You might be a grown woman, but you know I don't tolerate no back-sassin'."

She dropped her head back on her shoulders, exhaling a long breath, and closed her eyes. Later tonight, after she'd downed an entire bottle of wine, she was going to laugh about this day. She hoped.

"Sorry, Daddy, that wasn't meant for you." She shut her car door and hustled toward the front steps of town hall, trying to make up for the time her father had cost her. "Now, what can I do for you? You should be enjoyin' that conference instead of worrying yourself with calling here."

"I wish I wouldn't have to call you, but you haven't given me much reason to trust you can take care of Havenbrook on your own, now have you?"

No, not much. Only five years of her life, not to mention restoring a failing downtown while she was at it. But none of that mattered in her daddy's eyes. Mostly because—as far as Willow could tell—she simply wasn't her older sister. Or born with a penis. And, unfortunately, there was nothing she could do about either one of those.

"No need to fuss," she said. "We're doing all right here, even without the mayor."

He snorted in that arrogant way that set Willow's teeth on edge. "Avery said it's a mess there, just a mess."

With every word out of his mouth, it was getting harder and harder to bite her tongue. Especially when they both knew what he said was a pile of horseshit. There was no way her assistant and best friend would throw her under the bus. Even if it was the truth. Town hall *had* been a mess since Richard Haven had gone out of town. A mess he'd left her with, but one for which he'd criticize her endlessly, constantly comparing the somehow lacking job she did to her older sister. Never mind the fact that Perfect Rory had never held a job in public service—or at all, for that matter. That didn't matter to Daddy. Rory did no wrong, and Willow did nothing *but* wrong.

She was twenty-seven years old, had been doing this job for five years, and she was fed up with her daddy's constant nit-picking. She'd done the job better than anyone in the past decade, and yet she was critiqued on her performance on a daily basis.

After a lifetime of it, she should be used to it, but the truth was it still stung.

"Town hall is running fine, Daddy. Nothing to worry about. I've got it all under control."

"Funny you say that, seein' as how you're on the phone with me instead of tending to your first appointment."

The urge to look over her shoulder was strong just to check and make sure he didn't actually have cameras on her. How else could he be thousands of miles away and still know the ins and outs of her day like some kind of bloodhound?

She pulled open the front doors and stepped inside, sighing into the cool relief of the air conditioning as she hurried toward her office. "I'm headed in there now. I had to run out to my car and grab some paperwork for it."

He grunted, and she could just see him smoothing his tie over his slightly rounded belly, his lips pulled down in the corners. "I need some information on the little party you've got comin' up."

The *little party* to which he was referring was the annual Fourth of July parade—something that took a full year of planning and preparation to pull off. In fact, for the past five years, she'd allowed herself a couple hours of celebration on July fourth, and then on the fifth, she dove straight back into planning the following year's parade—or *little party*, according to the town's mayor.

"All right," she said, working hard to keep the frustration from seeping into her tone. "What sort of information?"

"Well, I don't know, now do I? I'm not the one who plans all these frivolous gatherings. I need somethin' to show at this meeting, is all. Just send me whatever you've got, and do it quick. It's startin'."

Without waiting for a response from Willow, her father hung up, giving her absolutely no details on what he needed, how much of it he needed, or where to send it. But then again, that was her daddy. Expected other people to do the work for him without giving them heads or tails of what he needed, then berated them for doing a subpar job.

Yeah, she was definitely drinking an entire bottle of wine tonight. Maybe two.

She shuffled her way to her office in her too-high heels she could only hope no one would notice didn't match. Her messenger bag thumped against her hip as she hurried down the hall, careful not to spill the coffee gripped in one hand. Sliding into her office sixteen minutes late, she darted her eyes around, breathing a sigh of relief when no one waited inside. Finally, the dominoes had stopped crashing into each other.

Avery looked up at her and smiled. "Nola's already in your office."

"Dammit." Willow's shoulders sagged. Of course she was. Willow wouldn't have been lucky enough to have her appointment be late too. She blew a wayward strand of hair out of her face. "How long's she been here?"

"About ten minutes."

"*Dammit.*"

Avery waved a dismissive hand and shot Willow a smile. "Don't worry about it. I brought in a couple glazed croissants from The Sweet Spot and got her all set up with some fresh coffee. Then we discussed the glorious specimens of men on display over at the firehouse, weighing the pros and cons of a runner's body versus a linebacker's. She's fine."

"You're a godsend," Willow said. "An inappropriate godsend, but a godsend nonetheless."

Avery grinned. "Indeed, I am."

Willow huffed out a laugh and rolled her eyes as she juggled the items in her hands so she could turn the knob to her office. "Hey, Nola. I'm so, *so* sorry——"

"No big deal," Nola cut her off, offering a smile. With the pink ends on her long, platinum blond hair, a nose ring, and more tattoos than Willow could count, she would have fit better in a big city like Nashville than she did in the tiny town of Havenbrook. She no doubt got looks anytime she went out, but it didn't seem to bother Nola at all. Though, as far as Willow could tell, nothing much did. "Avery hooked me up with some croissants and a coffee."

"I heard y'all also debated the merits of tall and lean or big and beefy." Willow tsked in mock disappointment. "Our first responders are more than pieces of meat, you know."

Nola grinned, her eyes sparkling. "If they don't want us talkin' about them, why are they always out washin' the fire trucks without any shirts on?"

"Excellent point." Willow set down her messenger bag, dropped her purse in her bottom drawer, and settled behind her desk. So damn thankful Avery had more forethought than she did. All the paperwork she and Nola needed to go over at the meeting sat paper-clipped together on top of her desk. "Congratulations, by the way. I don't think I've had a chance to tell you that since you bought Pete's old place. I had no idea you were interested in business ownership."

Nola shrugged, taking a sip of coffee. "Thanks. An opportunity presented itself, so I snatched it up."

"You mentioned wanting to start construction over there this week. We've got a bit of paperwork to fill out before y'all get going on that, but I don't think anything'll hold y'all up." Willow pulled the paper clip off the stack and sorted through the papers to find the ones she needed.

"Actually, my business partners should be here any minute. We'll probably need to wait for them to go over everything."

Willow cocked her head as she stilled her hands. "Business partners?"

"Yeah, I couldn't afford it by myself, so I wrangled some old friends into buyin' it with me."

Willow tried to remember if that information had been on any of the paperwork that'd crossed her desk. It might've been, but the truth was, she hadn't had a chance to even glance at it, let alone familiarize herself with the ins and outs of Nola's venture. Her daddy had her running around like a chicken with its head cut off, trying to take care of Gloria's unattended work on top of Willow's already precariously balanced workload. "Oh, I apologize. I must've assumed it was just you."

Nola shrugged. "Most people do." She glanced at her phone, typing out a quick text. "That's them now. They grabbed a coffee at Higher Grounds and are on their way over."

Willow took a healthy swallow of her coffee, nearly sighing as the good-as-gold elixir worked its way through her system, thankful for the wake-up. "So, what made y'all want to start up a boutique?" she asked.

Nola's brows shot up on her forehead. "A boutique?

We're not startin' a boutique." She tossed her head back and laughed, slapping her hand on her thigh. "Lord, the thought of the Thomas boys running a boutique is funny as hell. Can you imagine?"

Willow's lips curved at the corners, Nola's laughter contagious. "Oh, I just thought—" She froze as Nola's words finally caught up with her.

It'd been a long time since she'd heard those two words together—*those* Thomas boys *are nothin' but trouble. Why you runnin' around with one of 'em, Will?*—and she had to remind herself to breathe.

Just breathe.

Maybe Nola didn't mean who Willow's memory automatically called up. And of course that'd been where her mind had gone—after the dream and then the false sighting, it was no wonder she had Finn Thomas on the brain.

It'd been so long since he'd left, it was easy to forget Nola and the Thomases had run around together in high school. But that didn't mean anything. Surely, they weren't still in contact. Finn hadn't been back in ten long years, and he sure as hell hadn't called or sent so much as a letter, despite claiming he'd been desperately in love with her. Certainly it'd been the same for everyone else in town, hadn't it?

"Who—" Willow cleared her throat, smoothing a hand over the papers on her desk. Bracing herself for the answer she feared. "Who exactly are you partnering up with?"

"Oh, you remember—"

A knock cut off Nola as Avery pushed the door open and poked her head through the crack. "Willow? Miss

Nola's partners are here." She widened her eyes and mouthed *Holy shit, there's two of them* while fanning her face. Then she pushed the door open the rest of the way, allowing the two men to walk into Willow's office.

And her whole world stopped spinning. Just froze entirely.

History in the form of heartbreak strolled right through her door. Willow couldn't talk—could barely breathe. Her eyes landed first on the man closest to her—the one, she realized, she'd seen walk into Higher Grounds only fifteen minutes earlier. He was tall, dark, and handsome, just as he'd been years ago. Nothing short of drool-worthy, as her assistant and best friend had pointed out.

But he wasn't the one who drew her eyes. He wasn't the one whose very presence was a magnetic pull Willow couldn't ignore no matter how hard she tried. No, that belonged entirely to the man who stepped in behind his twin.

While only minutes before she'd been almost saddened at the thought the spark between them could somehow be gone, she now *yearned* for that separation. Because it was damn embarrassing sitting in front of the man who'd stomped all over her heart with her nipples noticeable from a fifty-foot distance. She tried to appraise him with cool, detached professionalism, but that was a joke. There was no denying the zing of awareness that always flared in her body at his nearness. And damn it all to hell if it hadn't lessened any with time.

Looking like a near mirror image to the man Willow'd seen across the street, Griffin "Finn" Thomas stood in front of her for the first time in a decade, the breadth of his shoulders blocking out the harsh sun from the window at his back. His dark hair was shorter than it'd been when they were younger, cropped close but still carelessly messy. At least a day's worth of stubble covered his jaw, probably more like two or three. The cotton of his T-shirt stretched over muscles that'd popped up since she'd known him, worn jeans encasing strong legs. Strong, *long* legs—he'd somehow gotten even taller since she'd last seen him when he'd been just nineteen, and Lord have mercy, had he filled out. Where once he'd been tall, almost rangy, now he was fine-tuned with solid, carved muscles, the kind men worked hard for—either at the gym or at life. And if Willow knew anything at all about Finn, she'd place money on the latter.

A memory of work-roughened hands sliding up the insides of her thighs, fingers brushing over the brand on her hip, breath hot in her ear, and lips soft against her neck flashed in her mind before she blinked it away. Memories didn't have any place here—certainly not *those* kinds of memories.

"Hey, Willowtree," Finn said, his voice just as rich and smooth as she remembered.

His old nickname for her set her on edge, tightening her nipples *and* her jaw all at once, snapping her composure like a twig. He'd given it to her all those years ago, before they'd become a couple, saying she'd always looked sad like a weeping willow. And then he'd pulled her into his orbit, and her sadness had lifted because for the first time in her entire life, someone had seen her for exactly who she was. Seen her, and apparently concluded the real her wasn't worth sticking around for.

Oh, he had some nerve coming back here, strolling into her office like he hadn't made her fall in love with him only to take her heart, chain it to the hitch of his car, and drag it behind him as he'd peeled out of town, never to be seen or heard from again. Like he hadn't upended her plans, hadn't changed the course of her life when he'd so callously bailed on their future. Like he hadn't disappeared like a ghost without so much as a backward glance.

In the past ten years, she'd had a lot of time to fantasize about what she'd do if she ever saw Finn Thomas again. What she'd say, how she'd look. What she'd be wearing and how she'd act. In her daydreams, she'd always had on her best outfit—something that minimized her ample booty and maximized her barely there breasts. Her hair was always salon-day perfect, her makeup flawless. Sometimes, she'd give him a piece of her mind, tear him up one side and down the other. Sometimes, she'd be with another man— someone infinitely good-looking who'd dote on her. They'd laugh and joke, lean in for a kiss as they passed Finn. Sometimes, she'd walk by as if she didn't recognize him.

But never, not once in all the scenarios she'd dreamed up over the years, did she sit there looking like hell warmed over, wearing two different colored shoes, no makeup, and dirty hair pulled back into a ponytail, just…staring.

Silence reigned for far too long, blanketing the room until it nearly smothered her. Only when Avery cleared her throat did Willow manage to pull her head from her ass.

She clenched her teeth, fisted her hands… Tried to bite

back the words that were on the tip of her tongue, because they certainly weren't professional. And Lord knew she'd already been unprofessional enough for one morning, strolling into an appointment fifteen minutes late, without a clue as to the details of said appointment. Besides that, the words certainly weren't *Willow*. She didn't lose her temper. She didn't snap. Those qualities belonged solely to her daddy.

But, truthfully, after the *spectacular* start to her day, there was really no holding back anything. Not when her worst memory greeted her as if nothing had happened to cause that painful ache in her chest. "You've got some nerve showing up in my office after all this time, asshole."

chapter two

Finn Thomas could've spent every day of the past ten years preparing for this reunion, and it still would've knocked him on his proverbial ass. From the day all those years ago when he'd walked into the animal shelter they'd both worked at as teens and saw Willow Haven standing there, something had sparked between them. She'd been everything good and pure in his dismal life—sunshine and light, happiness and home-cooked meals, porch swings and a dip in the lake on a hot summer afternoon. It was a wonder she'd ever given him the time of day, never mind actually letting him get close enough to taste all that heaven.

But he'd gone ahead and fucked it up, hadn't he? He'd blown it all to hell when he'd left all those years ago. Forget the reasons he'd bailed—they didn't mean shit, not in the grand scheme of things. They could've been the noblest of reasons, and it would've meant fuck-all if Willow hadn't benefitted from it—if his leaving hadn't made her happy, made her life better in some way.

Truth was, though, his reasons hadn't been noble at all.

Not really. He'd run, plain and simple. When faced with reality—with what it'd mean to him *and* her if he stayed—he'd turned tail and gotten the hell out of dodge. Not stopping until he was all the way in California, as far away from Havenbrook, Mississippi as he could get.

He'd have been lying to himself if he said he'd thought his and Willow's first introduction after this long would've gone any smoother than the reality. Honestly, he was damn lucky she'd only tossed that handful of words in his direction instead of the coffee currently clutched in her hand. And she wanted to, too. Wanted to toss that hot liquid right in his face. It was written all over hers. Probably wouldn't have second thoughts about it, either. Not with how she white-knuckled the travel mug, her restraint evident in every rigid inch of her body.

And even though it made him every bit the asshole she'd called him, he couldn't stop his eyes from roaming over that body. From taking in each detail of her, starved for her when he'd been denied her presence for so long. Where she'd once had a fresh-faced innocence about her, a bomb-shell now sat in front of him. She'd done some growing up in the time he'd been gone, her curves filling out so much his fingers begged for a test drive. No longer were they the ones he'd once had memorized with his hands. And his tongue.

Her hair was pulled back in a ponytail exposing her long, slender neck, her cheeks flushed and alive, her eyes bright with...okay, yeah, that was definitely fury lighting those green irises. Couldn't say he blamed her.

Her words rang in his ears, the first ones he'd heard

from her lips in far too long. And he couldn't even find fault in them.

"Always did have a mouth on you, didn't ya, Willowtree? Least, around me you did." His lips kicked up on the side, unable to keep the taunt to himself. Christ, he was a jackass.

His gut twisted when she narrowed her eyes, clenching her fists against her desktop. But then she took a deep breath, and he could practically see her armor clinking into place, piece by piece. Something he'd forgotten she'd even done—how could he have forgotten something like that? He'd thankfully never been on the receiving end of it, though. No, she'd put up that shield for one person and one person only—her father.

Finn had watched it more times than he could count, each instance she'd felt the need to do it, to cover up the real Willow in deference to what her daddy expected her to be, making Finn hate him a little more. Which had been a damn hard feat, considering Finn held the devil himself in higher regard than Richard Haven.

Finn watched as a false calm settled over Willow. It no doubt fooled Nola and his brother—would have probably fooled most. But not Finn. He could still see the anger humming beneath her surface. He'd always been able to read her, as long as he could remember. Looked like no amount of time had changed that.

And it seemed she knew it, too, if the narrowing of her eyes was any indication, the tick of her jaw as she clenched her teeth. No, she definitely wasn't greeting him with open arms—not that he'd expected any different.

"Drew," she said, nodding to his brother. Of all the

things to get worked up about, her saying his brother's name before his should *not* have been one of them, and yet there they were. "Griffin." She spat his full name like it was a piece of gristle and she couldn't stand the feel of it in her mouth. "If y'all'll give me just a minute, I'll get the correct paperwork drawn up so we can get this done as quickly as possible." Her *so you can get out the hell of my sight just as quick* went unsaid, but Finn didn't have any problem reading between those lines.

As soon as Willow left the room, it was clear Drew hadn't had a problem picking up the not so subtle tension either, his eyebrows hitting his hairline as he looked at the now closed door to Willow's office.

Nola let out a low whistle, shaking her head. "Damn, Finn. Can't believe you made sweet Willow Haven cuss. I'm not *entirely* certain, but I don't think she's forgiven you quite yet."

"You don't think?" he asked, scratching his chin. "Went better than I expected, to be honest."

"What the hell did you expect?" Nola cocked an eyebrow. "A kick to the nuts?"

He shrugged. That very scenario might have crossed his mind a time or two.

"Maybe it was a front," Drew said, settling in the chair to the right of Nola. "She's probably out there now planning a welcome home party for you."

Finn didn't bother responding as he glanced around Willow's office, just lifted a certain finger in his brother's direction, letting it drop once Drew rumbled out a laugh.

Willow's office was devoid of anything personal—no art

on the walls, no vase of flowers on the side table, no framed photo of her with friends or her sisters on her desk...nothing. To anyone else, it probably looked like she preferred to keep it professional, sleek. No clutter, no mess. But Finn knew better. Knew her deepest fears and her greatest insecurities—or he had at one time. And he'd bet his left nut she kept her office sparkling and pristine, lacking any personal touches, so her father couldn't use it as a weapon against her while she tried to perform this job under his command. So he couldn't turn it into some kind of weakness on her behalf, as he'd been known to do a time or twenty.

Jesus, what had made her come back here? Not just here to Havenbrook, but *here* to town hall, to an office twenty feet away from her daddy. To a career working for a man she'd constantly butted heads with. A man who'd made it his mission to make her feel less-than. One who never, *ever* saw her worth.

Nola cleared her throat, drawing his attention. She stared at him with expectation, eyebrows raised.

"What's up, Xena?" he asked, settling in the chair on her other side.

"Look, I don't know all the details of whatever went on between y'all"—Over Nola's head, Finn met Drew's eyes and exchanged a look loaded with gravity. No, she didn't. Not many did—"but this is my life here. I don't want y'all's history messin' with things. It's already gonna be hard as hell runnin' this by myself after y'all leave, 'specially in this town filled with good ol' boys. The business—"

"Is ours too," Drew cut in.

"No, I know that." She divided a look between him and

21

Drew. "Of course I do. Keepin' in touch while y'all've been gone is one thing, but for y'all to come back and do this with me… Well, I appreciate it, 'cause you both know I didn't have the capital by myself."

Nola's proposition for them to go into business together couldn't have come at a more perfect time. Finn had been itching to do *more* for a while, and though it'd been logical to move toward ownership of the bar he managed in California, it hadn't felt right. Not like this did. "You know we were happy to—goin' back to diapers, we've been a team," Finn said. "Always had your back. Always will."

She elbowed him—her version of a hug. "Same goes. But that doesn't change that y'all'll be leavin' soon, and I have to stay here, you know? Just…" She sighed and shot him a look out of the corner of her eye. "Just go along to get along, okay? Don't make waves for me where you ain't droppin' your anchor."

With a nod, Finn agreed, because he couldn't do much else. He and Drew had flown back to Havenbrook with plans to stay only long enough to help settle things with the new space. Nola, Drew, and Finn had purchased it together in a 20-40-40 split respectively, going into a partnership with Nola when she'd presented them with an offer too good to pass up. Of course he loved that he and Drew were able to help out one of their oldest and closest friends, but *this* bar in *this* town meant so much more than that. After all, it wasn't every day he got to stick it to someone he despised. First bar in a town Richard Haven had spent his life working tooth and nail to keep *pure*? The poetic justice was too good to resist, especially considering his and the mayor's history.

The plan had been for the three of them to get the paperwork settled, sign his and Drew's names where necessary—much as Nola hated it, two male names carried more weight than hers ever could, especially in the backward town of Havenbrook with a mayor like Dick himself—approve the blueprints and construction plans, and then bail again. Head back to California, back to their lives...

Truthfully speaking, though, despite living there for the past ten years, they didn't have much of a life on the west coast. No matter what they did, how many roots they planted there, it had never felt like home. Not like Havenbrook had.

"Sorry 'bout that." Willow slipped back into the office, not a chink in that armor he'd watched her put on, and settled behind her desk, fake smile spreading her lips. She straightened the stack of papers in her hand, brightly colored flags popping out along the edges. "We've got just a few things to take care of then y'all can be on your way. Shouldn't take but a minute." Yep, that armor was perfectly in place, but she wouldn't look his way. Instead, she spoke to Drew. "If you'll just sign right by the flag." She pointed to a spot on the paper, handing Drew a pen. "Then go 'head and pass the stack on down so we can get everyone's signatures."

She shuffled through more papers on her desk, avoiding any and all eye contact, with Finn in particular. "Looks like Nash has already filed for the proper permits to get started on construction, so y'all're all set there."

Jesus, was there anything worse than listening to her small talk, go on about some nonsense like they were two random strangers? Like he didn't know the weight of her body on his own, didn't know the taste of her on his tongue, didn't recall the exact tenor of her moans? He hated it, absolutely fucking hated it.

And he had no right to. None at all.

He'd given this up—*he'd* been the one who'd walked away, never mind that he hadn't had much of a choice in the matter. It wasn't fair of him now to demand things, to want to know everything that'd happened while he'd been gone. To want answers to all his questions—why was she here? Why was she working for her father? Why wasn't she in Tennessee like they'd planned? But even knowing he didn't have a right to those answers, it didn't stop the burning in his gut, the suddenly overwhelming urge to know everything boiling up inside him.

"Since the permits have—"

"Why aren't you in Nashville?" Shit. He hadn't meant to just blurt it out like that, but he couldn't deny it was the single question that'd plagued him for far too long—*years*. Since Nola had let it slip about long ago that Willow'd been back in Havenbrook for a while. Had started working for her daddy. That was a far cry from her original plans of going to art school and becoming the creator he knew she was, deep in her bones. So far from the buttoned-up professional sitting in front of him in her tailored suit—which, yeah, looked hot as hell on her, but didn't belong on her nonetheless. He wanted to pop the buttons on that fitted suit jacket just to see if she'd kept a tiny bit of her old self under this facade.

The thought of one of her paint-stained tanks under her professional clothes had his lips tipping up at the corners.

No matter where she'd been or what she'd been doing, she'd used to wear an old tank, perpetually stained with every color of the rainbow, beneath her clothes. In case the urge to paint hit her, she'd told him once. Jesus, those white slips of fabric covered with paint spatters with the tiny little straps had driven him and his teenage brain crazy. They'd fit her like a second skin, clinging to every inch of her body.

"Why aren't you wherever the hell you ran off to?" Willow snapped back, her temper flaring before his eyes. Her cheeks flushed, her eyes flashing, connecting with his and giving him that contact he craved, even if only for a second before she took out her anger on the papers in front of her.

A not-so-discreet elbow jab and a pointed stare from Nola had him keeping his mouth shut for the rest of the meeting, scrawling his signature above the line indicated by the blue flags. As soon as his name was on the last paper, Willow snatched the pile from him and stood, making it clear in no uncertain terms it was time for them to get the hell out.

"I'll let y'all know if there're any problems, but I don't foresee anything," she said with false cheer, not moving from behind her desk. "In the meantime, let me know if anything comes up, Nola."

"Thanks, Will," Nola said.

"'Preciate your help, Willow." Drew gave a short nod in her direction, tipping his baseball cap up, before stepping aside to let Nola out the door ahead of him.

Finn stood, rapping his knuckles twice on the desk. For the briefest moment, Willow's eyes met his, and sparks went off under his skin. Just like always. "I'll see you again soon, Willowtree."

She huffed out a disbelieving laugh, shaking her head to break the spell. Then she dropped into her seat, twisting her chair around until her back was to him. "Goodbye, Griffin. And don't worry, I won't hold my breath."

He wasn't going to win this battle, no matter what he said. So he stood there for another moment before turning and walking out of her office. Nola and Drew waited outside, the hot May sun beating down on them.

"That went well," Drew said on a laugh, shaking his head. "I don't think I've ever seen Willow that mad. And I was there when Billy sprayed her white shirt with water in high school—you remember that?"

Yeah, he remembered. And thinking about it now wasn't going to do anything but get him half hard again, just like he'd been while sitting across from her.

"Y'all, quit it. I'm serious now. Stay out of her way," Nola all but pleaded. When Finn didn't respond, she wrapped her hand around his forearm, digging her short nails into his skin hard enough to leave indentations. "Griffin Reilly Thomas, I mean it."

With a laugh, he peeled her fingers from his arm. "Shit, Xena, quit reminding me why we gave you the nickname in the first place. I'll give her space, promise."

She narrowed her eyes, but Drew changed the subject, like a good twin. "Damn, never imagined I'd forget what May in Mississippi's like, but I think California made me soft." He lifted his baseball cap off his head and ran a hand

26

through his hair before replacing it again, shading his eyes from the brutal rays.

"Don't worry. Y'all'll be back there in no time." Nola patted Drew on the cheek. "Though, you might want to get some sunscreen so you don't burn all this pretty, delicate skin."

One second Nola was walking between Finn and Drew, and the next Drew held her planked across his shoulders, spinning round and round.

"Oh my God! Andrew Brennan Thomas, you better put me down right this second!"

With a laugh, Drew finally set her on her feet, chuckling as he jumped out of the way to dodge a slap to the chest. "Damn, girl, what's with you throwin' around middle names all willy-nilly? I can't believe you three-named me."

"You're lucky those are the only names I called you."

Laughter bouncing between them, the three walked across the street, striding toward the building on the corner —*their* building. The town square was quaint and well kept, considering how run-down it'd been the last time Finn had seen it. But he shouldn't have been surprised at the...*life* that was now evident. Not since he knew Willow was responsible for it.

He could see touches of her wherever he looked. The new streetlamps, flower baskets filled with bright pops of color hanging from the wrought-iron posts. Park benches every few feet, the back rungs decorated with paintings he immediately recognized as hers. So she *hadn't* quit paint-ing... Maybe she'd decided she hadn't needed to go to art school to be happy? Maybe she'd found a way to do both—

27

working on her art while staying in her hometown, a compromise of sorts. Maybe she was happy here, working for her daddy?

That was all Finn had ever wanted, was the main reason he'd left in the first place. More than anything, he wanted her happy, living the life she deserved. He just had to trust she was. And he hoped he'd be able to see even a sliver of it in the few short days he and Drew would be in Havenbrook.

chapter three

Willow stewed at her desk for long moments after Finn left her office, her heart racing like a jackrabbit, beating so forcefully she could feel it in her lips. It was like someone had lit a sparkler and set it under her skin, lighting her up from the inside out. That'd always been what it'd been like being in Finn's presence—intense and raw and all-consuming.

Thankfully, she was older now. Wiser. Had a hell of a lot more life experience under her belt than that naïve seventeen-year-old girl who'd fallen for him in the first place, or the equally naïve eighteen-year-old she'd been when he'd left her. She wouldn't make the same mistake again, wouldn't get caught up in his orbit. Wouldn't *allow* herself to.

"Holy shitballs." Avery wasted no time hurrying into Willow's office as soon as the trio of new business owners left. "It's not often we get eye candy like that in here, but to get *two* of them at once? Damn, girl. It was like *Christmas*." Her eyes sparkled, her smile huge.

Willow feigned nonchalance, dropping her gaze to the

papers on her desk. "Oh, were they good-lookin'? I didn't notice."

Avery snorted so loud, she slapped a hand over her mouth, her eyes dancing with laughter. Shaking her head, she dropped her hand as she fell into the chair in front of Willow's desk. "How long have we been friends, Willow?"

Avery knew exactly how long they'd been friends, so Willow just raised a brow. "You gettin' at somethin'?"

"Um, yeah," Avery said with a sharp nod. "How about the fact that you're lying through your teeth? There's history there—that wasn't the first time you'd seen those fine-ass specimens. So, spill. I need details, and I need them right-fucking-now."

Since Avery was a transplant to Havenbrook, having only lived in their little pocket of paradise for a bit less than three years, she hadn't witnessed the presence of the Thomas boys. And being Willow didn't like to talk about the boy who'd flipped her whole world upside down, ripping her heart out of her chest in the process, Avery—even as one of Willow's best friends—had no hope of knowing who Griffin Thomas was. Least of all, who he was to Willow.

Willow stared at her best friend, seeing the resolve on her face, and sank back into her chair. As much as she definitely didn't want to rehash the abysmal history, she couldn't deny it'd be nice to have another ear, besides her younger sister Mackenna, to listen. "All right. I'll give you a condensed version right now, but all the gory details'll have to wait until I've got at *least* three glasses of wine under my belt."

Avery's eyes brightened as she rested her elbows on

Willow's desk, leaning forward. "I'll bring the wine. And I can deal with condensed right now. Although there was nothing condensed about either of those boys, am I right?" She waggled her eyebrows, bringing a levity to the situation that Willow desperately needed.

With a laugh, Willow shook her head. "How can you make me laugh when I'm ready to crawl out of my skin?"

"One of my many redeeming qualities."

"Too true." Willow bit her lip, then let out a long sigh. "You remember me telling you about my high school boyfriend?"

Avery nodded. "The one who bailed after he took your virginity? Hard to forget that story. What an asshole."

"Yeah, well. Now you know why I called him that."

"Wait, what? Those guys...?" She widened her eyes and slapped a hand down on Willow's desk. "*No.*"

"'Fraid so."

"Which one? Baseball Hat or Gray T-shirt?"

Willow tried and failed not to think about the gray material stretching over the broad muscles of Finn's chest, the sleeves banding tight around thick biceps. She heaved a sigh. "Gray T-shirt."

Avery's mouth dropped open. "Damn, girl, you hit the virginity jackpot. That boy is *fine*."

"What I hit was the asshole jackpot."

The awestruck look dropped from Avery's face, and she frowned. Reaching over, she patted Willow's hand. "I'm sorry, hon. We'll save the rest for after you're good and toasted. Wine and pizza tonight. Sound good?"

Willow honestly couldn't think of a better end to this

truly awful day. Except maybe a chance to go back in time and avoid it entirely. "Sounds fabulous."

"Okay, but can we talk about how you actually *called* him an asshole? Is that discussion on the table? Because I have questions. Like, were you maybe having an out-of-body experience? Do I need to perform an exorcism on you?"

"Shut up." Willow laughed.

"Seriously, I don't think I've ever heard you swear around…well, anyone but me and Mac."

Mackenna was going to have a freaking coronary when she found out Finn was back in town. Which, according to Havenbrook standards, was going to be in, oh, about seven minutes. Nothing much stayed silent in their sleepy little town, especially not gossip as juicy as the Thomas boys being back. Them being back *and* opening the very first bar Havenbrook had ever seen? Yeah, that was going to spread like wildfire. Her daddy was going to be madder than a hornet when he found out. He'd fought the wet county law tooth and nail, had heavily rallied against it, saying it'd *sully* their town. And even though it'd passed, he'd thus far somehow managed to keep any restaurants in town from carrying alcohol.

But a brand-new bar in Havenbrook owned by *Finn Thomas*? Heaven save them all. Her daddy had never been Finn's number one fan—had, in fact, done all he could to keep Willow and Finn from seeing each other. In the end, he hadn't needed to do anything. Finn had left all on his own.

"He definitely brings out the worst in me," Willow finally said.

"I don't know about that." Avery stood from her chair,

shifting toward her desk in the outer office as the phone began to ring. "I sort of loved seeing that fire in your eyes. Rage looks good on you, Will."

As Avery answered the phone, Willow straightened her shoulders, arranging the paperwork on her desk into some semblance of order. Her day had been upended, and it wasn't even noon.

"Hey, Will?" Avery called.

"Yeah?"

"I'm gonna run and grab a couple of cupcakes from The Sweet Spot."

Willow's mouth immediately started to water. They had the best cupcakes in Havenbrook. The menu changed with the season and with the day. A Wednesday in May meant Triple Chocolate Raspberry. The divine chocolate concoction, topped with heavenly ganache and filled with chocolate raspberry buttercream, was her and Avery's guilty pleasure, reserved for the very worst of days. And today *definitely* qualified.

Willow smiled her first genuine smile of the day. "You're a mind reader. I could use one. Or a dozen."

"You sure could. Especially when I tell you Rory's on line one."

Apparently, Willow's original guess of the gossip taking seven minutes to spread through Havenbrook had been a bit generous. She dropped her head back on her shoulders and closed her eyes, exhaustion cloaking every inch of her. After her morning, she didn't know if she had the strength to put on a good face for her older sister. But she didn't have much of a choice. She'd learned long ago not to let Rory see her sweat.

"Of course she is," Willow said to the ceiling. "Maybe later the grim reaper'll show up to take me to lunch."

Avery laughed, grabbing her purse and waving as she headed out to grab the treats. "Be right back with enough sweets to keep you in a sugar coma for the rest of the day."

Willow took a deep breath before picking up the phone and pressing the button to connect the call to her line. Pasting a smile on her face, she answered like she had no idea what would prompt her sister's call. "Hey, Rory. How're you doin' today?"

"Will, you're never gonna *believe* what I just heard," Rory said, diving in without pleasantries. Very unlike her, which meant she deemed the gossip juicier than usual. She wasn't wrong. "Mrs. Thompson was out waterin' her flowers— honestly, she waters them fifteen times a day just so she makes sure not to miss Edna with the daily gossip." She tsked, despite the fact that it was the same reason Rory sat in her porch swing all day, even when it was twelve thousand degrees outside. But as it was Rory, of course her hair always looked perfect, her makeup precisely applied, neither daring to step out of line despite temperatures rivaling hell. "*Anyway*, you'll never guess what she heard."

Oh, Willow probably had a couple good ideas.

Without waiting for Willow to say anything, Rory continued, "Rumor has it, the Thomas boys are back in town."

"Yep, they sure are."

"They got in—wait, what?"

"I said, yep, they sure are. The Thomas boys are back in Havenbrook. You heard right." The number of times she'd thought about saying those words... Lord, she'd dreamed about it for months after Finn had left. That it had all been just a misunderstanding, that he was coming back any day. She'd spent her time daydreaming about it. But at some point, she'd stopped dreaming about it, stopped hoping. And she could honestly say she hadn't ever thought she'd be uttering them ten years after the fact.

"How do you know that?" Rory asked.

"Because they just left my office."

"What in heaven's name were they doin' in your *office?*"

Willow felt every ounce of disdain Rory put into the word office, like Willow having dared to pursue a career instead of finding a nice man and popping out babies was akin to peddling drugs on the elementary school playground. She took a deep breath, knowing it was a delicate balance, playing this game with Rory. Especially when their daddy did *not* need to be informed of all the plans just yet. But word was going to get around to Rory one way or another, whether Willow delivered the news or not. It might as well be the truth coming straight from the source... "You know Pete's place in the square?"

"The old soda fountain?"

"That's the one. I thought it was just Nola who bought it, but it turns out Drew and Finn are her partners." She paused, closed her eyes. "They're opening a bar."

Rory gasped. "A *bar?* For heaven's sake, Daddy's gonna throw a fit. Does he know?"

There wasn't a doubt in Willow's mind he had no

idea, because if he did, there was no way he'd have been gone at his conference this week. He'd have done everything in his power to make sure he was there to keep an eye on the Thomas boys while they ran around in his town.

"No, and I'm not tellin' him. Neither are you."

Rory made a sound that managed to project irritation and superiority all at once. "I can't believe you'd ask me to lie to Daddy, 'specially on account of them."

"I'm not askin' you to lie, Rory." Willow rolled her eyes. Their daddy wasn't even there to see Rory suck up, and still she did it. "I'm just askin' you not to say anything right this second." Willow would rather pull out each of her eyelashes, one by one, than admit defeat to her perfect older sister. Because of that, she couldn't tell Rory how challenging her job had been lately, how letting their daddy in on this was going to do nothing but make her life even more of a hell than it had been the past few weeks. So she fibbed. "Daddy needs to focus on this conference. It's important. He can't afford any distractions. And the Thomas boys are a big one."

Rory hummed. "I suppose they are. Especially *Finn* Thomas. At least where you're concerned."

Willow didn't say anything in response—didn't need to. Of course Rory knew about Willow's history with Finn—at least the basics. Daddy had made sure everyone in the family knew of her misguided path...and how far she'd fallen when the boy she'd thought was the love of her life had bailed without so much as a Post-it note stuck to her window.

"You're not gonna do anything stupid again, right?" Rory asked.

Again. Because of course Rory wouldn't let an opportunity pass to remind her sisters of all their multiple failings, and Finn would forever and always top Willow's very long list.

And do something stupid? Like falling head over heels for a boy who had trouble written all over him? Yeah, she'd been there, done that. And she had absolutely no desire to do it again. Not as long as she lived.

She took a sip of her coffee in an attempt to hold back the heated reply sitting on the tip of her tongue. When she was sure she wasn't going to bite her sister's head off, she said, "No, I plan to stay away until they do their disappearing act again."

Rory hummed. "You don't think they'll stay?"

The words Finn had said to her so long ago—words she'd worked damn hard to forget—came rushing back. *Be very sure of what you're saying right now, Willowtree, because if I take these last steps between us, it'll take Jesus himself to tear us apart.*

Apparently, their Lord and Savior had made a trip to Havenbrook that day all those years ago because from her vantage point, it'd seemed like Finn had left with little thought to what—or whom—he was leaving behind. So, did she think he'd stick around now? Not a chance in hell. He'd do whatever he'd come here for—to make sure Nola was set up with the building and the construction plans were on track, then go back to being a distant partner, just like Willow had caught Drew mumbling about as they'd been signing papers.

She shrugged to no one, as if talking about the only boy ever to break her heart didn't cause the old scars to rip open at the seams. "They don't have a reason to. Their life isn't here anymore and hasn't been for a long time. We'll see the dust of their rental car as they drive off in a day or two. Mark my words."

chapter four

For as long as Finn could remember, Nola had been in his and Drew's small circle of friends. In Havenbrook, there were the haves and the have-nots, with very few in between. Growing up in the trailer park on the outskirts of town, Finn and Drew fit neatly into one particular category. And Nola had been right along with them, her trailer just a couple doors down for their entire childhood.

So it hadn't been a surprise when she'd called a few months ago, going on about a great opportunity to buy the old Main Street Soda Fountain and renovate it. At the time, Finn had been contemplating making an offer on the bar he managed in California for the ready-to-retire owner—not because he loved that space or because it was a particularly good investment, but because it'd been time. After managing the business for the better part of five years, it'd seemed like the next logical step to take over ownership, especially when he had the means to do so.

Thanks to his goddamn genius of a brother, the two of

them and their momma had been lucky, sitting on a nest egg Drew had been able to cultivate. So Finn had the financial means to do it—something he, his brother, and their mother had been without for the first twenty years of his life. But it had been more than just that. He'd wanted to *do* something with his life. Wanted to be something more than a bar manager. He wanted something of his own.

And now he was getting it…two thousand miles away from home.

It'd been so long since he and Drew had been in Havenbrook, Finn hadn't remembered exactly what the old soda fountain had looked like, but they'd trusted Nola to make a sound decision for the three of them. Now that he stood in front of it, it was like he'd blinked and been transported back in time, to when he was nineteen. Most of the other buildings in the town square had had facelifts in the time he'd been gone, their storefronts and signage new and updated, matching with the rest of the renovated square. Not their place—or maybe their *hole-in-the-wall* would have been a more apt description.

It was the only unoccupied building of the newly revived downtown, a two-story brick storefront on the corner, complete with a crumbling front walk and peeling paint on the window casings. The dark red bricks made it appear classic, but the rotted front door and sign hanging above it screamed of neglect.

Finn cringed, thinking about what they'd find on the inside. It hadn't been in his and Drew's plans to stay more than a few days in Havenbrook, so he hoped the interior was up to snuff. The space had been empty for going on two years—was why the three of them had been able to get it at such a steal. Because of that, they had a bit of extra money to put into the renovation. And, from the looks of things, they'd need every penny.

The three of them stood out front, Drew and Finn flanking Nola as they all stared toward their future.

"What do y'all think?" Nola asked, dividing a look between them.

"I think we're gonna use every bit of our budget." Drew shook his head. "Maybe more."

It was no surprise Finn's knee-jerk reaction matched his brother's. Finn stared up at the building, toward the grimy windows of the second story, remembering Nola had said it had an apartment they could possibly rent out for some additional income. One positive in what he feared was a money pit.

"What time's Nash meeting us?" Finn asked about the contractor they'd hired.

As soon as the words left his mouth, a faded red truck, beat to hell and somehow still running, came to a stop along the curb in front of them, KING CONSTRUCTION in bold letters on the side. A man Finn didn't recognize stepped out. But of course, it could only be one person. It'd been a long time since he'd seen Nash King, and he'd changed by leaps and bounds. He'd been a couple years younger than them in school, so they hadn't hung out much—or at all, really. But in a town as small as Havenbrook, everyone knew everyone. No longer was Nash the scrawny teen Finn remembered.

Now he stood as tall as Finn, his skin-and-bones stature filling out no doubt thanks to his chosen line of work. The younger kid wasn't a kid anymore.

"Well, if it ain't the Thomas boys, as I live and breathe," Nash said as he stepped toward them, a smile stretching his lips.

"Hey," Finn said, extending his hand for a shake. "Barely recognized you. Good to see you, man."

"You too." Nash shook Drew's hand as well, grinning at them both. "Y'all gettin' along okay?"

"I guess we'll see once we get inside." Finn nodded toward Nola who pulled out a set of keys.

"It's actually not as bad as you'd think," Nash said. "I walked it with Nola before y'all bought it to make sure we weren't lookin' at anything structural or any big-ticket items." Nash grabbed the door at the top once Nola unlocked it and held it open for everyone. "With the exception of needing new electrical and a whole new HVAC system, it's a solid building. A good investment, in my opinion."

Original hardwood floors covered the space, several planks damaged or missing. A few fixtures had been left behind, as well as the bar and stools where the soda fountain had been. The walls, coated in months of grime, were a faded blue. Cobwebs and dust covered every square inch. Even if it was in good working order, it was going to take a shit-ton of elbow grease to get this place gleaming again.

"After talkin' with Nola about what y'all wanted in here, I drew up a couple different floor plan options." Nash walked to the counter, unrolling the plans and laying them across the dusty surface. "Anything can be changed, of course. This is just to give y'all an idea of space constraints and such for everything y'all want included. If possible, I'd like to get these finalized today, so I can get my guys in here tomorrow and get started. I know y'all won't be here for long, so I want to fit in as much as possible. Save Nola some of the headache of dealin' with any issues that come up after y'all leave."

"What kind of issues?" Nola asked.

"Various things that come up here and there as we uncover possible issues with the space. You'll also need to get started on picking out specific pieces—furnishings, fixtures, flooring, those kinds of things."

"But that won't take much time, right?"

"Did y'all hire a designer?" Nash asked.

Finn, Drew, and Nola shared a glance, he and his brother shrugging. Coming from a bare-bones bar that had nothing more than a bar top, stools, and a few high-top tables, Finn hadn't even *thought* about hiring a designer for the space. Had no idea they'd need one.

"I'll take that as a no." Nash laughed. "In that case, it's gonna take up a good bit of time. At least in the beginning. Once y'all get everything decided, your involvement will be less frequent, though there are always small details to contend with and building issues I'll need approval for."

"Any chance this can all get done within the next few days before Finn and Drew leave?" Nola asked with a hopeful smile.

Nash's bark of laughter caused that smile to drop from her face.

43

"Shit." Nola blew out a breath, running a hand through her hair. She turned to Drew and Finn. "I love y'all, and I know this whole thing was my idea, but I've still gotta work until this place is up and runnin' and bringing in actual cash. I can't afford to quit. And I sure as shit can't afford to get fired because I'm runnin' over here every fuckin' day to pick out wall sconces."

"What the hell's a wall sconce?" Drew asked, scratching his jaw.

"And y'all thought you didn't need to hire a designer?" Nash asked with raised brows.

Shit. She was right—they both were. This was going to take a lot more time than they'd bargained for, and Nola didn't have it to give. Wasn't fair to make her either. Not when she didn't have the security of a solid savings account to fall back on like he and Drew did.

"All right, just hang on a second," Finn said, running a hand through his hair. "Gimme a minute to think." He glanced around the room, his gaze catching on a dark alcove toward the back, stairs beyond it no doubt leading to the unoccupied space above. A plan started forming in his head, the itch under his skin he'd first experienced in Willow's presence spreading until it was too much to ignore.

"Hey, Xena, you said the space upstairs is an apartment?" he asked.

"Yeah, two-bedroom. Cute little thing. If I wasn't in the middle of my lease, I'd move there in a heartbeat and save money on rent. Pretty sure they even left some furniture in it."

Finn's question had been innocent enough, but neither

of the brothers had ever been able to get anything by the other, and this was no exception. Drew's brows shot up in an unasked, *what the hell are you gettin' at?*

Finn rubbed a hand over his rough jaw. "I was just thinkin'…"

Drew blew out a heavy breath and shook his head. "Bad idea, man."

"You don't even know what I'm gonna say."

"Twins," was all he said with a tap to his temple.

Nola divided a look between them. "What am I missin'?"

"You *were* in there, right?" Drew asked him, ignoring Nola's curious looks as he hooked a thumb over his shoulder toward town hall on the other side of the square. "Did she seem real open to havin' you around for a while?"

"This isn't about her." *Lies.* "You heard Nash—someone's gotta be here dealing with this shit, at least for a little while. Nola can't do it."

"And we can?"

"We have the means to take extended leave if we need to."

"Wait." Nola placed a hand on each of their forearms. "Y'all're stayin'?"

"No," Drew said, his eyes never leaving Finn's.

"Maybe." Finn crossed his arms, widening his stance.

Drew could deny it all he wanted, but the truth was they needed to hang around—at least for a little while—to get things squared away, and they both knew it. They had enough money so they could go a bit above their budget, but there was still no way they'd be able to hire an interior designer to deal with everything—especially not considering there wasn't anyone in Havenbrook who'd fit the bill, which meant they'd have to shuttle in someone from Memphis or Jackson. Dollar sign after dollar sign kept adding up, and while they *did* have a savings account to pull from, they'd already taken a huge chunk of it out thanks to the building and renovations. And, truth be told, Finn didn't have a whole lot of interest in going back to his childhood days where they scraped for every penny and had survived mostly on boxed mac and cheese with cut-up hotdogs. He wasn't going to use up all the money just because they had it available to them.

Which meant sticking around, living in the apartment they'd already paid for, and taking care of this stuff on their own was the most logical and economical thing to do. And if it gave him the opportunity to hang around and make sure Willow was all right, well, that was just the icing on the cake, now wasn't it?

He couldn't get that buttoned-up version of her out of his head. She didn't belong there—not behind that desk and not in Havenbrook—and he needed to know why she'd given up all of her dreams to move back.

Nola narrowed her eyes at Finn. "Is this about Willow?"

"Of course," Drew said with a snort. "When is it about anything else?"

"Just because we shared a womb doesn't mean I won't beat your ass."

Drew's relaxed stance remained, his hands stuffed in the pockets of his jeans. "If I had a buck for every time you said that to me, I'd be a mighty rich man. And yet my ass has remained unbeaten."

"Maybe this time I should follow through."

"Are y'all about done?" Nola asked with an eye roll. "Can someone please let me in on whatever the hell y'all are goin' on about? Not everyone here has shared a womb."

Before Finn could open his mouth to say anything, Drew beat him to it. "Romeo here thinks there's some chance with the girl he ran away from. Wants to stick around and find out. And, if I'm not mistaken, wants us to hunker down in that apartment above the bar while he does it." Drew turned to Finn, eyebrows raised. "Did I get that about right?"

"No, you didn't, smartass," Finn said. "This isn't about Willow. Nola can't be around every day while we get these details figured out. Who else are you proposing do it? Our fairy godmother?"

"So, what, you're just gonna leave Sammy in the lurch? You know he can't run the bar without you."

"The bar'll run fine. I'll let him know we'll be back in two weeks—three, tops." Finn didn't need his brother telling him this was a bad idea—he already knew that. He didn't know what the hell he hoped to accomplish by staying. Didn't know what he *could* accomplish. But he wanted to try. Even for just a little while.

"What about you?" Finn asked Drew. "What've you got goin' for the next bit?"

"Nothin' I can't do from here, and you know it."

"So then hanging 'round for a couple weeks shouldn't be a problem."

"Jesus." Drew took off his cap and scrubbed a hand through his hair before replacing the hat, no doubt reading every ounce of hope and apprehension that dripped from Finn. Drew stared at him for long moments then sighed and shook his head. "All right, I'm in. Let's see how this shitshow plays out."

chapter five

I t had been a couple days since Willow's world had capsized. Since the ex-boyfriend from hell had popped back into her life. And she'd done a damn good job of pretending it hadn't happened. She'd replicated the life of a hermit, diligently avoiding most public spaces—and thus avoiding the gossip mill. She had at least seven voice mails from Rory to tend to, but she just didn't have it in her yet, wanting instead to keep her head buried in the sand a bit longer.

The prediction she'd made to Rory a few days before rang through her head, how the Thomas boys would peel away from town before the people of Havenbrook could blink. She didn't know one way or another if they had—she'd asked Mac and Avery not to mention anything about the twins, and she'd studiously kept her head down and her nose to her work.

The thought of Finn still being in Havenbrook sent her stomach into a tailspin. More concerning, though, was the fact that the thought of him leaving without a word, going back on his promise of seeing her again, sent a whole flurry of other emotions swirling in her belly. And since there wasn't enough wine in the world to explore that particular issue, Willow avoided examining it further. Pulled the proverbial blanket over her head and ignored. She went to work and then straight home, usually forcing Mackenna to run and grab supper and bring it back to the house so Willow could stay hidden away.

She just had to ride out the few days until Finn and his brother bailed again—and she was already two days into it. She could hold out through the weekend. By Monday, the Thomas boys would once again be just a distant memory.

She squinted at the painting she'd been working on for the better part of the day. Definitely needed more red. She'd just dipped her paintbrush in a deep, blood shade when the phone rang. Without setting the brush down, she reached for the phone with her other hand. "Hello?"

"Please tell me you're doing something other than sitting in front of your easel, wastin' the day away," Mac said.

Willow froze, paintbrush suspended in mid-air. Her sister was creepy sometimes, but Willow wasn't going to tell her she was absolutely right. Though she wouldn't consider this "wasting the day away." "'Course not." A lie didn't count through the phone, right? "What'd you need?"

"Avery was thinkin' about Chinese for supper. That sound all right to you?"

"I could go for Chinese." What she could go for was not leaving the house, and having her sister and Avery deliver it to her certainly fit that bill.

"All right. We're just finishin' up a few things, so it'll be a bit."

"'Kay. See you later."

Willow didn't know how long "a bit" was, but she planned to use it to her advantage and brought the paintbrush back to the canvas. Some mindless TV droned on in the background, but she didn't pay it much attention. Instead, she focused on the canvas and threw all her frustration into it. The painting—a mix of colors and patterns with no rhyme or reason—was raw and wild and a great big mess. Exactly like Willow.

She'd been using paint as a means to express herself for as long as she could remember. Even after Finn had left, she'd managed not to allow her favorite pastime to be dampened by his memory. Which meant her having flashbacks now didn't make any sense, but yet there she was. Every instance over the past few days when she'd picked up her paintbrush, snippets from her teenage years, from her time with Finn, would rush to the forefront of her mind. The first time she'd shown him one of her paintings, the look of awe and pride on his face. How he'd never made her hobby seem like a waste of time like her daddy had. When he used to sit behind her and play with her hair as she painted, his arms a solid weight around her, making her feel safe and secure, like she'd never felt before.

It had all been lies, of course.

She didn't know how long had passed before Mac and Avery found her there, both their eyes narrowed.

"You liar," Mac accused as she tossed her purse on the side chair, setting down boxes from Wok This Way on the coffee table in front of the couch. "You said you weren't still doin' this."

"And you believed me?"

"'Course not. I hope you know you're in the same exact place we left you. *Hours* ago."

Willow raised an eyebrow and spared her sister a glance. "At least I'm not moping on the couch. Besides, I'm not sure what you thought I was gonna do. I'm not exactly in hostess mode." She gestured toward her ensemble of frayed sleep shorts and a faded, paint-splattered tank top she'd had since high school.

"This is getting ridiculous, Will," Mac said.

"What is?" Willow could avoid with the best of them.

Avery snorted, plopping on the couch as she grabbed her takeout container from the table. "How long do you think you can stay holed up in here? Avoidance will only get you so far."

Avoidance seemed to be doing her just fine, thank you.

Mac went to the kitchen, bringing back silverware for them before taking a seat in one of the side chairs. "I hope you've enjoyed your little game of hide-away, because it ends tonight."

Willow rolled her eyes as she put down her paintbrush and went to wash her hands. If there was one thing that could pull her away, it was mediocre Chinese food. "How do you figure?"

"As soon as you finish that Kung Pao Chicken your lovely, beautiful, devoted sister brought for you, we're heading out to Ropers," Mac said.

Before Willow could express her displeasure at the

thought of going out, Avery held up a hand. "Don't even try to argue. Mac's right. You've had a shit week, and no one would blame you for inhaling seven cartons of ice cream."

How dare she. It'd only been three.

"But it's time to get out," Mac said. "You deserve to have some fun. Have some drinks, dance a little. Enjoy yourself. And since Ropers is a half-hour away, it lessens the chances we'll run into anyone from town, which keeps you out of the gossip mill."

That was the problem with having a sister for a best friend—she'd been there their whole lives and knew Willow almost better than she knew herself. The fact was Willow hadn't just been avoiding *Finn* in town, but also the busybodies of Havenbrook, every one of them having had a front row seat to her heartbreak ten years prior. She'd lived through one round of the pitying stares, the whispers people thought she couldn't hear. She had no interest doing it again.

And she couldn't deny she could use a night out with her best friends, especially after the week she'd had. There was no doubt in her mind she'd have a good time—she always did when the three of them hit the town.

"Fine," Willow said as she sat next to Avery and dug into her container. "But drinks are on you both."

Avery glanced at her out of the corner of her eye, her mouth turned up at the corners. "Don't you worry about drinks. No work tomorrow and me as D.D. means we're getting your ass drunk. And once you change out of all this —" she gestured to Willow's ensemble with a lip curl "— we'll be getting free drinks all night long."

Willow's nightly glass of wine hadn't done shit to stop her mind from traveling back to places it was better off not going. Maybe getting good and buzzed was exactly what she needed.

An hour later, they walked into Ropers, the closest bar Havenbrook had—at least, for the time being. Willow and Mac had spent many a night there in their early twenties, rebelling from their daddy in the tamest way possible. It was already packed, which was to be expected on a Saturday night, too many bodies crowding the bar and the tall tables set up around the space. A live band played current favorites at the back of the room, the dance floor separating them from the rest of the tables. As much as Willow loved to dance, it would take a few drinks to get her inhibitions low enough to venture out there. But as Avery thrust a Long Island Iced Tea into her hands, she figured she'd be out there within the hour.

"Drink up while I scope the place," Avery said, her gaze already roving over the available men in the bar. Her eyes lit up, and she tilted her chin toward Willow's left. "Couple hotties have all eyes on you."

Willow raised an eyebrow, taking a sip of her drink, trying not to cringe at the heavy alcohol. It'd been too damn long since she'd had anything but wine—maybe getting a good buzz going wouldn't take long at all. "Or they have eyes on *you*." Her best friend was gorgeous on a normal day, but when she put effort into it like she had that evening? She had to beat off the guys with a stick.

"I'm not the one with my legs on display," Avery said.

Willow glanced down at the short shorts she wore—

shorter than her standard, but when Avery had thrust them at her, lending them to Willow from her wardrobe, she'd figured what the hell. She'd paired it with a thin, gauzy tank that dipped down low in the front and back, and wedge sandals that made her average-length legs look a mile long.

"No, but your boobs are saying hello to anyone with two working eyeballs." Willow tipped her chin toward Avery's ample cleavage on display.

Avery just shrugged. "Work with what you've got—that's my motto. And we all know my boobs are my best asset." She gave a little shake of her shoulders to punctuate her point, pulling laughs from Mac and Willow. "Yours, my lovely friend, is your legs. Mac's is her ass, which is why I put her in those tight as hell jeans. Honestly, you both act like I'm an amateur."

"After this long, neither of us doubts your powers," Mac said, taking a swig from her bottle of beer.

"Well, good. You shouldn't. Remember the last time we went out? We had those guys eating out of the palms of our hands." Avery winked. "Stick with me, girls, and I'll make sure the free drinks keep coming."

"This wasn't free." Willow held up her glass, the contents nearly gone.

"It was more important to get you well on the way to Drunkville than it was to wait for a freebie." Avery bumped her hip against Willow's. "Speaking of, how're your lips, girl? Tingly yet?"

Mac smiled around the mouth of her bottle, both of them knowing Willow's first tell of being tipsy.

Willow held her fingers close together, squinting her eyes as said tingly lips lifted up at the corners. "Li'l bit."

Avery threw her head back in laughter as Mac grinned her approval. It'd been a while since Willow had let loose like this, setting out for an evening with the sole purpose of getting good and drunk. It'd been a while since she'd *needed* to. The main focus of her frustration was usually relegated to her daddy or Rory, and she'd had years of practice dealing with those two. This week had been the usual multiplied by seven thousand, and it'd left her floundering.

As Mac launched into a rant about the lack of available men in Havenbrook and her dismal dating life, Willow glanced around the bar, her gaze skating over the swarm of bodies stacked upon each other, the space having filled up even more since they'd arrived. As she sucked the last bit of her drink through the straw, her eyes skittered over a trio standing by the front door, then snapped back, her body stiffening as she took in who'd just walked into the space. Even thirty feet away, there was no mistaking exactly who it was. There was also no mistaking the way her stomach bottomed out at the same time her heart started galloping like a racehorse.

Finn stood by the door, Nola and Drew on either side of him. As he surveyed the room, Willow took the opportunity to survey *him*, the unabashed ogling something she'd tried to rein in when he'd been in her office and had been watching her. Now she had the opportunity to stare with him unaware.

His hair was mussed, like he'd been running his hand through it. The scruff on his jaw had grown in even more since the other day, and she nearly sat on her hands to hold back the urge she had to feel it against her palms. He was casual in a white T-shirt, the material clinging to huge muscles that looked both strange and completely at home on his frame. He tucked his hand into the pocket of the dark jeans hanging low on his slim hips, causing Willow's eyes to trail all the way down his body.

"Hello?" Mac snapped her fingers in Willow's face. "What's got your attention?" Before waiting for Willow to answer, she looked over her shoulder, her head snapping back almost immediately. "Well, shit."

"What? What's up?" Avery asked, turning in the direction Mac had looked. Once she spotted who they'd been looking at, she whistled low. "Damn. Looks like we picked the wrong place to drink."

"What do you want, Will? You wanna leave?" Mac asked, setting her empty bottle on the table. "We can try Rudy's instead?"

Rudy's was a dive bar a few miles farther down the road, just a bar top and some high tables inside, no frivolous extras—like clean bathrooms—to be seen. It was a place you went strictly to get shit-faced. And while that sounded pretty good right about now, Willow's drink was already working its magic, the alcohol flowing through her veins. She'd spent the past several days avoiding Finn, staying holed up in her house or her office. But she'd be damned if she let him run her out of here too.

"What I want," Willow said, tearing her eyes away from Finn, "is another drink."

Avery and Mac exchanged a look, then Avery nodded. "You got it, sweetcheeks. Be right back."

One thing Avery had mastered was getting the bartender's attention almost immediately, her cleavage going a long way to shorten the time frame. Less than five minutes later, Willow had another Long Island Iced Tea in her hand.

She worked hard to avoid tracking Finn's movements, instead counting on Mac and Avery to take care of it for her. Every once in a while, she'd catch Mac's eyes narrowed at some place over Willow's shoulder, but she never looked. Told herself she didn't want to. Didn't need to. She was here to have fun, and she wasn't going to let Finn Thomas ruin that for her.

"You ready to move this out on the dance floor?" Avery asked as Willow finished her second drink.

Willow scrunched up her nose, the tingly sensation from her lips having spread to most of her face. "Maybe."

"If there's one thing that'll get your mind off this week, it's a hot man who rocks a cowboy hat and whose ass looks sinful in a pair of jeans."

Willow laughed, trying to suck up one last sip of her drink. "That was oddly specific."

"Yeah, well, prepare yourself. Mr. Oddly Specific is headed this way."

A few seconds later, three guys surrounded their table. Every one of them was a good-looking country boy—and each of them knew it too.

"Evenin', ladies," the first guy said, tipping his hat. "How 'bout y'all come out and dance with us."

It wasn't a question but rather a statement, cockiness

rolling off him in waves. Arrogance usually turned Willow off, but it wasn't like she was going to start dating the guy. Hell, she wasn't even going to take him home for a night of fun. She'd come here to forget about Finn and the mess he'd tossed back on her doorstep. Alcohol went a long way toward helping her do that. Dancing with this guy would go even further.

Avery and Mac deferred to her, and after a short nod from Willow, the girls both grinned, hopping off their stools and leading the way to the dance floor. Mr. Oddly Specific settled in behind Willow, his hands on her hips as the band played a current radio hit. His body was a little too close for her liking, but she ignored it, instead focusing on letting the music flow through her. She raised her hands above her head, swiveling her hips to the beat as she closed her eyes and tried to forget the fact that her ex-boyfriend hadn't fled Havenbrook like she'd assumed he would. Tried to ignore the fact that he was mere feet from her, somewhere in the bar.

Tried to ignore the way her nipples tightened at the thought, a low hum running through her body, the tattoo at her hip tingling with memories.

Moments later, she knew exactly why her body was buzzing. Even though she didn't look behind her, she recognized the second Finn replaced Mr. Oddly Specific at her back. The air around her grew charged, the fresh scent of him wrapping around her like her favorite childhood blanket. How, after so long, did he still smell the same? More importantly, how did she *remember*? And why did it transport her back to years ago, to memories of sunsets watched from the bed of his old truck, long walks along forgotten trails, and hidden moments in her childhood tree house, every single one of them heavily weighted with comfort and security?

Finn didn't say anything, didn't announce his arrival or that he'd somehow gotten rid of the other guy, just placed his hands on her hips, exactly as the man before him had.

But this felt different. Though it always had with Finn.

Heat spread through Willow's body, pooling low in her belly. For all intents and purposes, Finn's touch was chaste. His hands rested over the denim of her shorts, and though she could feel the heat of him against her back, none of his body touched hers. And yet even with that minuscule touch of just his hands against her, it lit her up more than some men had been able to do while lying naked beside her.

It was the first touch the two of them had shared in years, and her body warred with itself, half of her wanting to flee, to find Mac and Avery and get the hell out of the bar. But the other half wanted to press back against him, wanted to lean into him and feel those newly developed muscles along her back. Wanted to pretend for a while they didn't have history, that he hadn't stomped on her heart. That she wasn't the brokenhearted sweetheart of Haven-brook. Wanted to pretend he was just some guy who could make her body hum simply by his presence.

So that was exactly what she did.

She continued dancing like she hadn't noticed the change in partner, though how she managed was a damn miracle because her entire body felt like it was on fire. Finn kept his touch subtle, but the tips of his fingers scorched her even through the layers of fabric separating their skin. And even though she was burning up inside, feeling like there was a neon arrow above her head, pointing straight down at her, the people around her were oblivious. Avery and Mac were somewhere on the dance floor, though she couldn't see them. Which was probably for the better. If either of them saw her and Finn dancing together, they'd drag her out by her hair.

When the music switched to a slower, grittier song, the undercurrent of the beat and lyrics blatantly sexual, she and Finn didn't pull apart. Instead, he closed the last couple of inches between them, settling along her back as he slid an arm around her waist and tugged her against him, brushing his palm across her stomach along the way.

The lights were dim, the dance floor packed with so many people it felt like they were hiding in plain sight. Maybe that was what allowed her to relax back into him, her ass settling into the cradle of his hips. She caught her breath at what she felt behind the fly of his jeans, how hard he was for her, and couldn't stop her eyelids from fluttering closed, her head lolling to the side as it rested against his chest.

Finn leaned closer, running his nose along the column of her neck, and it was so easy to forget everything when he touched her so reverently. So easy to block out all the horrible memories they shared when he held her like she *meant* something. So easy to shove aside all their history.

At least, until Finn rubbed a circle against her hip over the material of her shorts, his fingers in the general vicinity of the brand she'd had put on her ten long years ago.

"You still have my bird on you, Willowtree?" His lips pressed against her ear, his voice a quiet rumble that ricocheted through her entire body, first sending a shiver down her spine before snapping it straight.

The tattoos they'd gotten on her eighteenth birthday had been one of her last acts of rebellion. And, unfortunately, had become a daily reminder of how much she'd misjudged someone she'd thought she'd known better than anyone. A daily reminder of her failures, one she couldn't run from.

As his words charged the space between them, she didn't pause to think—didn't turn around and give Finn a piece of her mind, didn't so much as stomp on his foot. Instead, she plucked his hand from around her waist and walked off the dance floor without a backward glance, ready to get the hell out of this bar. What had started out as a night to forget everything Finn had brought to her doorstep ended up only serving as a reminder of exactly why everything about him was a bad idea. He had trouble written all over him, and if her reactions were anything to go by, she couldn't trust herself around him, not even with their sordid history.

If Finn wouldn't stay away from her, she'd make damn sure she stayed the hell away from him.

chapter six

L ate May in Mississippi was not the time to be working on renovations in a closed-in space without a functioning air conditioner, but they didn't have much of a choice. The stale, thick air hung in the former soda fountain, the humidity nearly choking Finn. He wanted nothing more than to spend the next hour in a walk-in freezer, but that wasn't going to happen.

"Jesus," Drew said, swiping his arm across his forehead. "It's hotter than two rabbits fucking in a wool sock."

Nash barked out a laugh, shaking his head as he hauled in a few replacement planks of wood for the floors. "Y'all've gone soft on me. It hasn't even hit ninety yet. Quit your bitchin'."

Ten years in California probably *had* made Finn go a little soft, but facts were facts. And the fact was it was hot as hell in there. "Drew's right. When can we get some ceiling fans in here? And get that new AC installed?"

"AC is on order. As for the fans, soon as we get the

ceiling done up. Y'all decide for sure if you want them covered in that old barn wood I've got?"

Finn nodded, thinking over what he, Drew, and Nola had discussed over the past few days. They'd spent the weekend sizing up the competition, seeing what their interiors looked like, what kind of vibe they gave off. It'd turned out the three of them were in agreement on one thing: they had no interest in going the typical honky-tonk route. Instead, they wanted something with an industrial vibe— old, reclaimed wood and corrugated steel all blended together.

The only problem they were having was figuring out how, exactly, to incorporate it all. Finn didn't know a sconce from a hole in the wall, which meant it felt like he had his head up his ass most of the time. He could pick out what he liked for all the different pieces they'd need, but he had no idea if it'd all flow together well or look like a hodgepodge of randomness. They really should've budgeted for a designer, because he wasn't so sure the three of them could pull it off without help, and this place was too important to wing it.

Friday night, they'd headed to a place in Parkersville, almost an hour away. The bar had been a bit of a dive, but then again, there hadn't ever been much competition around the area. The people of Havenbrook had always had to go outside the county lines to get to a bar of any sort —and it was clear those bars hadn't had to do much at all to bring in customers.

Saturday night, they'd narrowed their search, coming closer to town and closer to their more immediate competition. Finn's first impression of Ropers had been mediocre at best. Nothing about it had stood out to him—at least, not until he'd spotted Willow across the bar, sitting at a high-top table. She'd been with her assistant from work and a girl who, based on his memories, looked a hell of a lot like Willow's younger sister Mac. Shock at seeing Willow there had faded into that ever-present attraction as he'd stared at her, noticing the low dip of her shirt and how much of her legs had been on display in those nearly indecent shorts she'd worn.

After that, Finn had had no hope of noticing anything *but* her. He'd kept his eyes glued to her as he'd followed Drew and Nola around the place, pretending like he was paying attention to what they'd been saying about the decor, the band, the beer selection. Truth was, he'd been thinking only of Willow. His body had been wired into her presence —that hadn't changed over the years. And even with twenty feet separating them, he'd felt the buzz in his veins.

That pleasant hum he'd always welcomed in Willow's vicinity had turned into an unmistakable surge of jealousy when some dickhead had taken her out on the dance floor. Finn knew he'd had no right to feel it, knew it wasn't his place. Knew it made him an asshole for it too. Even worse, though, had been when he'd told the other guy to fuck off and had taken his place behind her, allowing himself the pleasure of putting his hands on her.

It'd been a chaste touch, only his hands on her hips, but the sensation had shot straight to his cock, hardening it like steel. Willow had done a good job of pretending not to notice when Finn had stepped up behind her, but there was no denying how *aware* she'd become as soon as his hands had settled on her.

Having her tight little ass pressed right up against his cock had brought him nearly to the brink of insanity. But *Jesus*, what a way to go. And then, because it hadn't been enough for him, he'd had to push. Too damn hard, too damn fast, and off she'd shot like her ass had been on fire, fleeing from him as fast as she could.

And he'd done nothing but spend the past few days thinking about what an idiot he was.

"All right then," Nash said, placing the wood planks in the corner and pulling Finn back to the present. "I'll get those boards hauled in tomorrow and start workin' on that so we can get some ceiling fans in place for you sissies. Until then, I reckon I'll run over and buy some box fans so you delicate pansies don't wilt."

Drew just laughed as Finn gave Nash a one-finger salute. Finn's phone buzzed in his pocket, and he pulled it out to find a text from Nola.

Willow needs some paperwork signed. Can you swing over to town hall?

Finn glanced down at himself, bare chest covered in a sheen of sweat, patches of dirt caked on his skin. No, he wasn't exactly town hall appropriate.

Can you check if Willow can bring it by instead?

He went to put his phone back in his pocket, but Nola's response came right away.

Uh, no. If you want Will to be your errand girl, grow some balls and tell her yourself. Godspeed.

Willow's number came through a second later as a contact attachment. Finn chuckled, shaking his head. His charms hadn't been tested this much in a while, and he knew damn well they'd get a workout when it came to Willow. Knew, too, it was probably a really bad idea to call her and ask this. Still, he dialed the number Nola had sent, waiting for Willow to answer.

"Hello?" Her voice was wary, probably because his number was one she wasn't familiar with.

"Hey, it's Finn."

There was a brief pause before she asked, "Why're you callin' me on my private number?" Her voice was tight, that anger he'd only recently seen come out simmering under the surface. He'd never had that anger directed at him before— had never given her a reason for it to be. And he shouldn't like it as much as he did, but there was no denying Willow was hot as hell when she was fired up.

"Ah, sorry," he said. "Nola sent it to me. Said you had some paperwork that needed to be signed."

Willow made an impatient huff. "I'm still not seeing why that involves calling my cell phone, Griffin. I have an office phone for a reason, especially considering this is *office* business."

He closed his eyes and scrubbed a hand down his face,

hating every time she uttered his full name. Knowing damn well she was using it as a way to put up imaginary bricks between them. She could keep putting them up all she wanted, and as long as he was there, he'd keep knocking them down.

Finn ran a hand through his hair. "Drew and I are workin' in the bar today with Nash. We're not exactly dressed for town hall. Any chance you can swing that on by?"

Nothing but silence came from her end, and he could just imagine her in her office, her jaw tight, paperwork clenched in her fist. He waited for her to tell him to try his hand at skydiving, minus the parachute.

Instead, she snapped, "Fine." Then the line went dead.

He slipped the phone into his pocket and glanced up at Drew, who was watching him intently.

Drew raised a brow. "How's that plan of yours workin'?"

"Fuck off," Finn said and turned his back on his brother.

Drew's laughter followed Finn as he went back to pulling off another section of baseboards. The truth was he didn't *have* a plan, not when it came to Willow. And maybe that was the problem. All he wanted to do was make sure she was happy here, that his leaving had served a bigger purpose. But it seemed like any time they got around each other, all common sense fled his head.

He didn't know what he'd have to do to get through to her, to get her to actually have a conversation with him, but he wasn't giving up just yet.

HOURS LATER, Finn was spackling a bit of plaster by the ceiling, Drew and Nash having just slipped out to wheel a few salvage loads from the back room out to the dumpster. He'd managed to stop checking the clock a while earlier, but that hadn't made the time go by any faster, wondering when Willow would get over her anger and stop by.

He heard her before he saw her, the click of her heels on the sidewalk outside drawing his gaze toward the opened door where she walked through, taking a tentative step into his building.

And damn. *Damn.*

While he would always prefer the more casual Willow— the girl who was at home in paint-stained tank tops and cutoffs—he couldn't deny how well she pulled off a suit. The tight, mid-thigh length skirt clung to the tantalizing curves of her hips...hips he'd had under his hands mere days before. She wore a bright red sleeveless top tucked into the waistband of her skirt, no doubt having shed her jacket in her office in deference to the heat.

Her dark hair hung down her back, loose waves framing her face. Cool detachment was written along every inch of her body and a fake smile on her pouty pink lips. At least, until she took in the space around Finn, no doubt a mess in her eyes, and realized no one else was around. It was just the two of them. That fake smile dropped like an anchor.

"Hey, Willowtree." He climbed down from the ladder, setting the plastering trowel and mud pan on the old counter.

"Stop calling me that," she snapped. She closed her eyes and took a deep breath, like she was trying to get herself under control. Trying to rein in that temper that only intrigued Finn. When she opened her eyes again, she looked anywhere but at him, taking in the place that was in utter disarray. "Where're Drew and Nash?"

"Around." He hated how his gut twisted when she asked about the other guys, one of whom was his brother. But Nash...shit, for all Finn knew, Willow and Nash had dated at some point. It wouldn't be so farfetched, considering the small pool of available people their age in Havenbrook. Nash was a couple years younger than her, having graduated with the youngest of the Haven girls, Natalie. But that didn't mean anything.

"Why, you need them for somethin'?" he asked. As if he could wipe the make-believe images of Willow and Nash together from his mind, he plucked the T-shirt he'd tucked into the waistband of his shorts and used it to wipe the sweat from his brow. That did fuck-all to get thoughts of Willow with some other guy from his mind—which was dumb as hell because of *course* she'd been with other men while he'd been gone. It'd been ten years. And besides being stunning as hell, she was smart. Funny. Kind. Generous. She was everything any sane man would want by his side.

And Finn had just walked away.

He'd kicked himself daily for that over the past ten years, but he'd stayed away. He'd managed to keep himself from running back because, while the circumstances surrounding his departure hadn't left him much choice in the matter, he'd been sure he'd done it for her benefit. That his being gone had allowed Willow to become the person she was meant to become instead of being weighed down by him.

Shaking those thoughts from his head, he ran his shirt down his chest to wipe away the sheen of sweat and glanced back at Willow, realizing her eyes were trained on his hand as it brushed the cloth across his abs.

"Willow?" he asked.

"Huh?"

"Why'd you want to know?"

"What?" she asked, snapping her eyes to his. "Oh, just wondering." She averted her gaze and crossed her arms over her chest, but not before he caught sight of her nipples straining at the material of her shirt, dark shadows beneath all that red. And since it sure as shit wasn't cool in here, that meant one thing.

Willow was still attracted to him.

And it might make him an asshole, but if that was what he had to use to get her to come around to talking to him, so be it. He'd pull out every obnoxious play in the book if she'd just tell him about her life.

She cleared her throat and thrust the paperwork in his direction. "I just need your signature on these. You missed a couple pages last week."

He stepped closer to her, trying hard not to smirk when she stiffened. Then he brushed his fingers over hers as he pulled the papers from her hand. "Happy to give you anything you need, Willowtree."

Her nostrils flared, the anger she was suppressing clearly written over every inch of her. But instead of chastising him for using her nickname from when they'd been teenagers, or for lacing his statement with an innuendo he was certain she'd picked up on, she just squared her shoulders. "You can go ahead and drop 'em by later today."

"Much as I'd love to visit you in your office again, I'm afraid I'm not fit for public viewing for the foreseeable future." Finn gestured to himself, the sheen of sweat he'd wiped away already replaced thanks to the heat.

Her eyes dropped to once again take in his appearance, a flush working its way up her neck and to her cheeks. Just as quickly as her eyes had dropped to observe him, they darted off to the side, staring instead out the grimy front windows. "I'm sure you can find another shirt."

That much was true, especially since Finn and Drew were staying upstairs in the apartment for the time being. "C'mon, it'll just take a minute," he said. "I can sign them now. I was gonna break for lunch anyway." He strode toward the stairs at the back of the space, intent on heading up to slap together a sandwich. He looked back at her and tilted his head in the direction of the stairway. "If you come on up, I'll share with you. I'll even make it for you—peanut butter and banana sandwiches, your favorite."

It was only a brief moment where her expression changed, but he saw it—saw how her eyes softened the tiniest bit at the mention of her old favorite. The night before he'd left, they'd had a picnic in her tree house, one he'd prepared for her himself. Other girls might've wanted candlelight and fancy restaurants, but Willow had always been satisfied with anything, so long as they'd been together.

The memory was bittersweet, tugging at his chest. He watched as the same emotions played out over her face.

That softness in her eyes lasted for only a moment before she hardened her features once again.

"I do not want to share your lunch, Griffin. As lovely as the offer is." Sarcasm dripped from every word, her sweet Southern front dialed to ten. "What I'd like is for you to sign the papers so I can go back to work."

He nodded, knowing when not to push. Tossing the papers down, he glanced around under the guise of looking for a pen, hoping if he couldn't get her upstairs to talk, she'd be up for sharing a bit right there. "How're you liking it?"

"You wastin' my time?" she asked. "Not at all, actually."

Finn shot her a smile over his shoulder. "I meant workin' for your daddy."

"I like it just fine," she said, arms crossed and spine straight.

"Better than painting?" He didn't stare at her as he waited for the answer, hoping if he pretended his attention was snagged by the paperwork in front of him rather than her answer, she'd be more inclined to respond.

She was silent for so long, he finally glanced over his shoulder at her in time to see her shake her head at him. "Look, I'm not sure what you think is happenin' here, but you lost the right to ask me questions like that when you left town without a word. Ten freakin' years ago. If you want insights on my life, you're gonna have to ask around town, because you're sure as hell not gonna get any from these lips."

He dropped his gaze to said lips, flushed and pink, the barest hint of moisture there, as if she'd just licked them. He remembered what it'd been like to have that mouth on him.

Remembered in great detail, actually. While he'd always liked to call up those memories in previous years, it had gotten ridiculous over the past week. Thoughts of Willow had been his morning companion in the shower as he'd taken his cock in hand and worked himself to completion over the fantasy of her under him. Astride him. Bent over in front of him. Dozens upon dozens of different ways, only one of which he'd ever actually had the pleasure of experiencing. Because he'd bailed.

And as he stared at her, still stuck in her hometown, no apparent desire at all to have followed the dream she'd talked about for so long, he couldn't help but wonder what the hell he'd left for. The whole point had been so she could achieve her best life without the stain of his name holding her back. But from where he stood now, it looked like she'd held herself back just fine without his help.

He wanted to know why. Was desperate to find out what had snuffed out the bright, vibrant flame of the Willow he'd coerced out of her shell all those years ago. And she could shoot as many dirty looks his way as she wanted, but he wasn't going to stop until he found out why his spirited Willowtree was back here again, under her daddy's thumb. Living a life less than she deserved.

chapter seven

First her office, then Ropers, then right across the street from town hall. And not just across the street, but across the street while half naked, ripped chest and corrugated abs glistening from him working so hard…

Whew, was it hot in here?

Finn was unavoidable, that much was clear. No matter what Willow did, he kept popping up again, leaving her on edge every minute of the day because she just couldn't escape. And now she had those images from earlier burned into her brain, the sight of him on that ladder, his back muscles flexing, ass looking delectable in a pair of worn jeans, haunting her every waking moment.

After her workday was done, she stormed into her and Mackenna's place, slamming the door behind her. The walls of the guesthouse on their parents' property rattled, but she couldn't muster up an ounce of care. She tossed her purse behind her without concern for where it landed before chucking her heels to either side, grumbling under her breath the entire time.

"Will?" Mac called from upstairs. "Is Ella with you?"

"No," she snapped.

"No? What's all that bangin', then?"

Yeah, okay, so she was acting like their seven-year-old niece. Point taken. Still, she couldn't get her feet to let up as she stomped upstairs and into Mac's room.

"All that bangin' is me losing my ever-lovin' *mind*." Willow threw herself facedown on Mackenna's bed.

"Umm…"

"Umm?" She turned to glare at her sister where she sat with her back against the headboard, magazine forgotten against her chest. "My world is ending, and all you have to say is, 'umm…'?"

Mac rolled her eyes, then poked Willow in the side with her toe. "I hardly think your world is ending, Will. Dramatic much?"

"Sure as hell feels like it. Especially when Finn won't stay out of my life!"

"Uh oh…you had another run-in?"

Saturday night at the bar, Mac and Avery hadn't questioned Willow's urgent plea to bail immediately. They had, however, cornered her the following day and asked what the hell had happened. She'd spilled all the details, cringing as she'd relived every minute of having Finn's body pressed against her own. Avery's and Mac's faces had been sympathetic, and they'd agreed they'd do what they could to minimize the time she'd need to see Finn while he was in town. So freaking much for that plan.

"Yep. Bastard made me go over to his building so he

could sign some papers. He's just tryin' to mess with my head."

"Oh, honey, c'mon now. I love you, but you've gotta get a grip. I highly doubt that's what's goin' on. We didn't tell anyone where we were goin' on Saturday, so him bein' there was just a coincidence. And today...well, I'm sure it was innocent enough."

More snippets of a bare-chested Finn flashed in her mind, and no. There was definitely nothing innocent about that man. He'd been downright *indecent*. He'd managed to render her speechless, her jaw nearly unhinging as she'd stared at him dragging that old cotton shirt across his muscle-packed chest, down the washboard ridges of his abs...

"Um, Will? I know we're close and all, but I don't wanna know what your sex face looks like, so I'm gonna have to ask you to stop thinkin' 'bout whatever you are." Only a second passed before Mac gasped, her eyes going wide as she flew up from her reclining position. "Did you sleep with him?" She hissed the question, like they were seventeen and eighteen again, back in their parents' house while divulging all the sordid details of Willow's whirlwind romance with the bad boy of Havenbrook.

"Lord, no." Willow squeezed her eyes shut against the remembered flush of awareness that'd flooded her body in Finn's presence. Mac didn't need to know the thought had crossed Willow's mind too many times to count since he'd made his appearance back in town. Honestly, she didn't even want to admit it to herself, let alone say it aloud to someone else.

"Okay, then everything's fine." Mac waved a hand in the air. "There's no need to panic. I know Havenbrook's small, but that doesn't mean you're gonna be running into him every day or anything."

Except, if the past week was anything to go by, she would be. She took a deep breath and sat up, tucking her ankle under her leg as she faced her sister. "He seems hell-bent on making that happen. And since Gloria's on maternity leave until August, I'm the one and only person he'll be in contact with as they renovate. I don't know how long they're plannin' on staying, but according to Rory's latest voice mail, the Thomas boys have taken up residence in the apartment above the storefront."

"Oh shit."

"Yeah, oh shit." Willow pushed up from the bed and walked across the hall to her own room as her sister continued with platitudes that were doing exactly nothing to reassure her. She whipped off her sleeveless blouse, then unzipped and tugged off her skirt. As she went to her dresser to grab a pair of yoga pants and a tank top—screw doing anything tonight but bingeing on Ben & Jerry's—she caught a glimpse of herself in the floor-length mirror that stood in the corner of her room. A tiny fleck of black peeked out of the waistband of her low-cut bikini panties, and she tugged them up her hip—a force of habit as she hid the last bit of Finn Thomas she still had in her life.

The tiny bit of Finn Thomas she'd carried on her skin every day for the past decade.

And maybe that was the problem. Maybe that was why he still affected her so much—because no matter what she told herself, no matter how many different men she'd tried to have a relationship with, she'd always had this *what-if* in the back of her mind, courtesy of the brand she wore of his.

You still have my bird on you, Willowtree?

She closed her eyes against the whispered words he'd said to her in Ropers, wanting desperately to blink and have this thing off her body. She walked over to stand in front of the mirror, then tugged down the front of her panties until the entire tattoo was visible.

It might've happened ten years ago, but she remembered it as clear as if it'd been last week. The weeks leading up to it, all the planning that'd gone into them—both hers and his. Sketch after sketch after sketch until she'd gotten them just right. This act—getting tattoos together—was symbolic of so much more than the actual symbols on their bodies. It was the physical representation of them starting their life together, taking the leap with nothing but their love and a few prayers setting the foundation.

What a fool she'd been.

She'd willingly marked her body forever for a boy it turned out she'd never really known at all. Because when he'd walked away, he'd negated every word he'd ever said to her, every whispered confession of love, every promise of a future.

So now, when she looked at her tattoo—a bird in flight on her hip—instead of reminding her of everything she should soar for as intended, it only served to remind her of all the flying Finn had done to get away from her.

Well, no more of that. She'd lived with this for far too long, and it was time to do something about it. She snatched her phone from the pocket of her discarded skirt, then queued up Ty's name—Finn's friend who'd done the tattoo in the first place—and shot him a quick text. She hadn't talked to him other than a hello around town for so long, she hoped it was still his correct number. But she hadn't needed to worry. His reply came almost instantly, letting her know she could swing by his place tonight and they'd talk about her options.

Whether she covered it up with something else or removed it completely, she didn't care. As long as it got the image of Finn's bird off her body once and for all.

LORD, why was she so nervous? This was her choice—a decision long overdue, to be honest. She'd lived with that black mark on her skin for too long, and now that she'd finally decided to do something about it, butterflies battered her insides. Placing one hand over her stomach hoping to quell her nerves, she clutched Mac's hand with the other as they walked up the front path to Ty's house.

"I feel like we're doing some kind of shady drug deal, going to his house after hours instead of the tattoo shop," Mac said.

"Yeah, well, you know as much as I do if I even stepped foot in that shop, the entire town'd be talkin' about what Willow Haven was doing in a seedy place like that. It'd get back to Daddy in a heartbeat."

It was a miracle she'd managed to keep her little act of teenage rebellion a secret as long as she had. The handful of souls who knew about the tattoo she'd gotten with Finn were Mackenna and the men Willow had been intimate with—which, admittedly, hadn't been many.

"Yeah, yeah. Gotta keep up the image," Mac said. "I get it."

As one of the middle Haven girls, Mac *did* get it. It was what made the two of them so close. Rory soared far above her sisters, the picture-perfect woman in their daddy's eyes, married to her college sweetheart and raising two flawless children. And Nat, their youngest sister, hadn't given a damn about this town or what their daddy thought, soaring in a different way and getting the hell out as soon as she'd graduated high school.

Willow and Mac stopped on the front stoop, both of them staring at the door. The blare of a television, interrupted sporadically by murmured voices, seeped out from inside.

Finally, after standing for long moments, Mac squeezed Willow's hand. "Ready?"

Not even a little bit.

"Yeah," Willow managed to get out through the invisible fingers wrapped tightly around her throat. She didn't have to actually *do* anything tonight, but at least when she left there, she'd have a plan one way or another.

Mac raised her fist to knock but paused and glanced over, giving Willow one last chance to back out. When Willow didn't speak up, Mac brought her knuckles down on the door in a quick rap.

"It's open," someone called from inside.

"No going back now." Mac turned the doorknob and stepped over the threshold.

While Willow was friendly with everyone in town, she wouldn't exactly say she and Ty were friends. As such, the last time she'd been to his house had been ten long years ago, and he'd done some upgrading since then, moving on from the trailer he used to have to a small ranch home. It was cleaner than she'd expected it to be, nicer too. A TV mounted on the far wall blared a video game, and as large as it was, it looked nearly minuscule compared to the massive couch that took up the majority of the room.

Ty sat sprawled out on one side, and Willow lifted her hand in a wave before glancing to the other occupant. Her hand froze in midair along with the smile on her face, her feet refusing to move.

Lord, couldn't she catch a freaking *break*?

The person sitting all the way on the other end, smiling up at her, was none other than the man who'd dominated nearly all of her thoughts. Finn *freaking* Thomas. He looked so relaxed there reclined against the back cushions, his legs spread, fingers loosely wrapped around the neck of the beer bottle resting on his knee, like he hadn't teased her with his body and his words earlier in the day. Like he hadn't rocked his erection against her ass on the dance floor mere days prior.

Willow's stomach bottomed out, seeing him there as if he didn't have a care in the world when the tornado of butterflies in her stomach just got kicked up to a Category five hurricane. She tightened her grip on Mac's hand until her sister let out a squeak of protest and dug her fingernails into Willow's skin in retribution.

"Looks like I picked the right night to stop by," Finn said, his eyes stuck to Willow.

Willow blinked and shook her head. "Stop by..." She narrowed her eyes at Finn, who only returned her glare with a smile. Of course, she'd known Ty and Finn were friends—they had been their whole lives. Really, it was her own damn fault she hadn't anticipated this, especially considering the past few days. Ropers may have been a coincidence, but there was no way this was. No freaking way. She had half a mind to stomp her foot right there and cuss Ty out.

Instead of doing that, she settled on shooting daggers his way, a finger jabbed in his direction. "Tyler Owen Kenning Junior, you traitor. Your momma know what you get up to with boys like him?"

Ty laughed, resting an arm against the back of the couch as he tipped his beer bottle toward her. "My momma thinks I'm an angel and doesn't listen to nothin' anyone might say otherwise."

"Mm-hmm," Willow said, dropping Mac's hand to cross her arms over her chest. "So this is the kind of professional you are, huh? When someone asks for an appointment, you invite all your friends to the show?"

"Appointment for what?" Finn asked, watching her like a hawk. Did she imagine how his eyes flicked down to the vicinity of her hip and the black bird hidden under layers of clothes?

Ty held up his hands in surrender and spoke as if Finn hadn't said a word. "Hey, you said you just wanted to talk about your options. Didn't think it'd be a problem when Finn said he was gonna stop by, too."

"What kind of options?" Finn asked.

She couldn't tell if he was playing dumb, or if he really didn't know her reason for being there. Either way, ignoring him was in her best interest. To Ty, she said, "And I bet his stopping by had nothing at all to do with me being here, huh?"

Ty looked away from her, focusing on the TV. "I don't know nothin' about that. That's between y'all."

"*I* don't know nothin' about what you're doing here," Finn said. "Someone wanna fill me in?"

Willow ground her molars together. "I told you earlier, you weren't gettin' anything out of me, Griffin."

He clenched his jaw, no doubt over the use of his full name. Good. It was dumb and childish, but at that point, she needed to hold on to every bit of distance she could put between them. "You thinking of getting some more ink on that pretty skin?"

She ignored the shiver his words sent down her spine. "How do you know I haven't already?"

His gaze heated even more, and she wanted to slap herself for being such an idiot, for walking right into his trap. He lifted one eyebrow and did a slow sweep of her from head to toe. "Guess I don't. You offering to show me, Willowtree?"

Those handful of words coming from Finn's mouth— the seductive, almost lilting way he said them—had the temperature in the room rising at least ten degrees. And she wasn't the only one who felt it if Mac's reaction was anything to go by.

"Oooookay." Mac side-stepped Willow and plopped down next to Ty on the couch. "You two kids work out whatever you need to work out. I'm gonna play this game until you're done."

What the hell? Willow had brought Mac along for support, and as soon as the temperature got cranked up, she bailed. Some freakin' wing-woman she was.

"We don't have anything to work out," Willow said. "All I need to know is—" She cut herself off. Why was she discussing this when Finn was sitting right there?

More importantly, why did she *care* if he was there when she did?

Steeling herself, she straightened her shoulders and addressed Ty, doing her best to ignore the way Finn bored holes into the side of her face with his eyes. "The tattoo you gave me. I want it gone. What're my options?"

As much as she tried to ignore Finn, she couldn't help the way her eyes darted over to him as soon as the words left her mouth. The crack in his facade was subtle, but it might as well have been a flashing marquee for as loudly as it screamed at her. He was good and pissed if the tightness in his jaw and shoulders was any indication. But, really, what did he have to be pissed about? *She* was the one who'd been left behind.

"All right," Ty drawled, glancing at Finn out of the corner of his eye before focusing back on Willow. "Well, you can always do a cover-up. Your original tattoo's not very big, so it'd be pretty easy to do."

"And if I don't want it there at all?"

"There's always laser removal, but, Will, that'll—"

"I have a few options you should consider," Finn said.

Willow's eyebrows shot up her forehead as she looked over at him. Was he for real? "I'm not all that interested in your opinion, considering you're the reason I'm here in the first place. Now, if you don't mind, I'm gonna listen to what Ty thinks is best since he's the professional."

Finn stood then, setting his beer on the side table, and took a step toward her, then another and another. And, all right, it probably didn't help her case the way she took equal steps back for every one he took forward, but she couldn't be that close to him again—*could not*. Except she didn't have a choice because soon her back was pressed against the wall, and he wasn't stopping—*didn't* stop until he stood directly in front of her. So close, she could feel the heat emanating off his body, could smell his delicious Finn scent. She snapped her spine straight and commanded her body to hold herself upright so she didn't do something horribly embarrassing like faint at his feet.

And then she did something she absolutely shouldn't have. She took a deep inhale of him—fresh and clean, like the air on a summer day—and just…looked.

Lord, he was pretty. He'd hate that descriptor, but it was accurate. His eyes were like butterscotch candies surrounded by the lushest eyelashes she'd ever seen, a total waste on so much masculinity. His nose wasn't perfect—he'd gotten in too many fights for there not to be a bump or two—but it was perfect on him. The scruff was new to her since he'd stayed mostly clean-shaven when they'd been together, but she could admit she liked it on him now. It made him look even manlier—which was nothing but trouble, because Finn certainly didn't need any help in that department.

She begged herself to stop cataloguing his features there, but her eyes didn't listen as they continued their path of no return until they reached his best feature—his mouth. His lips weren't overly full, but the curve of his top lip begged to be traced—and she had too. With her fingers. And her tongue.

Low, so low she wasn't sure Mac or Ty could even hear him, he said, "Stop lookin' at me like that, or I'm gonna start thinkin' you want more than you're sayin'."

"I don't know what you mean," she said, her eyes glued to his lips.

Said lips kicked up a notch on the side. He leaned closer—how was that even possible when it felt like they were as close as they could be while in mixed company? "C'mon, Willowtree, let's go down the hall and discuss your options. Alone."

His words shattered her trance, reminding her exactly why she shouldn't be in such close proximity to him. She crossed her arms over her chest, desperate to hide her reaction. The last thing she needed was for him to think she was still attracted to him.

Even if it was the painfully obvious truth.

"Funny, I didn't think you were a tattoo artist," she said. "Though, to be fair, I guess I really have no idea what you've been doin' with your life since I haven't heard from you in a *decade*."

He reached up and rubbed his fingers over his jaw,

studying her. "I didn't want to have to bring out the big guns for this."

She set her shoulders, narrowing her eyes at him. "Oh yeah? What're those?"

He leaned even closer, his breath a whisper of air against her mouth. "Either go back there and listen to what I have to say, or I'm gonna tell Mac and Ty the sound you make when you—"

She yelped and didn't even think about it as she slapped her hand over his mouth, her eyes wide in horror, darting over to where her sister and Ty sat, oblivious to what was going on between the two of them. "You wouldn't," she hissed.

Along with a raise of an eyebrow and a nip to her fingers currently pressed against those perfectly shaped lips of his, everything about his body language said, *try me.* She studied him, wondering if he was bluffing. The sure and steady way he stared back at her indicated he absolutely wasn't. Not even a little.

She shoved her hand harder against his mouth, pushing him toward the hallway off to the left. "I hate you."

He stepped back with a smile and led them down the hall and into an unoccupied bedroom. "Knew you'd see it my way."

"Not like you gave me a hell of a lot of choice."

"Aw, I think you and I both know you just needed an excuse to come back here."

"You are such an arrogant jack—"

The word cut off on her tongue as he reached out, his fingers hooking around her hip, his thumb pressed to the space where the black bird was permanently marked on her skin. After all this time, how did he remember the exact location? His touch burned through the thin layer of her shorts as he rubbed the area in tiny circles, her nipples hardening almost painfully at the intimate touch.

"Why're you thinkin' of getting this removed, Willowtree?"

She swallowed and tried to think about anything other than what it felt like to have his hands on her. She failed. After ten years, it'd been easy to brush off the connection she'd remembered between them. To wave it off as childish infatuation. Pretend she'd built it up in her mind and it hadn't been as electric as she'd once thought. But now? Now that he was eliciting reactions in her with a single thumb that other men hadn't been able to garner with their whole bodies and hours of time, it was clear she'd only been fooling herself. The two of them together were a perfect storm.

"Because I don't want to see it anymore," she said, forcing herself to speak through a throat clogged with desire.

"Is that right? Seems to me you might need a little reminder to fly."

Oh, that was rich coming from him. Her days of flying were long gone. "Yeah, well, there was a flaw in your plan. Because when I see this bird now? All I think is how *you* flew, Finn. So forgive me if I don't want that reminder on my skin every day for the rest of my life."

His grip on her hip tightened as he tugged her until their fronts pressed together. And—whoa, momma—she wasn't the only one heating up at their nearness if the hard ridge pressing against her stomach was any indication.

"You think I don't have the same damn reminder? That you were here the whole time without me? These are your roots on me, Willowtree," he said, pulling up his shirt and giving her a glimpse of the tattoo on the side of his rib cage he'd gotten the same day as hers. The one she'd drawn for him so long ago. The top was obscured by his shirt, but she knew what'd be there—the wispy leaves of a willow tree. The trunk twisted and contorted until it widened at the base, the roots spreading like outstretched fingers near his hip. Had there always been so many? She couldn't remember.

Finn reached down and grabbed her hand, pressing her fingers to his skin. His muscles rippled under her touch. "These are your roots on me, and no matter what's happened between us, I'd never want anything to erase what we had. Because what we had was *real*, Willow, and you know it. Don't forget that. Don't discount it."

She opened her mouth to tell him all they'd experienced was puppy love, but the words wouldn't come. They were frozen in her throat because they'd be the single greatest lie she'd ever told in her entire life. Without any conscious thought, her fingers started tracing the lines of ink on Finn's skin, and all she could do was watch. He was so solid and warm under her fingertips, his puffs of air growing faster and faster against her neck, then her cheek, then her lips.

And even though it'd been a long time, she knew what was coming a split second before he pressed his mouth against hers. Her sound of protest was lost in the space between their mouths as he swiped his tongue against her lips. And then there was nothing but Finn and his sinful mouth and his body flush against hers. He swept his tongue inside her mouth, and *Lord*, had he always tasted this good? Had he always *kissed* this good?

Never breaking away from her mouth, he walked them until Willow's back was pressed against the wall, and then he just sort of…settled in. His hips held hers against the wall, the length of his erection pressing into her, proving this wasn't at all one-sided as his hand continued its maddening path along her hip. But then—Lord, then he slipped his thumb under the waistband of her shorts until there was nothing between his rough fingertip and the part of her body forever marked as his. If it were possible, the soft caresses had her melting even further into him.

He kissed her like he was a starving man feasting on his first meal in a month. She'd forgotten how he'd always put his whole body into it, the heat and solidness of him pressing against her, making her feel safe and secure. Finn groaned into her mouth as he deepened the kiss even more, and all she could do was clutch him, one hand fisting the front of his shirt and the other pressed against his side where her tree was eternally imprinted.

"You feel so damn good," Finn said against her lips.

Willow murmured her agreement into his mouth because there was no denying it. Her body was on fire, her nipples hard points pressing against his chest, her skin lit up from the inside out. And then Finn's thumb, rubbing maddeningly against her tattoo, slipped to the right until he was as close to the Promised Land as he'd been in a long time. He didn't try to push it any further, just ran his thumb back and forth right above where she was wet and ready for him until she thought she'd die.

After a blink and an eternity, his heated mouth slowed until he pulled away, kissing along her jaw, flicking his tongue against that spot behind her ear that'd always made her knees weak. Then he brushed his lips against the shell of her ear, his words just a breath. "You feel that?"

She didn't think he actually expected an answer—which was a good thing, since all of her brainpower was being used to keep herself upright.

"I know you do," he said. "I know you've felt it every day since I came back. Think about this before you do anything, all right? Think about *us*, Willowtree. That's all I'm askin'." He scraped his teeth along her earlobe, and then…then he removed his thumb from her shorts, removed every inch of his body from hers, and stepped back.

His face was flushed, his eyes molten as he stared at her. His chest heaved with breath, and she didn't have to look down to know the evidence of his arousal would be apparent in his jeans, but she wanted to. Lord, she wanted to more than anything. Wanted to pull him back to her, wanted to strip him of his clothes and see what other changes had been made to the body she'd once known so well. And that thought scared the ever-loving hell out of her.

With his hands clenched into fists, as if he were physically restraining himself from coming toward her again, he gave her hip one last look, and then he left.

As she stared at the door Finn had gone through, her fingers pressing to the lips he'd so thoroughly kissed, she wanted to call out a thousand things at his retreating form. Most of them pertained to the fact that he had no right to ask that of her when he clearly hadn't thought of the two of them when he'd left.

But then she remembered his willow tree tattoo, prominent and untouched, when the rest of him had been inked up over the years—tattoos she hadn't given herself permission to catalog, but ones she would've had to be blind to miss—and the ache in her heart grew. Which only worried her more, causing the ache to turn into panic. Finn wasn't supposed to elicit those kinds of reactions from her. Not anymore.

When she had her bearings enough that she trusted herself around mixed company, she walked out to the living room to find Mac and Ty still playing the Xbox. They both looked up at her entrance, and Mac's eyes flitted to the front door, where Willow assumed Finn had fled through only moments before.

"What'll it be, Will?" Ty asked.

So much for having a plan when she left there tonight, because now her brain was all jumbled, and even if she could've made a decision, she wasn't sure she'd be able to trust herself.

"I'm gonna think it over, and I'll let you know," she said, her voice shaking only a little. "Mac, you ready?"

"Uh, yeah, sure." Mac got up from the couch, tossing the controller to Ty. "Thanks for the game."

"Anytime. See ya, Haven girls."

Mac headed out onto the porch, but before Willow

stepped over the threshold, she turned around to address Ty. "Don't mention my decision to Finn, all right?"

"What decision?" he replied with a wink.

"Exactly," she mumbled, then stepped out, shutting the door behind her as she sagged against it.

"Girl, what the hell happened in that back room? Finn looked like he was ready to combust when he came out."

That made two of them.

Willow shook her head as they walked to the car. "I'll tell you as soon as I figure it out myself."

chapter eight

Finn couldn't say he hadn't participated in some ground-shaking kisses in his time, but he could say, unequivocally, he'd never experienced one like he'd just had with Willow. At least, not in the time since he'd left her.

As he headed back to his temporary apartment, his lips still tingled from touching hers, her taste still lingering on his tongue. *Jesus*, the things he'd wanted to do to her. So much more than just kiss that tempting mouth of hers. He'd wanted to spin her around to the empty bed in the room, press her into the mattress and lay himself on top of her. Grind his cock into all that welcoming heat between her legs. Trail his mouth down every inch of her and find out if she tasted as good as he remembered.

But instead, he'd left. He'd *had* to. Kissing her had been about showing her there was something to them. That her removing the tattoo on her hip, removing a part of their history, would be a mistake.

And, shit, hearing her saying she'd wanted that part of herself changed? *Erased?* As if it'd never happened? It'd nearly wrecked him, especially considering the tattoo he bore of hers was as much a part of him as his fucking heart.

The willow tree she'd drawn for him—the one she'd sat by him for hours as it'd been inked on his skin—was the only thing he'd had tethering him to her for all those years he'd been away. And he'd made sure it'd done its job, not allowing himself to forget about her, even when she'd probably thought he hadn't given her a second thought after he'd left.

Truth was, he'd thought about her every damn day.

And every year on her birthday—the same day they'd gotten tattoos in the first place—he went and got another root added at the bottom of the tree. He might've spent years being thousands of miles away from her, but she'd been stamped on his heart—and his body—forever, her very essence permeating down to his bones.

After that kiss in Ty's house, after how she'd responded to it, melting into him, her tongue meeting his stroke for stroke, there was no doubt left in Finn's mind that Willow knew what still crackled between them. And didn't just know it, but *felt* it, same as he did.

He'd be damned if he wasn't going to push her to explore it with him.

He walked up the stairs to his and Drew's apartment, unlocking the door and walking into their temporary home. Nola had been right—it was in okay shape, all things considered. It was smaller than their place in California, but it worked for now. It had the same hardwood floors that ran through the main floor, though these weren't nearly as worn as the ones downstairs. They'd needed to give it a good scrubbing and vacuum a few thousand dust bunnies, but it was in working order now.

And thanks to their handful of friends who still lived in the area, they'd been able to fill it with castoffs. Someone's cousin/momma/friend had had what they'd needed sitting in unused guest rooms. Southern hospitality at its finest.

Finn tossed his keys on the counter in the small kitchen as he strolled into the living area and found Drew on the phone. He tipped his chin in Finn's direction before speaking to whoever was on the other line. "Yeah, we got the box. We're doin' all right otherwise. Ty's momma spotted us a few things, and we got most of the rest from Nola's cousins."

If Finn had to guess, he'd place bets it was their momma, calling to check in on them, same as she'd done every day since they'd been gone. The separation was getting to her, that much was clear. It was the longest the three of them had been apart in...well, ever. If that made him and Drew momma's boys, so be it. But the three of them were all they had, so they stuck together, through thick and thin. And there'd been a lot of both over the past twenty-nine years.

"He's fine. Just walked in," Drew said, glancing Finn's way, his eyes doing a quick sweep over his brother. Even though Finn was certain nothing in his body language said anything about what had happened with Willow, he also knew his brother would know something was up. Same way Finn had known when Drew'd lost his virginity to Lexie May sophomore year of high school. Sometimes it was awesome being a twin; sometimes it was a little awkward and damn inconvenient.

Finn fell into the corner of the couch, throwing an arm across the back as he waited for the phone.

"All right, Momma. I'll let y'all talk. Love you." Drew tossed the phone in Finn's direction before getting up and strolling into the kitchen.

Finn brought the phone to his ear. "Hey, Momma."

"Hey, sweetheart. Y'all gettin' on okay there?"

With one hundred percent certainty, Finn knew she'd asked Drew the same thing. But every time she asked, she did so with such sincerity, he couldn't fault her for it. He wasn't sure if the concern was because she wasn't used to being away from them, or if it was because she was worried about the reception they'd receive in Havenbrook. When they'd left, he and Drew were only a year or so out of their rebellious teen years where they'd gotten up to everything from petty vandalism to property damage. Add that in with being from the wrong side of the tracks, born to a teenage single momma, and they'd had *outcasts* and *troublemakers* branded on them from birth.

"Doin' fine here. Spent today doin' demo and working on some repairs on the plaster. Things are movin' along."

"So y'all think you'll be comin' back soon, then?"

"I'm not sure." The thought of leaving now, before he'd had a chance to explore whatever this was between him and Willow, left him with a rock in the pit of his stomach. "We haven't even begun to pick out the finishes for the space yet. And Nola can't be dealin' with all that while she's still workin' at the auto shop. She didn't have as much money put away as we did."

"How's that sweet girl doin'? Haven't talked to her in ages. You tell her to give me a call, would you?"

"Yes, ma'am."

"Now what's this I hear about you talkin' to Willow Haven?" she asked.

Finn blew out a breath and shot a glare at his brother who'd taken a seat on the other end of the couch. Drew's only response was to shrug as he took a swig from his beer.

"I've gotta talk to her, Momma. She's in charge of things at town hall now."

"Mm-hmm," she said, her displeasure hitting him like a ton of bricks, even through the phone line. "What exactly do you think's gonna happen between y'all, with your history?"

Honestly? He had no fucking idea, but he sure as hell wasn't gonna tell his momma that. He knew what he *wanted* to happen. Could finally admit to himself he didn't just want to see Willow happy, but he wanted to see her happy *with him*. A connection like theirs was once in a lifetime, and he'd be damned if he let her pretend it wasn't there. He just had no idea how to go about getting her on board with it.

"I know what I'm doin'," he said.

She tutted. "From where I'm sittin', you don't know much of anything. Honestly, Griffin… Stringin' that poor girl along. I raised you better than that." Silence hung from her side of the line for a moment. "Unless…unless you're thinkin' about stayin'?" she asked, her voice tinged with something that sounded an awful lot like hope. But that couldn't be right. Why would him moving back to Haven-brook make her *happy*?

She'd wrung her hands when he and Drew had told her of their plans, so worked up over the two of them going back to a place that'd done nothing but try to force the three of them out. A place that'd never, ever welcomed them into its fold, despite years of trying. Despite their momma being an active part of the community. True, she hadn't been a doctor or a lawyer, hadn't been on the school board or the PTA. But she'd paid her bills, had tried her damnedest to keep her boys out of trouble—though it'd been hard as a young, single mom, working two or three jobs to keep a roof over their heads and food on the table.

Even if she'd been home more, Finn and Drew would've found trouble anyhow. It was in their blood. But it wouldn't have mattered anyway. They could've followed every ridicu-lous law in Havenbrook, could've played along with the do-gooders of the town, and it still would've done fuck-all to change the minds of many of the residents of Havenbrook. The Thomases, along with their friends, had been branded *wrong* simply because they couldn't afford a lot of their own or a house with a foundation instead of a single wide trailer.

Which was why opening up this business with their own money, no help at all from the Bank of Havenbrook, felt so damn good.

"I already called Sammy and let him know what was goin' on. Right now, the plan is to stay for a couple weeks," he said, hating how the words lit a fire in his gut, burning all the way up to his chest. He couldn't imagine leaving so soon. Not now...not after having Willow under his hands again. Not since having her taste on his tongue after ten long years without it.

"Mmm…plans change," his momma said.

They did. Situations changed…people changed. He could only hope he could get Willow to see that.

After a few more minutes of conversation and a promise to call tomorrow, Finn hung up and dropped his head back on the couch as he scrubbed a hand down his face.

"You wanna tell me why you came in practically whistling before talkin' to Momma?" Drew asked.

"Not really."

"Sounds like I'm shit outta luck, then. I'll never be able to crack the unbreakable code that is Griffin Thomas," Drew said, his voice ringing with sarcasm.

Finn rolled his eyes, standing to grab himself a beer. "If you already know, why'd you ask?"

Drew didn't say anything. Not until Finn sat back on the couch, beer in his hand. "You start somethin' with her?"

Finn thought back to the kiss, to her hips under his fingers, the lush curves of her pressed up against every inch of him. Lord had he wanted to. He shook his head. "Not yet."

"Well, somethin' happened."

"You didn't ask if somethin' happened. You asked if I started somethin' with her. And I haven't."

"Yet."

"Yet," Finn confirmed with a nod.

Drew just stared at him before shaking his head. "She's got you all kinds of fucked up, you know that, right?"

He did, but what the hell was he supposed to do? He'd

walked away from her once, and it'd been the single greatest mistake of his entire life. He'd be damned if he made the same one again, if he walked away without giving this thing between them a chance to actually become something. Not now that he was older, wiser... Now that he wouldn't allow her asshole of a father to stand between them as he had back then.

"Nothin' I can do about that," he said.

"So, what's your plan? We stayin' here indefinitely, or what?"

Drew had exactly as many ties to California as Finn did. Namely, zero. As long as they got their momma back to Havenbrook, they'd be fine. And whether or not Drew agreed with what Finn was doing where Willow was concerned, he'd stand behind his brother, have his back every step of the way. Where Finn went, Drew followed, and vice versa.

Knowing that made it easier to move forward, since Finn didn't know what the hell was coming. If he'd be in Havenbrook or California...New York or Nashville. Right now, he had one goal, and that was to get in the good graces of one Willow Haven.

"My plan is to find out if I can make her see me as more than just the asshole who left. Everything else will come after."

Drew snorted, shaking his head. "Man, you're a damn idiot. That girl does nothin' but spit fire when you're around."

"She wasn't spittin' fire when she let me kiss her tonight."

Raising an eyebrow, Drew said, "Maybe not. Doesn't mean you don't have a shit-ton of work ahead of you."

Didn't he know it. But that was all right. Finn hadn't fought hard enough for her in the first place. Hadn't stuck it out when he was pressed between a rock and a hard place. So if that meant he had to work harder now, so be it. Willow deserved every bit of sweat on his part, and he was trying hard to be worthy of her.

chapter nine

A couple days after the kiss that'd rocked Willow's world, she was still doing her best to forget about it. Okay, she was doing her best to *try* to forget. So far, it wasn't going well. Or at all, really. She'd done little but think about what it'd felt like to have Finn's lips on hers again, to have every inch of his body pressed against hers, all that heat directed solely at her.

There was no denying it anymore. Over the years, she *hadn't* inflated their chemistry in her mind. It was there, and it was real, and it was every bit as potent as it'd been when they'd been only teenagers. Maybe even more so. Which meant she was well and truly screwed.

"Will." Rory stood in the paint section of the local hardware store, holding up two white samples. "Which one do you like better?"

Normally, Willow could debate paint colors with the best of them, but she could barely focus on her own name let alone the varying shades of dove and moonlight. "Um… that one." She pointed to the one in Rory's left hand.

Rory scrunched her nose, her lips pursing as she considered it. "You don't think it's too yellow?"

"What room is this goin' in again?"

Rory narrowed her eyes. "Have you been listening to anythin' I've been sayin'?"

Well, actually...no. No, she hadn't been. As if Willow didn't have enough to think about after that kiss with Finn, she also had to contend with the fact that her daddy was coming home from his conference at the end of the week. She wasn't sure how she'd managed it, but as far as she knew, he was none the wiser about the new Havenbrook residents. And if he'd gotten wind of it, she had no doubt he would've called her immediately, demanding answers. Since she hadn't received any five a.m. wake-up calls, she figured all was good. Which was nice in the present, but it only postponed the inevitable blowup when he came back and found out what had been happening in his precious Havenbrook during his absence.

"Sorry, Rory. Tell me again?"

With a huff and an eye roll, Rory held out the white and white paint samples in front of Willow's face. "I'm repaintin' the study."

"Didn't you just do that a couple months ago?"

Rory lifted a single, perfectly groomed eyebrow. "Yes, I did. But I don't like it. It's too dark for the space, closes it in. I want to go light this time, with pops of color in the accent pieces instead. I'm thinkin' crimson and teal." She waved the paint sample Willow had picked in her face. "So, do you think this one is too yellow for that?"

She shouldn't have been surprised at Rory's whim

when it came to redecorating her house. Sean, Rory's husband, worked as an attorney at his daddy's firm, which meant long hours for him and even longer hours for Rory at home taking care of their two daughters all by herself. Willow didn't know the ins and outs of their marriage—Rory wasn't one to discuss that kind of thing, so Willow didn't push—but it seemed to her Sean didn't put up a fuss at the constant changes Rory made because she didn't put up a fuss when he had to work late for the sixth night in a row.

"No, I don't think it's too yellow," Willow said, though she still hadn't more than glanced at the samples.

"Hmm…" Rory turned around, moving to the different light sources the hardware store offered to see the variances in color. "I'm just not sure."

Willow plucked a deep blue sample from the display. The shade would be perfect if she painted an ocean scene at sunset. "So Sean's workin' late again?"

"Mm-hmm."

"He seems to be doin' that a lot lately. He workin' on a new case?"

"You know his daddy trusts him the most, Will. Doesn't like any of the other attorneys to help him with his cases, which means long hours for Sean." Rory's response came out sharper than usual, an undercurrent in her tone that had Willow glancing up. But before Willow could question her on it, Rory's smile was back in place.

"Did you hear about what happened to Brenda Nokes?" Rory asked, her eyebrows raised.

"Can't say I have." Willow replaced the blue sample and

grabbed something in a light orange—perfect for the glow of the sun.

"It's a shame, just a shame. She caught Bill with Susanna Jenkins! Can you believe that? Poor thing, her husband and her best friend." Rory tutted, shaking her head. "According to Edna, she's not leavin' him either. They're gonna try to work it out."

"That's good, I guess."

"*Good?*" Rory laughed humorlessly. "I wouldn't say there's anything good about the situation. Can you imagine havin' to decide between divorcing or sticking it out with a man who wants someone else? Bless her heart, I just feel so bad for her."

Despite being a gossipmonger, Rory's sympathy was genuine. Without letting Willow get a word in, she continued, "At least they don't need to worry about people talkin' for long. All the commotion around it'll die down in a bit. Honestly, all anyone can talk about is the Thomas boys anyway." She looked at Willow over her shoulder. "Did you get my voice mail about them moving in to that little apartment over their building? No one's been able to figure out if it's permanent or temporary. But heavens, can you imagine the Thomas boys living here again?"

Rory laughed, shaking her head as if the idea were preposterous. As if Willow hadn't been imagining that very thing since she'd been swept off her feet by a kiss that definitely shouldn't have happened. "I haven't had a chance to swing by yet, but I'm plannin' to. Just to check in on them, of course. See how they're doin' and welcome them back into town. Maybe bring 'em some muffins."

Uh-huh. A welcome that came with a side of spying and information mining. Willow saw right through Rory's bull-shit story, but she didn't call her on it. What was the use? Besides, if Rory's attention was snagged on something else, maybe she'd stay off Willow's case for more than a day.

"Before I can do that, though, I need to figure out which of these I like better..." Rory continued comparing the stark-white and slightly less stark samples, so Willow slipped over to the unoccupied paint counter, leaned against it, and prepared for a long night. The last time she'd agreed to come with Rory, they'd spent three hours in this damn store, most of which had been spent looking at door hooks. *Door hooks.* Only Rory would put that much effort into perfection.

After that unforgettable experience, Willow had sworn to herself she'd never come again. And then tonight had happened. She and Mac were supposed to watch their nieces while Rory and Sean went out to dinner. Instead, he'd had to work late, which meant Rory was slated for a night of seclusion. But when she'd dropped the girls off, she'd looked a bit frustrated at her husband's disappearing act—a crack in a perfect facade. It was so unlike Rory, Willow had taken pity on her and asked if she could come with.

And now she was bored out of her ever-loving mind, debating the merits of painting a room dove or moonlight. That was what she got for trying to be the nice one. Mac had only waved with glee as Willow and Rory had left. Never mind the fact that she was on the hook as solo care-taker for their seven- and nine-year-old nieces. Apparently, that was far superior to being stuck with their eldest sister for any amount of time.

Rory was mumbling about cyan versus cerulean throw pillows and which would look better with moonlight when a laugh drew Willow's attention down the aisle toward a small display of lighting fixtures. Two people stood below an array of ceiling fans, and it took Willow only half a second to realize it was Finn and Nola. The same time the realization hit her, an invisible fist clenched around her stomach and squeezed.

She hadn't seen him since their kiss—had done all she could to avoid him, to be honest. If any of them had needed help with something at the building or had questions about a regulation, she'd had Avery run interference. Maybe not her most professional move, but she hadn't been able to face him just yet. Not when the kiss still had her all jumbled up inside.

Rory's nonstop stream of conversation faded into the background while Willow watched Finn and Nola laugh, Finn's head tossed back and a huge smile on his face. And, yeah, she could say the fist squeezing harder around her insides was just the shock at seeing him when it wasn't part of her plan. But she'd done an awful lot of lying to herself since he'd come back to town, and she was tired of it.

As much as she'd tried to avoid it, as much as she'd done whatever she could to believe something else, there was no getting around it. She was attracted to Finn. Desperately. Her mouth tingled as she remembered how he'd pressed her up against the wall, had slipped his tongue between her lips and feasted on her like she was the best thing he'd tasted in years. And now? Seeing him laughing and so comfortable with another girl kicked her straight in the heart, jealousy seeping out of her pores. Which didn't make any sense. She'd never been jealous a day in her life, so why the hell would it start now when she wasn't even *with* Finn?

"All right, I think I decided on moonlight," Rory said, stepping up next to Willow. "What's got your attention?"

Before Willow could straighten and look in the opposite direction of where Finn and Nola stood, her sister turned and glanced down the aisle. Rory's eyes narrowed when she saw who stood there, and she hummed low in her throat. Her gaze was calculating, which meant Willow had about three seconds to get her sister out of the store before Rory did something that would no doubt humiliate her.

"Are you about ready?" Willow asked, keeping her voice quiet as she pushed away from the counter.

"Not quite." Rory grabbed Willow's hand and dragged her down the aisle, closer to Finn and Nola. "Need to get some new paintbrushes too. What do you think of these, Will?" she asked, far louder than she needed to.

At the sound of Willow's name, Finn's head snapped up, his laughter cutting off. He looked in their direction, a slow smile spreading across his lips when he caught sight of her. *Lord*, why did that make her stomach flip?

And, damn, now he was coming toward them, Nola at his side, and the single tumble of Willow's stomach turned into a series of somersaults with no end in sight.

"Rory," Finn said with a nod. "Good to see you. How're things?"

Finn might've asked the question of Rory, but his eyes strayed almost immediately to Willow. And then he did a slow sweep of her from head to toe while Rory went on about everything amazing that was going on in her life—two kids on the honor roll, heading up the PTA, the multitude of fundraisers she'd done for Havenbrook residents in need, her husband being promoted to partner in the firm. It all blurred into background noise as Willow's body heated up simply from Finn's gaze. The way he allowed his eyes to trace over every curve of her was as good as a caress on her naked body. Everything tightened, her nipples going stiff and the warmth in her lower belly spreading until it was all she could focus on.

"But enough about me," Rory said, placing a hand on his forearm. "I heard y'all bought the old soda fountain. Gettin' it all fixed up?"

Finn finally dragged his eyes away from Willow and glanced at her sister. "We're tryin'. Between the three of us, we'll be lucky if it doesn't look like a flea market in there, though."

"Oh? What're y'all thinkin'?"

Nola shrugged. "We're still a little fuzzy on the details. We just know we don't want a typical honky-tonk vibe. Maybe something with an industrial flair instead?" She pulled out her phone and turned it to face Rory and Willow, showcasing a few pictures she had stored. "We were thinkin' something like this."

"*Together?*" Rory asked, her voice laced with horror. "Oh no, honey. No." Rory shook her head as she plucked the phone from Nola's fingers and swiped through the images. "Now I know this is y'all's baby, but I just wouldn't be a good neighbor if I didn't offer a few suggestions, now would I?" Rory's eyes were alight with excitement, no doubt over telling someone—anyone—what to do. She grabbed Nola's wrist and led her down the aisle back toward the lighting. "What I'd suggest is—"

Willow stopped listening then, because Finn stepped closer to her, choosing to stay with her rather than listen to Rory give a play-by-play of what they needed in the bar. He leaned a shoulder against the shelves at her back, curving his body toward her and bringing him far closer than was a good idea.

"Fancy meetin' you here," he said.

She slid him a look out of the corner of her eye, trying not to be affected by the warmth swirling in his gaze. Trying and failing. "If you're not careful, I'm gonna start thinkin' you're following me."

He smiled then, the sight nearly knocking Willow on her ass. "If I were following you, we'd run into each other a helluva lot more than we have been." He reached out, tucking a strand of hair behind her ear. Why did that tiny, innocent touch have her body lighting up? "I guess I've just been lucky these past few days."

Willow swallowed, attempting to maintain the facade of calm, when inside, she felt like she was on fire. "Is that what you'd call it?"

Once again, he let his eyes drop to take in every inch of her. And those eyes? They heated until there was no doubt in her mind he was mentally undressing her, imagining what every inch of her would look like bare. "Yeah, Willowtree," he said, his voice deep and rough, just a whisper in the space between them. "I call it damn lucky."

She swallowed. Tried to get her breathing under control. Failed miserably. "Quit lookin' at me like that."

"Like what?" he asked with a smile.

"Like *that*."

He leaned closer, dropped his voice even more. "Like I'm picturing what would've happened if I hadn't walked away the other night? If I'd been able to get you out of your shirt? See what you've got hiding under all these layers? Can't say I've *stopped* thinkin' about it. This is just the first time you've been present for it."

"Finn..." She tried to make it come out as an admonishment, scold him for being inappropriate, but instead, it came out breathless. Like a plea for more. Her entire body warmed, her cheeks growing hot, and there was no doubt in her mind everything was written all over her face.

She finally let herself meet his eyes, only to find his even more heated than before. Like it was taking all his strength not to grab her by the ass and hoist her up so she'd be wrapped around his hips—to hell if they were in a public place or not.

"It's nice to see your cheeks get red for somethin' other than you being pissed at me," he said, running the back of a finger down her warm skin. "Though I don't mind that either. As long as you're talkin' to me, I'll take what I can get."

His acknowledgment of her arousal only made the heat bloom more. She darted her eyes around him to where Rory and Nola stood, their attention focused on the lighting offered, paying her and Finn no mind. But all it would take was once glance in their direction, and Rory would see everything. And she would never, ever let Willow live it down.

Finn looked over his shoulder to where Willow's eyes were fixed, then he circled her wrist with two fingers and tugged her around the corner into an empty aisle. And, dammit, but that was both better and worse. She wanted to be in a crowded store, surrounded by people, as much as she wanted it to be just the two of them, hidden and tucked away where they could do anything they wanted.

And, *Lord*, did she want. No more lying to herself. Which meant she didn't trust herself around him. It was that simple. She'd proven time and time again she couldn't be trusted in his company, and the longer she was in it, the higher the probability she'd do something totally out of character for her. Something her sister—the sister who stood only an aisle over—would have a conniption over. Something she'd hold over Willow's head for eternity, right after sharing it with their daddy.

But Willow forgot about all that when Finn tugged her to him, sliding an arm around her to press against the small of her back. He didn't stop until their fronts were flush, an intimate touch that was absolutely inappropriate for the middle of the hardware store…and for two people who weren't a couple.

And yet Willow didn't push him away. With hands resting against his chest, she stood stock-still and stared up at him. His lips curved into the tiniest smile before he leaned down, bringing his face closer to hers. She panted—there was no other word for it. Her breaths came shallow and fast, her fingers curling into the material of the T-shirt covering all that muscled goodness Finn hid under his clothes.

He was going to kiss her again.

And…she was going to *let* him. She wanted that kiss more than her next breath, wanted to feel those warm lips of his against hers, wanted the sinful slide of his tongue along her own. He was so close, she could nearly taste the sweet tang of his tongue. But instead of pressing his mouth to hers, he brushed his lips across her cheek before nuzzling her neck as he inhaled deeply. She went boneless, certain the only thing holding her up was his arm around her, solid and sure.

Against her ear, he whispered, "You ready to stop ignorin' what's between us?" He pressed a light kiss on that heavenly place behind her ear—the one he'd learned at eighteen was her weakness. "Because I am. I'm here and ready whenever you are. I've thought about that kiss every damn second since it happened. Played it out a hundred different ways, and they all end the same, Willowtree. With me inside you."

The floor might as well have vanished beneath her, the aisle of decorative hardware surrounding her fading into nothing as she did the only thing she could. She *clung* to him. She gripped his shirt in her fingers, and he tightened his arm around her in response, holding her up and against him. They were as close as they could be in public, every hard inch of him pressing against her, and yet it wasn't enough. She wanted *more*. Despite knowing better, despite everything that'd happened between them, she wanted more.

"Will?" Rory called out from the other aisle, making Willow jump, the trance broken.

After another kiss behind her ear and a deep inhale, Finn stepped back. His eyes were heavy, his lips parted, and she couldn't stop herself from dropping her gaze to the front of his jeans where his arousal was clear as day as it strained against the denim. For her.

"I have to go."

He nodded once, just a slow dip of his chin, his eyes never leaving hers. Reaching up, he ran his thumb over her bottom lip. "Anytime, Willowtree," he said, his voice low and gritty as he dropped his hand and stepped back from her. "Remember that. Anytime."

And then he turned and walked away, down the aisle and around the corner before Rory and Nola could find them together. All Willow could do was stare at his retreating form.

Stare and daydream about what it'd be like if she actually gave in.

chapter ten

W illow had slept like shit the night before, her body
overheated and her dreams a constant reel of
what'd happened yesterday in the hardware store. At three
a.m., she'd been desperate, having jolted herself from yet
another dream before she could climax, and slipped her
fingers into her panties to get herself off. And though she
had finally gotten relief, that relief had come to thoughts of
Finn—something she hadn't done in *years*. Worse, though,
was that she'd woken for the day with him still on her mind,
the images she'd used of the two of them together as she'd
made herself come popping up at the most inopportune
times.

Like while she was at work.

She sorted the papers on her desk, trying to get her
mind on her schedule for the day instead what Finn's body
would look like now that he'd fully developed into a man.
She'd gotten a glimpse of it at Ty's house, but she wanted to
see more. Wanted to *feel* more. She had about a hundred
fifty-seven things to tend to before her daddy got back

tomorrow, and not one of them was Finn's dick, which kept flitting through her mind despite her attempts to block it.

"Hey, girl," Avery said as she strolled into the outer office. She powered on her computer and tucked her purse away. "I'll be right in."

Good. Maybe having her best friend in her office would stop Willow from picturing herself tracing the willow tree tattoo on Finn's side…with her tongue.

"Since you're here, I'll assume you didn't commit a felony against Rory last night." Avery sat in the chair across from Willow, prepared for their daily morning meeting with a pen and pad of paper in hand. "What did—" She cut off when she finally glanced up at Willow. "What's happening? What's going on here?"

Shit. Avery was too observant for her good. Or for Willow's good anyway.

Willow shifted in her seat, figuring playing dumb was her safest bet. "What do you mean?"

"I *mean*, what's with your face?" Avery gestured in Willow's general vicinity.

"Um…I tried a new blush this morning?"

Avery snorted then pointed her pen at Willow. "Bullshit. Something happened." She gasped and leaned forward, resting her elbows on Willow's desk. "With *Finn*?"

"*No*, not with Finn." Willow avoided Avery's narrowed gaze until she'd bounced her eyes onto every flat surface in her office. When Willow glanced back at her, Avery's eyebrow was raised in silent judgment. "Okay, fine. Yes, with Finn."

"Holy sh—"

Willow held up her hand. "But it's not a big deal."

"'Not a big deal', just like when he dry-humped you on the dance floor at Ropers? Or 'not a big deal' like when he kissed you within an inch of your life at Ty's?"

Dammit, why did she keep getting into these situations with him?

"Neither, okay?" Willow said. "It was neither. It was just…" She blew out a deep breath and closed her eyes. "I don't know what the hell is goin' on. I'd like to say it's all physical—"

Avery shot forward. "*How* physical?"

"Would you gimme a damn minute?"

"Right, sorry." Avery made a continue gesture. "Go on."

"I'd write it off as just this crazy physical pull between us, but then this mornin', this got delivered." She pulled the package from her drawer, showing it to Avery.

"Paints?" Avery furrowed her brow. "I'm not following."

"They're the same brand I used to use…back in high school."

"Okay…?"

"I didn't order them. They're from Finn."

Avery's eyes widened. "*Ohhhh.*"

There hadn't been a note in the box, but there hadn't needed to be. She'd known from the second she'd opened it they'd been from him, and it'd thrown her right back to ten years prior when he'd done the same thing. He'd worked hard to help his momma pay the bills and didn't have extra to buy a soda, let alone the expensive paints Willow had preferred. But when her daddy'd told her he was done footing the bill for her "frivolous junk," Finn had used his hard-earned money just to make her happy, sending them to her when hers had almost been out.

Willow shook her head. "I just...I don't know what it means. It's not even about the paints, exactly. I'm just not sure—"

"Will!" a voice boomed from the hallway.

The two of them froze, eyes wide as they stared at each other for half a second before Willow's eyelids slid shut, a long exhale leaving her. Because *of course* her daddy would come home early and unannounced. That meant one of two things. Either her momma was sick—and considering Willow had just talked to her yesterday afternoon, that wasn't likely—or he'd heard about the Thomas boys' plans within Havenbrook.

Richard Haven stomped into the outer office, red-faced and out of breath. Her momma hadn't mentioned him coming home, and she definitely would have. Which meant this trip back home had been an impromptu flight. If the wrinkles in his clothes were any indication, he'd caught the red-eye in and hadn't even bothered going home before showing up at town hall.

"Daddy!" Willow said, forcing herself to smile. "What're you doing back early?"

"I think you know damn well why I'm back. My office. *Now*, young lady."

Without waiting for a response—because he knew Willow would follow without hesitation—he turned around and stormed out of Willow's office suite, disappearing down the hall toward his.

"Well, this should go well." Willow pushed away from

her desk and stood, smoothing a hand over her hair, then her skirt. As if having a perfect appearance would help talk her daddy off the ledge.

"I'll be on standby to run over to The Sweet Spot," Avery said. "She's got triple lemon today."

"Maybe it won't be that bad." Willow slipped around her desk.

"And maybe I should just go ahead and place an order now…"

With those encouraging words from her best friend, Willow made the short trek out of her office and across the hall to where her daddy spent most of his days. Normally, he'd be in his inner office, his assistant seated in the outer office. But today, he occupied the main space, pacing from one end to the other.

This wasn't going to be pleasant. Still, she plastered on a smile. She could pretend with the best of them, and as far as she was concerned, everything was just peachy around these parts. "How was your trip, Daddy?"

He stopped as soon as she spoke, spinning around to glare in her direction. "How was my *trip*? My trip was fine. Finding out about those Thomas boys sullying up my town, on the other hand, was like getting eaten by a wolf and shit out over a cliff."

Internally, Willow rolled her eyes at his dramatics. *Sullying* was a bit strong of a word choice. Finn and Drew had been back for more than a week, and the town hadn't imploded yet. In fact, other than the mess going on in Willow's head—and, okay, her panties—not much had changed. Except that more Havenbrook residents now had work.

King Construction—the company Nash ran with his daddy—employed all kinds of tradespeople. Many of whom had either been traveling to nearby towns for work, or worse, had been out of it entirely. And right now, those people were earning a wage right there in Havenbrook. In a prime location on the square—the last missing piece in an almost revived downtown.

But there'd be no trying to convince her daddy of that. According to him, Finn Thomas and his brother had trouble written all over them, had from the day they'd been born. No amount of words on Willow's part would make him change his mind, so she wasn't going to try.

Instead, she said, "I'd hoped you'd be able to enjoy your conference before comin' home to that news."

"You didn't think it was pertinent information for the *mayor* to have? Sometimes I wonder what goes through that mind of yours…" He shook his head while Willow bit her tongue.

Deep breaths, in and out. Right then was not the time to get into it. What she needed to do was smooth his ruffled feathers, and then attack her mile-long to-do list. She'd planned to have the Fourth of July signage done up and posted before he'd gotten back, and that plan was now shot to hell. Plus, she needed to tend to the empty planters since Miss Clementine broke her hip and hadn't been able to fulfill her landscaping committee duties. Willow only hoped he was too preoccupied to notice. She wasn't sure she'd be able to keep biting her tongue if she got ripped into for that too.

He stepped closer to her, his mouth set in a tight line. Her daddy wasn't a tall man—well under six feet—but his presence filled up a room. Whether it was with jovial banter or scathing looks, the effect was the same: it was damn near impossible to ignore Richard Haven when in his company.

"What's this I hear about you helpin' get the paperwork all done up for those *boys*?" He sneered the word, as if he were talking about some rebellious teenagers and not nearly thirty-year-old men who were now business owners.

And she had no idea how to answer that question. Of course she'd been helping them. It was her *job* to help with paperwork, answer any questions new business owners had, and guide them through regulations, Thomas boys or not. And if she hadn't done her job, her daddy wouldn't have had any problem at all holding it over her head. Damned if she did, damned if she didn't, just like always.

She kept the smile on her face, though it felt brittle. "That's my job, Daddy."

"Your *job* is to make sure the mayor looks good. That's why I went against my instincts and hired you instead of Jeff, figuring you'd at least make sure the Haven name wasn't dragged through the mud." He huffed, smoothing a hand down his loosened tie, doing nothing to help the wrinkled shirt underneath. "You think having a bar in a prime location in the square shines a positive light on me and this town?"

Yes, as a matter of fact, she did. Willow'd had Avery pull some numbers over the past week in preparation for having this exact conversation with her daddy, comparing Haven-brook's information to the demographics of Parkersville, the next biggest town over. She'd hoped showing him the infor-mation in black and white would help calm him. But even if she'd had it ready and with her now, it wouldn't have mattered. She'd underestimated just how pissed off he'd be.

There was no denying the truth, though: the bar was the breath of fresh air their dying town needed. Havenbrook was hemorrhaging residents, mostly of the younger genera-tion, fewer and fewer of Willow's classmates or surrounding years' sticking around in a dead-end town with nothing keeping them there. And it was because they could get the same small-town feel with added benefits not far away. Why *wouldn't* they go? She wanted to stop that if she could, and she had a feeling this was a good step in the right direction.

This town was in her family's blood, and she loved it with all of her being. She loved the people who cared without question—even if they did get into her business more than she'd like—and she loved that she knew the story of every historical landmark in the square, and she loved that she couldn't go to the grocery store without running into at least one person who wanted to ask about her day. She didn't want Havenbrook to be perfect like her daddy did; she wanted it to *thrive*.

She wasn't naïve enough to think a single bar could do that, but it could go a long way in making sure the residents stuck around instead of spending their time and money in another county. Now, when they wanted a drink after work, they'd head into the square to get it. The bar would make money, and the trio of owners would pay their taxes, thus bringing in more revenue for Havenbrook. It was a win-win for them, even if her daddy couldn't see it just yet.

But he was blind to things like that, too stuck in his ways to believe things were changing. If they didn't change along with them, the town that was their namesake would continue to shrivel until it was just a forgotten dot on the map. She wasn't going to let that happen, even if that meant standing up for the bar coming into town, standing up for Finn. Even if that meant pushing back with her daddy.

She took a deep breath and squared her shoulders. "First of all, you hired me because I was better qualified for the job. Jeff is a janitor at the elementary school, and I'm sure he does a fantastic job there. But to have you say he would've handled this position better than me is insulting."

She wanted to say more, wanted to tell him she'd worked her ass off for him and this town for the past five years. And she'd done a damn good job of it. Would it hurt him to recognize that? But she had more pressing issues right then. "And I think having a thriving business bringing in both revenue and jobs—not to mention giving us an increase in taxes for things like new parks and better roads—is a good thing for the mayor, but more importantly for the town. No matter *what* the business is."

Her daddy jerked his head back, eyes wide. Probably because Willow could count on one hand the number of times she'd stood up to him, and most of them had been during her teenage years. He narrowed his eyes, his jaw going tight. "You know damn well I don't like that kind of business. Or that boy."

Understatement of the century. He'd tried to keep them

apart when they'd been teenagers, though he hadn't quite managed. Even if he'd done everything in his power to keep them from seeing each other, she and Finn had worked at the same place, and her daddy hadn't been able to stop that, no matter how powerful he was.

"That may be the case," she said, "but they've done everything above board. Went through the right paths, secured all the proper permits, even verified with the historical society about the items they'll need to be careful on to follow regulation. They're doing everything properly, Daddy."

She waited for him to argue more, but he only stared at her for a moment, his face getting redder, before he grunted.

"Now that I'm here, I might as well get to work."

"Don't you wanna go home and change?"

"Apparently, I don't have time since it looks like you didn't do much of anything while I was gone. Spend all your time paintin' your nails or what? Those damn toys from Tina's day care were all over the side parking lot, not put away like they're supposed to be. The tables at the cafe are blocking the sidewalks again. And for God's sake, when the hell are those planters gonna get filled? I thought that was supposed to be completed this week? If you don't get it done, I'll get someone in here who will." With that, he turned around and shuffled into his office, slamming the door behind him and dismissing her without so much as a word.

Willow stood there for a solid three minutes, staring at the dark wood of the door her daddy had shut between them, her hands clenched at her sides. It was getting more and more painful to bite her tongue around him. But she'd been raised with the knowledge that their family was as close to royalty as Havenbrook was ever going to get, her great-great-great-granddad founding it in 1867. Because of that, all four girls had been raised knowing there was an invisible line they needed to toe. And they were, under *no* circumstances, allowed to back talk their daddy—in public or private.

After twenty-eight years, it was ingrained deeply in Willow's psyche. But every time he said something like that, belittling her and cutting her down to size, she got a little more pissed.

And a little more determined to prove him wrong.

With a fire burning under her skin, she turned and stalked toward her office, stopping short when she got into the hallway to find she wasn't alone.

"Finn," she said, breathless. She glanced back toward her daddy's office, then at Finn's face—the tightness of his jaw, the rigid set of his shoulders. There was no doubt in her mind he'd heard what her daddy had said—she just didn't know how much. "What can I help you with?" she asked, polite smile in place.

What she desperately wanted to do was sweep her eyes down his body, take in the clothes he wore, decide if she liked them better or worse than what he'd been wearing last night. But she couldn't focus on holding it together in the face of her father's cutting-down if she got distracted by all of Finn's...*Finn*-ness.

"I see nothin' much has changed with your daddy. Still as much of a dick as his name implies." His response should've surprised her, but it didn't. The hate between the two certainly wasn't one-sided and had never been, and it apparently hadn't waned with time.

"Did you have a question about somethin'?" she asked, walking toward her office. The last thing she needed today was to have her daddy come flying out and get a look at Finn. That was an interaction she wanted to postpone as long as humanly possible.

"Yeah." He stepped close to her, closer than was appropriate for two business associates. Reaching out, he tucked a piece of hair behind her ear, let his finger drop to the side of her neck, resting against her pulse point. "I wanted to see if you got the delivery."

Her shoulders relaxed a fraction of an inch, the dormant butterflies in her stomach once again swirling to life when she thought about what the gift meant. Was he trying to tell her he hadn't forgotten about her, about back then? Or that he was disappointed she hadn't fulfilled her promise to go to art school? But that was a can of worms she couldn't afford to open right now. Instead, she said, "I did. Thank you."

"You still use that brand?"

Given he went out of his way to get them for her, she didn't have the heart to tell him no, so she just bit her lip and kept quiet.

He smiled, though there was still tension in his body. "Always so polite, aren't you? That hasn't changed." His jaw ticked as he glanced toward her daddy's office. "Is that why you let him talk to you that way? You deserve better than that."

She shrugged. "You know that's just how Daddy is."

"That doesn't mean—"

"Did you need anything else, Finn? If you heard him, I'm sure you know I've got a busy day, so I should get to it." She pasted on a fake smile, hoping like hell he bought it—or at least pretended to for her sake.

Finn looked like he wanted to say something, but instead, he clenched his jaw and inhaled deeply through his nose. He gave a quick shake of his head and dropped his hand from her neck. "Nothin' that can't wait."

"If you're sure." But Willow didn't wait for him to respond. Instead, she ducked her head and stepped around him, straight into her office where she had twelve hours of work she somehow had to stuff into seven.

chapter eleven

F inn wasn't sure he'd ever hated another human being as much as he hated Richard Haven. The man was everything Finn despised in a person—arrogant, pushy, narrow-minded, rude. And he'd been that way as long as Finn could remember. It'd been different then, though. Back when he'd been just a teenager, someone good ol' Dick could use his powers to intimidate and persuade and push exactly where he wanted.

It'd been a long time since anyone had been able to do that to Finn. Come to think of it, it'd been since the day he'd left Havenbrook behind. When Dick had made sure Finn had no choice but to leave, he'd sworn he'd never allow someone to do that to him again.

He only wished Willow could say the same.

It'd about killed him to hear her daddy talk to her like that. Finn had stood in the hallway, fists clenched, body nearly vibrating with the urge to *do* something. To step in and intervene. To tell Dick to fuck off once and for all. But if he knew Willow at all, he was certain she'd hate that.

His original intention had simply been to stop by and see if she wanted to grab lunch. See if his little talk at the hardware store had had any effect on her at all. Because it sure as hell had on him. Truth was, since he'd put it all out there, hoping she'd see things his way, he couldn't stop the runaway train known as his desires. He wanted her, with a single-minded focus. What he should've been spending his hours concentrating on was getting the bar up and running, not on the probability of getting another kiss from Willow.

But knowing with complete certainty she felt this pull too, that there was a possibility she'd give him another chance? Well, he couldn't think about anything else. And he'd be damned if he left again without giving this everything he had. Without giving them another shot. He couldn't live with the what-ifs for the rest of his life if he didn't.

"You gonna stand by the window all night like a goddamn creeper, or what?" Drew asked as he strolled out of his bedroom, tossing his keys in the air before catching them.

"She's been out there all damn day."

"Just doin' her job."

"I can almost guarantee planting fresh flowers isn't in her job description." Finn looked out the window again, finding Willow across the square at the cafe, attempting to shuffle the heavy wrought-iron furniture into some semblance of order. No doubt on her daddy's command.

"Yeah, well, her daddy's an asshole," Drew said. "Never did think a woman was good for much else than cookin' and makin' babies. He's probably made Willow sorry every single day that she took that job."

"I don't doubt it."

Drew clapped Finn on the shoulder, then turned to leave. "Gonna meet Nola at Rudy's. You wanna come?"

Go and have a drink while Willow busted her ass for someone who wouldn't even give her a grunt in thanks? Not if you paid him. "Nah. I'll see you later."

"All right then."

The door shut behind Drew, but Finn didn't take his focus from Willow. She still wore her favored business attire —a slim skirt and sleeveless top, the suit jacket she'd had on that morning tossed over one of the cafe chairs. Those siren red heels she still wore called his name. Her feet must've been killing her.

All day, he'd watched her from inside the bar. Watched as she'd flitted around like a hummingbird, her legs carrying her as fast as they could go. First posting flyers around the square for the annual Fourth of July parade she'd no doubt she worked her ass off to make sure was amazing, then filling all three dozen planters with fresh flowers. As much as he'd wanted to go out there and help with her duties, he knew her well enough to realize she wouldn't want it— would, in fact, bite off his head for even offering.

But now, long after he and the rest of the crew had closed shop for the day, she still worked. It was past eight in the evening, which meant she'd been working for nearly twelve hours. Not to mention, she was attempting to heft the heavy, wrought-iron cafe tables where they needed to go, in between wrangling the child-sized playhouses and toys strewn all about from the day care.

Well, he'd had about enough of that.

She'd probably give him a piece of her mind for helping, but he couldn't stand around and watch her bust her ass for another hour when he was perfectly capable of assisting her so she could get it done in fifteen minutes.

It was quiet on the square when he stepped outside. That was something he'd forgotten about, living in California for so long. At this time of night out there, many people were just starting their evenings. Getting ready to go to supper or out with friends. In Havenbrook? The entire town had been shut down for more than an hour already. If you wanted to go out after seven p.m., you did so in Parkersville. Of course, that'd all change once they opened their doors.

Willow was completely oblivious to Finn as he strolled across the square. Actually, she was completely oblivious to most everything but the table currently giving her grief. She mumbled under her breath, agitation and frustration etched in every clenched inch of her body.

Without a word, he went to the other side of the table and hefted his end off the ground. She stumbled a little now that the resistance wasn't there and stared at him, mouth agape. Jesus, even after a day of manual labor, after running around for twelve hours with barely more than a water break, she was still so gorgeous. Her hair was mussed, strands falling this way and that around her face. Her cheeks were flushed the same gorgeous shade of pink they'd been when he'd told her he'd thought of nothing but being inside her again.

And now there he stood, lifting one side of an iron table high enough to hide his hard as steel cock.

"Should I go ahead and move this myself?"

Willow shook her head then stepped into action, lifting her side of the table. "I didn't need your help, you know."

"I know." And he did. She'd spent so much of her life proving herself to people it was ingrained now. The thing was, though, she didn't have to prove anything to Finn. Never had. "Now, where are we movin' these to?"

She paused for only the slightest moment before lifting her chin to indicate an area behind Finn. "Daddy wants them out of the pathway, so they need to stay close to the building."

He had a hundred different things he wanted to say in regard to what her daddy wanted and exactly how few fucks Finn gave about what Dick desired, but that would only start up a shitstorm between him and Willow, and that wasn't how he wanted to play this. Not tonight. Not with her.

They worked quietly for a few minutes, but Finn had been starved for her for so long, the silence didn't last. "You may not use the same brand of paints anymore, but I'm glad to see you *are* still painting."

Willow's eyes shot to his, her brow furrowed. "How do you know I still am?"

He titled his head to the side as they shuffled another table closer to the building. Wasn't it obvious to every single person who walked through the square that Willow had painted the backdrops on them? He lifted his chin in the

134

direction of one awash in color, a single tree in a green meadow, a rainbow sunset as the backdrop. "Wasn't too hard to figure out."

"It's been a long time since you've seen anything I've done. How were you so sure it was mine?"

He smiled, just a slight curve of his lips. "You think I went even a day when I didn't think about your touch? Trust me, I can identify every single thing you've laid a hand on."

She froze for a moment, pausing with the table held a couple inches above ground. Then she shook her head and shuffled forward, her gaze locked on the ground. "That's quite a claim when you haven't been here in years. You don't know me. You *knew* me, once. Not the real me, though. Only the person I showed to everyone else because *I* didn't even know me back then."

"You don't really believe that. I knew you. I *saw* you. Saw everything you tried so hard to hide from everyone else. I wish you'd let me in again, because then or now, nothing much has changed. You're still my favorite."

She blinked at him, seeming to be at a loss for words. Good, he wanted to crack those walls she'd built up. Wanted to take a wrecking ball and knock them all over.

She forced out a laugh as she spun around and grabbed the closest chair to move. "Favorite, huh? I don't know about that. I seem to remember a certain stuffed monkey named Ralph who you absolutely treasured. He even had a better spot next to you on your bed than I did."

He didn't know whether to fall to her feet and hug her or hoot to the heavens. Because try as she might, she *hadn't* forgotten about them. About their history or the dumb little things that made them *them*. It gave him hope like nothing else had.

Making a big deal of looking around, he shot a worried glance over his shoulder. "Hush now, Willowtree. That's supposed to be just between us."

She pressed her lips together, clearly trying to rein in a smile, but it didn't matter that her lips never curved. The laughter sparkled in her eyes.

And he couldn't stay away anymore.

Not stopping until he was close enough to touch her, he did just that, tracing his finger from her temple down her jaw. "We had a lot of things just between us, didn't we?"

Her eyes connected with his, and for the first time since he'd been back, they were open and honest—like a wall had been knocked down right before his eyes. She seemed to realize it too because she turned away, freeing herself from his gaze. "I wouldn't recall. So long ago and all. You understand."

Oh, he understood, all right. Understood she was fighting like hell to keep those walls up. Well too damn bad. He'd knocked one down, and he wasn't going to let her build it back up. Not if he had anything to say about it.

Finn slipped his hands in his jeans pockets and sidled up to her as she walked toward her discarded suit jacket. "Were you able to grab anything to eat while you were workin' down here all day?"

She slid him a glance out of the corner of her eye, the apprehension he would've found yesterday thankfully absent. "You been watchin' me, Finn?"

Dipping his chin in acknowledgment, he met her stare.

"Every chance I get. Don't ever want to take my eyes off you, Willowtree."

The air crackled between them, and there was no doubt she felt it too. Not with how her lips parted, her breaths coming quick and shallow. Under the guise of grabbing her blazer, she dropped her gaze and draped the fabric over her arm. "Not yet. Hopefully Mac saved me some of whatever she made for dinner tonight."

"And if she didn't?"

She shrugged. "Then I guess it's microwave popcorn to the rescue."

The thought of her surviving on microwave popcorn after all she'd done today didn't sit well with him. Not at all. "Or you could come up to my place and I could whip up a couple of your favorites."

He could see the war going on behind her eyes, could see how much she was fighting with herself over her answer. He'd be damned if he made it easy for her to say no. "And, yes, I still remember the recipe—thin sliced bananas stacked on a generous portion of peanut butter with a drizzle of honey. And it just so happens I picked up a fresh loaf of bread today at the store."

She heaved out a sigh, shifting from foot to foot as if the pain had finally begun to register. "I have peanut butter and bread at home, Finn."

"I'm sure you do. But you don't have a Finn at home to make it for you." He reached out and slipped her jacket from her arm before draping it over his own. "Come on, Willowtree. After the day you had, let me make you a sandwich."

Glancing across the square to their new building, she bit her lip. "But Drew——"

"Is out with Nola. He'll be gone for hours."

"I don't know…"

"It's just a sandwich." The look she gave him said he wasn't pulling off that lie. It wasn't *just* a sandwich, and they both knew. "Okay, it's just a sandwich if that's all you want it to be."

She stared at him for the longest minute of his life until finally she dipped her chin in acquiescence. He couldn't stop the grin from spreading across his face, so fucking thankful he was making progress with her. He didn't know if it was because she was too tired to argue, if the thought of trekking home was too much to take, or if it was him…*them*. Honestly, he didn't care as long as it bought him more time with her.

He put his back to her and bent into a crouch. "Hop on." Glancing back in time to see her horrified expression, he laughed. "Hurry up, I wanna get you fed."

"I am not getting on your back, Finn. For one thing, I'm in a skirt. For another, I'm not twelve."

He raised an eyebrow as he stared at her over his shoulder. "Pretty sure we used to do this when you were eighteen, not twelve."

"Yeah, well, I'm not eighteen, either."

"No, you're not. But what you are is tired." He stood and tossed her jacket over his shoulder, then bent and scooped her right off the ground and into his arms.

Willow gasped, her hand flying to the back of his neck

to hold on. "Griffin Reilly, you put me down right this second!"

"What the hell is with everyone middle-naming me lately?" he asked as he took off toward his building. He tried not to think about how amazing she felt, how even after all this time, she still fit him like they were meant to join together. Like they were pieces of the same puzzle. And puzzle pieces, no matter how long had passed since they'd been put together, still linked seamlessly.

"Well, maybe you shouldn't act like a Neanderthal and you wouldn't get middle-named."

"How is me wanting to save you from how much pain you're in being a Neanderthal?"

By degrees, she began relaxing in his arms the closer he got to his building until she was nearly boneless, her fingers tracing small, subtle patterns on the back of his neck. He wasn't even sure she was aware she was doing it, but he was. And his cock *definitely* was.

"Who said anything about being in pain?"

"Don't insult me, Willowtree. Even though it's been a while, I still know you better than most. And I know those two lines between your brows mean you're in some kind of pain. With how you were shifting on your feet, I assumed it was those god-awful—but really damn hot—shoes."

She lifted one leg and glanced down at her red heels with a sigh. "They're my favorite, but they certainly aren't conducive to ten hours of manual labor."

"Why didn't you go home and change?" He shifted her enough to open the front door, then strode toward the back stairs.

"Honestly, Finn, I can walk." She clamped her mouth shut at the look he shot her. "And I didn't go home and change because you know Daddy. No sense in giving him any more ammunition than he already has."

Ammunition, his ass. Anyone else in Willow's job wouldn't have been able to pull off half of what she had. He was absolutely certain of it. He had to clench his teeth and force himself not to say anything about what, exactly, he thought of her asshole daddy. Finn wasn't going to open that can of worms, not now that he actually had Willow in his arms. Now that she was talking to him and not biting his head off.

Once inside his apartment, he strode straight to the couch and sat down with her in his lap.

"What—" Before she could finish her question, he slipped off her shoes, then pressed his thumb into the arch of one foot, rubbing in soft circles as he kneaded the tension away. "Oh Lord..." The words left her on a sigh. She tilted her head back, her eyes fluttering closed as she let out a moan.

And just like that, he went from half-mast to hard as fucking granite beneath her. She was perched directly on top of his cock, and there was no way she couldn't feel it. No way she didn't know exactly how much he wanted her. Though, that wasn't anything new. He'd made that clear at Ty's house and then at the hardware store. And now, if she gave him the chance, he'd make it *crystal* clear to her right there on his couch.

"Feel good?" His voice came out gravelly, the sound just a rough whisper between them.

There must've been something in his tone, because she lifted her head, her eyelids fluttering open so she could look at him. She met his gaze. And, Jesus, she was the most gorgeous thing he'd ever seen. He wanted to spend an hour just reacquainting himself with her lips. Wanted to spend an hour on every inch of her body, just to make sure he didn't miss anything new. Just to make sure he was as well acquainted with her now as he'd once been.

"We shouldn't be doin' this." But her hands didn't listen to her mouth as she reached out and traced his lips, scraped her nails through the scruff covering his jaw.

"I disagree. We should absolutely be doin' this."

"Everyone——"

"I don't give a single shit about everyone. I only care about you and me. You already know where I'm at with this. What I'm feeling." He slid his hand up from her foot, trailing his fingers along the curve of her calf muscle, kneading along the way. "Now I just need to know how *you* feel about it, Willowtree. So tell me what you want. You wanna try this thing with me? See if we've still got that spark?"

They didn't need to *see* anything. The truth was there, glaring as bright as a flashing neon sign. He knew it. She knew it. He just had to wait for her to admit it.

And then the fun could start.

chapter twelve

Oh Lord, what a day this had been. Willow had spent too many hours doing busywork just to please her daddy when she had about two dozen more pressing issues that still sat piled on her desk. Everything she'd had on her to-do list for the Fourth of July parade had been shoved to the back burner simply so she could tend to the issues her daddy thought were more important.

So she'd done everything no one else could be counted on to do. Her normal quitting time came and went, and yet she'd pushed on for hours. Hadn't even had time for more than a package of cheese crackers from the vending machine and a bottle of water.

And then Finn had happened.

She'd been struggling with those godforsaken tables that weighed a hundred pounds, and he'd come strolling along, calm as you please and looking like sex on legs. After the day she'd had, was it any wonder she hadn't put up much of a fight when he'd helped her, made her melt with his words, then hefted her right into his arms and carried her toward a gourmet dinner of peanut butter and banana sandwiches, like some kind of modern-day Prince Charming?

Willow had never needed a man to save her. Had, in fact, prided herself on being self-sufficient, if for nothing else than a passive aggressive jab at her daddy. But after twenty-eight years of being the only one she relied on, she couldn't deny it was nice to just...be. Couldn't deny it was sort of lovely having someone else want to take care of her. And not just want to, but actually push to be able to do so.

Which was obviously why she'd allowed Finn to. After the day she'd had, she'd been tired and exhausted and... weak. She'd said yes when she should've said no. When she should've gone home to her safe little guesthouse on Momma and Daddy's property and binged on Netflix with Mac or took out her sexual frustration on a new painting instead of into Finn's apartment where trouble was bound to turn up.

Trouble like sitting in his lap, being on the receiving end of a near-orgasmic foot rub while his erection pressed into her ass from below. While his breath ghosted over her neck. While simply being that close to him made her ache between her legs, made her clit throb with desire.

And now he questioned what she wanted? Ha! What she wanted wasn't good for either one of them, *especially* her. But Lord, would it feel amazing.

"The spark between us was never in question, Finn, and you know it." She rested her hand on his questing fingers hidden below her skirt, stilling them on her inner thigh. He traced microscopic circles on her flesh, heating her up from the inside out. Every inch of her felt that tiny touch. Every inch of her *yearned* for that same attention.

While they'd been intimate when they'd been teenagers, they'd only slept together once. And though it had been amazing because they'd been in love, she had no doubt he'd learned a few things in the past ten years. A few things she desperately wanted him to put into practice on her. He'd rock her world, undeniably.

"I do know it," he said. With a hand against the small of her back, he pressed her closer. Close enough so he could trail his nose along the curve of her jaw. Close enough to breathe her in before pressing a soft kiss to the space below her ear. "I just wondered if you'd finally accepted it was still there."

Accepted it? Of course she had. She wasn't happy about it, but there was really no getting around it. Their connection was plain as day, from the way her body responded to him to the way his did to her. And after restraining herself a torturous amount since he'd shown up in Havenbrook, she wasn't quite sure she wanted to ignore it anymore.

When they'd been younger, she'd always felt a sort of imbalance between them. He'd been more experienced, the bad boy of Havenbrook, while she'd been a good little Haven girl. And though he'd certainly never taken advantage of her or coerced her in any way, there was no denying he'd always been the one in the driver's seat while she'd simply been along for the ride.

And then he'd left, leaving her crumbling in his wake.

But now... Now, she held every ounce of power in this...whatever this was between them. Even though it wasn't the best reason to start something with him, she couldn't deny she sort of loved it. Loved that this thing would stop or continue based on only a single word from her lips.

And, maybe, after so long of pleasing everyone else, it was finally time she did something selfish. Something just for herself. Something she absolutely, without doubt, should *not* be doing.

The thought sent her stomach tumbling, but she swallowed down her nerves and lifted the pressure she'd used to still his hand. Guided his seeking fingers farther up her leg and deeper under her skirt. "There was never any denying it back then, and there certainly isn't any denying it now."

He sucked in a breath, the ridge of his cock beneath her seeming to grow even harder. His eyes were molten as he stared at her, his fingers at her back clenched tight against her skin while the ones on her thigh were soft. Careful. Tentative. His voice, when he spoke, was low and deep. Raspy. Raw. "Be sure, Willowtree."

Sure? She wasn't sure about a single thing other than the fact that if she didn't feel his hands on her, if he didn't use his fingers to make her come, she'd die. So with a subtle dip of her chin, she sealed their fate.

He dropped his head to her shoulder on a groan and guided his fingers up her thigh until he met the damp fabric of her panties. "*Jesus*, you're wet. You want my fingers, sweetness, or do you want my tongue? Can't say I haven't been dreamin' about tasting your pussy again. Every damn night."

With each word that left his mouth, he kept his touch

featherlight. Teasing her until she couldn't take it anymore. Until every inch of her ached with want and she was desperate to feel his fingers on her with nothing separating them.

"Anything…" she panted. "*Anything.*"

Finn scraped his teeth down the column of her neck, eliciting a shudder from her. "Careful, I might just take you up on that."

Heaven help her, she hoped so.

She gripped his shirt with one hand, the back of his head with the other as he finally, *finally* pushed her panties to the side and allowed them to touch skin-to-skin for the first time in ten years.

"Christ," he groaned, his forehead pressed into her neck. "I thought I remembered what you felt like, but my memories have nothing on the real thing, do they? You're soft as a rose petal. Soft and wet and warm and just aching for my fingers, isn't that right?"

Before she could answer him, tell him, yes, oh Lord, *yes*, he swiped a finger through her slit and used her wetness to trace slow circles around her clit. All the while he watched her with an intensity she didn't want to think about, didn't want to question.

It didn't matter, though. As soon as he slipped a finger inside her, both of them groaning at the contact, all thought promptly left her. Unable to stop herself, she guided his mouth to hers and slid her tongue against his as he pumped his hand beneath her skirt, working her slowly toward a climax.

She couldn't remember the last time she'd gotten off by

someone else's efforts. Months...more than a year, maybe. But even when it'd happened, one thing was certain: she'd never rocked herself so unabashedly against their hand. Had never ground down on them with a single-minded desperation to get herself off, unconcerned with what they'd think or how they'd respond to her wanton portrayal.

Of course, with Finn she didn't have to worry at all about what he might think. His body language said it all. The way he kneaded her ass, guiding her movements as she took his fingers deep inside over and over again. The way he whispered the filthiest things in her ear, how his cock seemed to grow harder with each passing second, with each stroke of his fingers between her legs.

"Come on now, Willowtree. Let me feel you come on my fingers. Let's get this first one out of the way so I can take my time with the rest of you." He sped up his hand as he spoke, his thumb flicking back and forth over her clit even as he pumped his fingers deep inside her. "I wanna spend an hour just kissing your breasts. Get you nice and worked up, then I'll spread those gorgeous thighs with my shoulders and make myself at home between your legs. Better get you fed first, though, because once I get my mouth on your pussy, there's no tellin' when I'll stop. Hours. *Days.*"

The desperation in his voice was what pushed her over the edge. Desperation for *her*. The thought of reducing this hulking man to his knees in front of her, his sole mission simply to please her with his tongue had her clenching around his fingers, his name a constant chant from her lips.

"That's it, sweetness. Give it to me." He groaned, brushing his lips against her collarbone as she did nothing but grip his shirt and hold on for dear life while the longest orgasm known to man or woman ravaged her body.

Finn slowed his hand, though he still pumped his fingers into her, still brushed featherlight circles around her clit as she shuddered and shook in his lap. Good Lord, she couldn't remember the last time she'd had an orgasm that powerful. Couldn't remember the last time she'd come that hard and yet still ached for something more. Still ached to be filled.

But she did. She couldn't deny that any more than she could deny her own name.

Willow knew exactly what kind of trouble she and Finn were stepping into here. There were so many unanswered questions—why did he leave? Why did he stay away? And, number one on the list, what the hell was she doing? But right then, she didn't care. It'd been too long since she'd allowed herself the freedom of doing exactly what she wanted.

In that moment? She wanted Finn. Wanted him with every ounce of her being. Wanted everything he'd promised her while he'd had his fingers inside her. Wanted his mouth between her legs, his cock filling her until she came from that alone.

And for once, she wasn't going to tell herself no.

chapter thirteen

Ten minutes and the separation of their bodies had done exactly fuck-all to settle Finn's raging erection. He was still hard as fucking stone, his cock throbbing behind the fly of his jeans at the mere memory of what Willow's body had felt like clenching around his fingers. His balls hadn't ached this much since he'd last been with her as a teenager. Those months before they'd finally slept together had been filled with fumbling exploration and more blue balls than he could count.

But Christ, it'd been worth it. Every single experience they'd had together had been, if only to see that look on her face as she came from his efforts. And she'd come. Every damn time, he'd made sure of that. If he had his way, she'd come half a dozen more times before the night was through.

Just as soon as he got her fed.

She sat on his counter, hands folded in her lap and legs crossed at the ankles—so prim and proper as if he hadn't just had his fingers inside her. As if she hadn't ridden his hand like it was the world's best toy. Her posture was the only thing prim about her, though. Her cheeks were flushed, their pinkness trailing down her neck to her chest. Her nipples were still hard beneath her silky top, and he wanted them in his mouth with a desperation he hadn't felt in a long damn time. Hadn't felt since he was last with her, actually.

After making her two sandwiches exactly how he remembered she loved, he handed her a plate. "Eat up, Willowtree. Gonna need your strength."

"Thank you. Let's see if your claim to remember how I like them is correct…"

"I think I already proved I remember exactly how you like it." With a wink, he turned away from her flushed face to slap together a sandwich for himself. This combination had never been a favorite of his, but in that moment, he didn't much care. He was going to need the fuel for what he had planned for the rest of the night. Now that he'd gotten a small taste of her, he didn't see himself stopping before dawn. He wanted to strip her down, lay her out on his sheets, and spend hours rememorizing every square inch of her body. Wanted to make her come enough times her moans became the constant soundtrack in his mind.

Willow bit into her sandwich, letting out a little hum of contentment as her eyes fluttered closed. She'd made a similar sound on his couch right before she'd come. Which was to say, the problem in his pants wasn't getting any relief.

"How'd I do?" he asked, his eyes locked on her lips as she slipped her tongue out to catch a bit of honey.

"Exactly how I love them." She took another bite as she stared at him, her head cocked to the side. "How'd you remember all of it?"

"Just because I wasn't here doesn't mean I forgot." He started on his sandwich, demolishing a quarter of it in one bite. "There's not a thing between us I don't remember."

Too much? Probably, if the look she gave him was any indication. But, hell, he couldn't keep his mouth shut about something like that. He wanted to tell her everything that'd happened, all the reasons he'd left and stayed away, but he couldn't do that. Not when she and her daddy were already at odds—and they were. Like nothing he'd witnessed before.

The reason he'd stayed away sat squarely on his shoulders, and he'd have to own up to that in time. But the circumstances surrounding his forced departure lay directly at her father's feet. Her knowing those circumstances would only serve to push her and Richard Haven further apart—possibly even cause irreparable damage. There were few things Willow loved more than her family. He wouldn't come between that, despite the disdain he held for her daddy.

But at the same time, he couldn't stand there and pretend she hadn't meant—*still* meant—the world to him. That he hadn't thought of her every day while he'd been gone. Hadn't wanted to come back to her dozens of times but stopped himself simply because he'd thought it'd been for the best.

What a fucking idiot he'd been.

"Why'd you come back here, Finn?" She held up her hand to stop him before he could answer. "And don't say because of the bar. You could've opened a bar anywhere in the country, and yet you chose Havenbrook. Why?"

He polished off his sandwich and loaded his plate in the

dishwasher, buying himself some time. But, hell, hadn't he just thought he wanted to tell her everything he could? If he couldn't be transparent with her about the reason he left, the least he could do was be honest with her now.

"You're not anywhere else in the country, now are you, Willowtree?"

She froze with her sandwich halfway to her mouth, her eyes wide as she stared at him. And while he was happy to lay his truth out on the line and reveal that part of himself, he didn't want to answer a dozen questions about it. Not just yet.

Besides, he had much better plans for his mouth.

Finn stepped in front of her, uncrossing her ankles and slipping into the space between her legs. Gripping her hips, he slid her closer to the edge of the counter. "I think I promised you some time with my tongue."

"But…" She swallowed, her eyes darting back and forth between his. "I haven't finished yet." She held up the remaining bite of her sandwich.

"And you go on and take as much time as you need finishin' it. I'm gonna feast on somethin' else for a while." Sliding his hands down her thighs, he hooked his thumbs under the hem of her skirt and pulled it up, exposing more of those luscious thighs every second. "Now tell me, sweetness. You still got on your panties under this pretty skirt?"

Goose bumps covered her flesh as she gave a slow shake of her head. "They were too wet, so I took 'em off."

Christ, she'd been sitting up there with absolutely nothing covering her pussy. Absolutely nothing separating them. No wonder she'd crossed her ankles, attempting to keep up a modicum of modesty. No need for that now.

"No panties...not very proper of you, Miss Haven." He tsked in mock disapproval when in actuality his cock positively throbbed inside its denim prison. He slid his nose along the column of her neck, feeling her panting breaths against the side of his face. Placed a kiss against the faint birthmark shaped like Africa just behind her ear. Goddamn, he'd missed that mark. "Can't deny it makes my job easier, though. You go on and finish your sandwich now. This won't take but a minute."

Without waiting for her response, Finn dropped to his knees, the counter the perfect height for him to be eye level with the heaven she held between her legs. He kissed one thigh, then the other, encouraging her to spread those legs a little with each brush of his lips against her. Hands cupping her ass, he guided her forward until she was perched at the edge of the counter, skirt bunched up around her hips, and her perfect pink pussy on display for him.

When they'd been teenagers, she'd only let him do this a couple of times, even when he'd assured her he'd loved it. At the time, she'd been too apprehensive of what she might smell like—*heaven*—and what she might taste like—again, *heaven*.

She wasn't apprehensive now, though. Didn't have a self-conscious bone in her pliable body. Nope, this time when he ran his tongue up her inner thigh, she didn't clamp her legs around his head and keep him at bay. Instead, she spread those beauties wider, welcoming his mouth.

So he gave it to her.

He took a swipe through her slit, soaking in every ounce of her taste. Groaning when her arousal hit his tongue. "Even sweeter than that honey I just had, aren't you, Willowtree? So fucking sweet."

The plate clanged to the counter, and then her hands were in his hair, guiding him, tugging him every which way. Like she wasn't quite sure if she wanted more or less of him.

Well, he'd settle that one for her. *More.* So much more.

Finn brushed his lips along her pussy, fluttering his tongue against her clit, all the while Willow chanted his name and rocked her hips up toward his seeking mouth.

He pulled back, replacing his mouth with his fingers. Tracing every inch of her before sliding them deep inside. "Gonna make you come all over my tongue right here in the kitchen. Then I'm gonna take you into my bedroom, lay you out on my sheets, and do it all over again. A dozen times if you want. A *hundred.* I'll never get tired of licking your sweet pussy. Never get tired of making you come with my mouth."

And then he did. Too worked up to draw this out any longer, he affixed his mouth to her, sucked her straight between his lips, and didn't let up. With his fingers pumping deep inside her, he flicked his tongue against her clit in a relentless rhythm until she bowed off the counter, her fingernails digging into his scalp.

"*Finn…*"

He groaned against her as she did exactly what he'd promised she would. Willow rolled her hips against his mouth as he guided her through her climax. As he drew out her pleasure for as long as he possibly could. And even after, he fluttered his tongue against her, loving how she shuddered under his hands, her fingers soothing in his hair, craving those happy little sighs of contentment falling from her lips.

But Christ, he craved so much more.

With another single kiss to her pussy, he stood, then hauled her into his arms, strode straight toward his bedroom, and kicked his door shut.

"I didn't finish my sandwich."

"I'll make you another one later." He dropped her on the mattress, then reached behind him and yanked his shirt off before tossing it to the side. "You've got me burning up, Willowtree. Got me aching for that sweet heaven between your legs. Need to get inside you before I go mad."

He popped the button on his jeans and slid the zipper down, sighing as his cock finally got some relief. But instead of shoving his boxer briefs down, instead of reaching inside and gripping his erection, he waited for Willow. Lord knew he had no idea why she'd agreed to this in the first place, and he wasn't going to take for granted the fact that she could put the brakes on at any moment. Was, in fact, going to wait for her to give him the go-ahead, no matter how long it took. Even if that meant standing there with balls the color of midnight.

Willow took her sweet time staring at him, her eyes taking a slow trail down his body as they catalogued every feature. And damn if he didn't love that she liked what she saw. That much was clear in how she bit her lip, how she ghosted her fingers across her collarbone. How her nipples were hard enough to be seen through the layers of fabric she wore.

When she finally lifted her eyes to his, hers were so full of desire, he nearly fell to his knees right there. "Well, come on, then. What're you waitin' for?"

WHEN WILLOW HAD WOKEN up that morning, she certainly hadn't anticipated this was where her day would take her. She definitely hadn't imagined she'd end it in Finn's bed after he'd just guided her to her second orgasm of the night, the most recent time with his tongue. And Lord almighty, what a talented tongue it was.

Tension vibrated in every inch of his muscle-packed, inked body, and that only made her feel even more powerful. This man had been waiting for her go-ahead. Waiting for her approval before he did anything. The control was heady, and she couldn't deny how much she loved it.

Now, though, she'd given him the green light, and he didn't hesitate any longer as he shucked his pants, leaving on only his boxer briefs. Though, they did little to conceal the monster tucked beneath. While she'd anticipated his body would fill out in the time he'd been gone, grow another inch or two and develop bigger, thicker muscles, she hadn't anticipated his cock doing the same. There was no denying it had, because Lord knew if she'd seen that beast at seventeen, she'd have run for the hills instead of letting him between her legs.

"You're the prettiest thing I've ever seen, Willowtree. I've never wanted anyone like I want you." His voice pulled her from her thoughts, the look on his face nearly doing her in.

She wanted to brush his words aside, but she couldn't. Not with the way he said them, like they were a prayer...the only truth he knew. And certainly not with how he looked at her, as if she were the only thing he ever wanted to see for the rest of his life.

It was too much and somehow not enough.

She needed to remind them both it was just about sex. She'd been down the heartache path with Finn before, and she had no plans of ever doing it again. "And yet I'm still dressed."

His lips kicked up on the side, though he didn't make any move to close the last step between them. "Gimme a minute, now. Been thinkin' about this for a long time. I wanna enjoy myself." He reached down and cupped himself through his boxers, the action shooting sparks straight to her clit. "You'll let me have my fun, won't you?"

He'd already given her two orgasms without even getting her naked. She'd let him have all the fun he wanted. And if he stood there and stared, that meant she got to do the same. She'd spent so much of her time since Finn had arrived in town fantasizing about what he looked like under his clothes, but those dreams had nothing on reality. His chest might as well have been carved from stone, and she wanted to run her tongue down the ridges of his abdomen. The only other place she'd seen such perfection had been when Mac texted her weekly Instagram models.

But Finn wasn't a model. He wasn't just a picture on her tiny phone screen. He was there in front of her in all his splendid, tattooed glory, and he was hard. For her. He'd covered his skin with several tattoos over the years—a compass low on his abdomen near his hip, part of it hidden beneath the band of his boxer briefs, a map covering from his shoulder down to his right pectoral, a series of numbers directly over his heart—and she found herself wanting to know the stories behind each of them. Wanting to know what he'd spent his time doing. A tiny ache settled in her stomach over the fact that there was a void of time where neither of them knew anything about the other.

And then there was her tree. Even though she'd spent more days than not hating his brand on her body, she couldn't deny how much she loved seeing hers on him. Now that there was nothing blocking her view of it, now that she wasn't incoherent like she'd been at Ty's house, she was certain there hadn't always been so many roots at the base of the tree. She'd drawn that willow tree for him, and she knew it like the back of her hand. He must've added to it in the time he'd been gone, but why?

"You're lookin' at me like I'm somethin' to eat." He pressed his knee onto the bed and crawled up her body until they were eye level.

"Sorry?"

He laughed, reaching up to brush aside a strand of hair. "I don't think you're sorry at all. Lord knows I'm not. You could look at me like that every day for the rest of my life, and I still wouldn't be sick of it. Just gonna make my job a little more difficult, is all."

"What job's that?" she asked, though she already had a pretty good idea. What, since he'd dropped his hand to the hem of her shirt and ran his fingers along the bare skin of her abdomen. Lifting that material right along with his seeking fingers until she arched beneath him so he could pull it up and off.

"It's a job I take very seriously, you know." His breath puffed against the swells of her breasts before he inched down the cup of her bra with his nose. Flicked her hardened peak with his tongue. "Worship every bit of your body, making sure I don't miss a single inch."

She reached for the back of his head, holding him to her, sighing as he engulfed her nipple in his mouth. "That might take a while."

He pulled back and blew against her wet skin as he lifted his eyes to hers, desire written plainly in their depths. "I'm countin' on it."

Taking his sweet old time, he unhooked her bra and tossed it to the side. Slid her skirt down over her hips until it joined the rest of her clothes pooled on his floor. And then she lay in front of him naked for the first time in so long. She thought she'd be self-conscious, being bare with him after so long. She wasn't the skin and bones teenager she'd once been. But from the look on Finn's face, he didn't mind one bit.

He didn't start at the bird on her hip, even though his eyes flicked there several times. Instead, he slid down the bed and lifted her foot, licking a circle around her ankle-bone before trailing his nose up the curve of her calf. He caressed every inch of her, like he could memorize her through touch alone. All the while, he whispered words into her skin—how beautiful she was, how much he'd missed her, how sweet she tasted. And others she couldn't quite make out, but from the way he'd closed his eyes, his lips brushing her skin as he said them, it was maybe better she hadn't been able to.

By the time he'd kissed every inch of her body except where her tattoo sat, she was a puddle of pure need. He ran his thumb over the mark, tracing the outline of it as he lay on his stomach between her legs.

"It probably makes me an asshole for sayin' this, but I love that my bird's still on you. Couldn't bear the thought of you gettin' rid of it. Not when I wear you on my skin too. Not when I look at it every day and see everything we had together."

And, really, what could she say to that? Hadn't she just thought the same exact thing about his tattoo? Before she could come up with a response, he plucked a condom from his night table and rolled it down his length as he settled between her legs.

"You don't wanna know how much I've thought about this."

Probably not. Especially when this was all starting to feel like a hell of a lot more than just sex. "Tell me."

He glanced up at her as he gripped his cock, ran his head along her slit in a slow, torturous circuit that made her quake with need. "It won't scare you off to know I've been thinkin' of it every day I've been gone? Or that I think of you in the shower and my bed? Every time I gripped my cock and got myself off, it was to thoughts of you. Memories of what we did. Fantasies of what I wanted to do."

Scare her off? Lord, no. It should have. It should've been a red flag that she was getting in over her head already, and they'd just gotten started. But though they'd merely begun, she was already in too deep.

"Show me."

He covered her body with his, notching his cock into her entrance. "As many times as you'll let me."

And then he pushed inside, just a slow glide of his cock into her, her body stretching to accommodate his size. Their moans mingled together, the delicious fullness overwhelming her as he continued to thrust inside. Slowly, at first, until she was relaxed enough to take every bit of him. And then, once she started lifting her hips to take him farther inside, he went faster. Harder. Drove into her so deep, she swore she saw stars.

"Finn… Finn." Willow couldn't say anything but his name, over and over again. It was like every other word had been plucked from her head, evaporated along with every other thought except them, together.

He rested his lips against hers, his words getting lost in the breaths mingling between them. "You feel how good we fit, Willowtree? There's nothing as perfect as this heaven, is there? *Nothing.*"

There wasn't, and there was no more denying it. For years, she'd wondered if she'd built up the connection she and Finn had had. Built it up into something so overgrown and complex that it was impossible for anyone else to stack up against. The truth was, though, she hadn't imagined a single bit of it. If anything, her memories had dulled what they felt together. It was magic, pure and simple. The kind of chemistry she saw in movies, read about in books. But it wasn't fiction. It wasn't just something to wish upon.

It was real, and it was them, and it was right there in front of her.

He hooked her legs higher around his hips as his thrusts sped up, his breath growing more frantic against her lips until he groaned and took her mouth in a heated kiss. Sliding his tongue against hers, he slipped a hand between them and thumbed her clit as he pounded into her hard enough to shake his bed.

"Come on, sweetness. Gimme one more. Let me feel you come around me." He nipped at her bottom lip then licked away the sting. "Let me feel what I do to you."

She couldn't deny him anymore. Was damn tired of denying herself. So she gave in. Fingernails digging into his shoulders, she allowed herself to be swept away by him, allowed him to push her up and over the peak, cresting even as he pumped inside her, groaning through his own release.

Minutes or hours later, she trailed her fingers up and down the expanse of his back as he continued to press kiss after kiss along any inch of skin he could reach. It was quiet between them—too quiet almost. As if they were both lost in their own thoughts. And her thoughts? Lord, they were a jumble. But the one thought that kept coming up over and over again was, *what kind of a mess have you gotten yourself into?*

A fine mess, indeed.

chapter fourteen

Willow must've been out of her mind, thinking her body would settle down after it'd had a taste of Finn Thomas. If anything, their being together had lit an insatiable fire beneath her skin, making her crave him when she had absolutely no business doing so. Like in the middle of a workday. In the middle of *every* workday.

After their amazing night together, she'd decided to throw caution to the wind and tiptoe her way into this thing between her and Finn for as long as he was in town. It was quite possibly the dumbest decision she'd ever made, but she didn't care. She was tired of only doing what she was supposed to. Sue her for wanting to do something that felt good…damn good.

Unfortunately, they hadn't been able to get together since the night she'd snuck out of his and Drew's apartment sometime in the wee hours of the morning. She couldn't remember the last time she'd done something like that, tiptoeing into her house like she'd been out doing something wrong. She was a grown woman, for heaven's sake. Did it really matter what she got up to on her own time and if she got up to it with one Griffin Thomas?

"You want me to make a copy of this paperwork before I get it sent off?"

She jumped at Avery's question, like she'd been caught with her hand in the cookie jar. Like her best friend could read all the thoughts—the super dirty, completely inappropriate thoughts—going on in her mind.

Willow cleared her throat. "Yes, please. Thank you."

"You wanna tell me why your face is bright red?"

She averted her attention to her desk and the suddenly very interesting mound of paper clips there. "Not particularly."

Avery snorted, but she didn't push. But, really, if Willow couldn't tell her best friend, what did that say? What was the big deal anyway? Maybe she'd pop over to the bar after work, say hi to Finn and see what kind of progress they'd made inside.

King Construction had been in and out of the building all week, hauling all kinds of material into the place, so she was kind of excited to take in the changes. She was...*happy* for Finn. And she was happy for her hometown. It'd been her mission to revive the heart of Havenbrook since she'd started working for town hall five years ago, and finally, after all this time, her mission was going to come to fruition. She was proud as hell she'd been the one to incite those changes. Made her feel like she was actually doing something with her life and job, actually bringing something back to this town she loved so much.

She couldn't wait to see the changes this brought in

Havenbrook, because she knew in her heart it was a change for the better. Whether or not her daddy saw it that way.

After their discussion—okay, argument—the day he'd come back into town, she hadn't attempted to broach the subject again. What was the use? She'd learned long ago to pick her battles, and that was one hill she wasn't willing to die on. Not since there was nothing her daddy could do about the bar going in. And certainly not since attempting to have a discussion with him was about as fruitful as talking to a brick wall. Except, at least brick walls couldn't talk back.

"Will?" Avery said, poking her head back in Willow's office. "It's about that time again…"

Willow sighed and pushed back from her desk. Mid-afternoon meant it was time to endure another daily meeting with her father. She'd come to dread the afternoons because of them. The meetings did nothing but eat out part of her day…and part of her self-esteem, if she were honest. In all the time she'd been working for him, he'd never once given her a job well done acknowledgment. Nope, all he'd given her was more work and dozens of migraines.

Since Gloria was still out on maternity leave, Willow went straight to his door and knocked, waiting for his bark of a response telling her to come inside.

"What took you so damn long? You're just across the hall, for God's sake."

Her daddy…such a pleasant, soft-spoken man. "After-noon, Daddy. This shouldn't take but a minute, and then you can get back to your business." Which, Willow knew, was absolutely nothing at all, unless you counted playing solitaire on his computer as something important.

"Let's get to it, then. I've got a lot left on the agenda today."

It took every bit of willpower she possessed in her body not to roll her eyes. She made his schedule, and there wasn't a thing on it.

She passed over a stack of papers she'd cleared off his desk yesterday and sorted through to make sure they were taken care of. She found staying three steps ahead of her father saved her a lot of hassles in the end. "We haven't discussed these yet, but I went ahead and got them taken care of. They just need your signature where I've indicated."

He grunted as he took them from her, barely glancing at the papers as he scrawled his name next to the flags. "Mighty nice of you to do something before I had to ask you to." Once he'd signed them all, he placed them off to the side and leaned back in his chair, hands folded over his rounded belly. "I'll have to look 'em all over, of course, but good job getting the jump on something. It's nice to see you workin' hard finally."

Well, would wonders never cease? It might've been back-handed as hell, but was that an actual compliment coming from her daddy's lips? Seemed after five years of busting her butt, he was finally paying attention.

"Um...thank you."

"Now, don't go lettin' it go to your head. I'm just pleas-antly surprised, is all. I thought for sure with those Thomas boys back in town, your attention might be...diverted."

Willow froze, her entire body going ice-cold. She and her father didn't speak about her relationship—past or present—with Finn. Which meant...had someone seen Finn and her together? Or worse, seen her fleeing his apartment well past midnight, which meant they'd been up to only one thing?

"But you're smarter than that now, aren't you?" he continued. "Wouldn't get mixed up with the likes of him now that you're not a dumb teenager, rebelling against her parents."

She breathed out a sigh of relief, realizing it wasn't based on anything but her father wanting to hold her past mistakes over her head. To him, that was all she and Finn had been—a mistake. An act of teenage rebellion, despite the fact that it had been love, plain and simple. An impassioned love her daddy had swept aside as a crush, or worse, an infatuation.

Had it really been less than an hour ago when she'd thought it wouldn't a big deal for her to swing by the bar, maybe go out to dinner with Finn? That was laughable. Her daddy would never let her live it down, would make her life even more unbearable if he even caught wind that something was going on between her and Finn.

The two of them hadn't discussed the details, but if they were going to keep seeing each other, they'd just have to do it on the down-low. Keep it to themselves and not involve everyone in Havenbrook. That'd be better in the long run anyway. Because no matter how she cut this, he was still leaving. At some point, once the bar was up and running and his job here was done, he'd get on a plane and fly back to California, once again leaving her behind.

This time, she just had to make sure he didn't break her when he left.

Having Willow's luck meant she could go all week never crossing paths with Finn, then make a decision to keep their interaction a secret, only to run into him half a dozen times in a single afternoon.

The first time had been the hardest. He'd spotted her and started strolling her way with that Finn grin she loved so much on his gorgeous face. Her daddy had been coming down the steps at that exact moment, and she'd panicked. Just spun on her heels and walked in the opposite direction.

And so it began. If Finn's facial expressions were anything to go by, he'd only gotten more pissed as the day had worn on.

She'd considered shooting him a quick text to give him a heads-up of the situation but figured that particular tidbit of information might be better delivered in person, where she could hopefully plead her case.

However, she did *not* want that in-person discussion to happen in her office, which was why she'd made Avery deal with Finn when he'd come in with a made-up excuse to see her, and why Willow was currently peeking out her office window, holding her breath as she watched Finn storm out of the building. Pissed as hell, thanks to her. Then, as if he could sense her watching him, he looked over his shoulder, straight up at her window.

With a yelp, Willow ducked out of the way just as her office door flew open and her best friend blew in without so much as a hello.

"Care to tell me why I just spent fifteen minutes with

one of the hottest men I've ever seen in real life, when I know for a fact you were perfectly able to take his impromptu meeting?" Avery asked.

Willow settled herself at her desk, straightening a stack of papers. "Um...not particularly."

"Tough shit." Unlike earlier in the day when she'd let Willow off the hook with that phrase, apparently, Avery wasn't going to be so easily appeased. She shut Willow's door, blocking them from the outside world and any chance someone would overhear. Never a good sign. "Your father's gone, and it's after five, which means it's officially quitting time."

"Well, all right then. I'll see you tomorrow."

"Nice try. You're not going anywhere until I get the scoop on whatever the hell is happening between you and Finn."

Willow opened and closed her mouth several times, just praying something intelligible would come out. Something that was sort of the truth, but maybe not all of it. She had to keep a few things just for herself, didn't she?

Okay, that wasn't it at all. What it really boiled down to was she didn't want to hear the *I told you so*'s when Finn up and left again. But it was different this time, wasn't it? She wasn't going into it blind. This time, she had her eyes wide open. She knew what she was getting into, what the end game was, and she wasn't going to be blindsided again.

Willow cleared her throat and avoided eye contact. "I'm not sure what you mean."

Avery gave her The Look. The one she could have trademarked that proclaimed loudly and very clearly that she was not here to take any of your shit. "Then it was just a coincidence that you turned tail and ran away every time you came across Finn today?"

"I did not!" She totally had.

"No? Never mind the fact that I actually saw it with my own two eyes, but your ex-boyfriend just ratted you out."

"Of course he did," Willow grumbled.

"Now, I know you, and I know something is up. Something happened between you two, and I wanna know what it is. And then I wanna know why I had to practically torture the information out of you." Avery's brows drew down. "I thought we were better friends than that."

Well, shit. This wasn't some information-mining mission like Willow would get from Rory. This was Avery, her best friend and biggest cheerleader, and Willow had unintentionally hurt her. Lord, a stake to the chest would've been less painful than knowing that. With anyone else, Willow would've assumed those words were simply a passive-aggressive guilt trip, but not from Avery. She said what she meant and meant what she said—it was one of Willow's most favorite things about her. She never had to wonder or worry about where they stood. And right now, she knew. She'd hurt her best friend.

Willow slipped around her desk and went straight to Avery, wrapping her arms around her. "I'm sorry. It's not you. Or us. I promise."

Avery returned her hug. "So you didn't tell Mac either?"

"Nope, and I have no doubt I'm going to pay for that tonight."

"Well, that makes me feel a little better. But I'm still going to need to know what's going on."

Willow pulled away with a laugh. "Of course you do."

"Seems only fair."

She paced around her small office, her lip caught between her teeth. She just needed to get this over with. Like a bandage. Rip it off and deal with the sting of pain rather than the slow torture of drawing it out. "I, um—"

"Oh my God, you *did* sleep with him!"

Willow spun around, her mouth agape. Was it written that plainly on her that anyone could tell? She'd worried about that when she'd given her virginity to Finn—that somehow, she'd be walking down the street and people would take one look at her and be able to tell. She hadn't thought she'd need to worry about it at twenty-eight, though.

"Don't crush my dreams and tell me he didn't get better with time," Avery said. "Is that why you've been avoiding him? He wasn't able to get you off, and now you can't face him?"

Willow choked on her spit at the same time flashes of their night together flickered through her mind. Oh, he'd definitely gotten better with time. Infinitely. "No, that's not it."

Avery's eyes got wide, and a grin spread across her face. "So he got *better?*" She fell into the chair and patted the one next to her, gesturing for Willow to sit. "Details. Now."

Yeah, it'd probably be better if she were sitting down for this. "It's only happened once..." Okay, that was a lie. It had only happened one *night*, but there had definitely been more than just one round. Technicalities.

"Just from looking at that man, I'd place bets he can do a *lot* during that 'once.'"

Willow tried not to let her memories sweep her away, but she couldn't help it. Not when they were so fresh in her mind. Not when they'd floated through her head more times than she could count—the first time on his bed, right after when he'd taken her in the shower after caressing every inch of her, even when they'd ventured out of his bedroom for a snack and he'd bent her over the kitchen counter and taken her from behind. Drew could've walked in at any moment, which, apparently, had only cranked Willow's engine a little hotter because she'd come so hard, she might've blacked out for a minute.

"Yeah, definitely don't talk about this with Rory," Avery said. "Your sex fantasies are written all over your face."

Shit. Rory. Willow hadn't even thought about telling her. While Mac would be pissed Willow hadn't come straight to her and told her everything, she'd get over it soon enough. With Mac, a conversation about Willow and Finn would be relatively painless. With Rory, it'd be a second version of hell.

"I don't think I have to worry about that. I'd rather strut down Main Street naked than discuss my love life with Rory. *Especially* when that love life contains one of the Thomas boys."

"I don't know—having that conversation with her might actually be easier than talking with Finn himself." Avery propped her feet up on the desk and leaned back in the chair. "He looked *pissed* when he came in here. Though I don't blame him—it was clear as day you were in here but avoiding him."

Willow blew out a deep breath. She wasn't looking forward to that discussion, but it'd have to happen sooner rather than later. She couldn't keep avoiding Finn like he carried the plague. And, truth be told, she didn't want to. But she also knew her original plan of carrying on like nothing was unusual, like she and Finn seeing each other again wouldn't register on the radars of the people of Havenbrook, was a pipe dream.

After five years of busting her ass and doing everything exactly right, her daddy had finally, *finally* bestowed a compliment on her. He was already waiting for her to screw up with Finn being in town. And if she did, he'd waste no time making sure Willow knew exactly how badly she'd messed up.

She wasn't going to go through that again. She'd had enough of it to last a lifetime.

chapter fifteen

E ven days after the best sex of his life, Finn still had a spring in his step. He smiled more freely, laughed a little louder, and felt more relaxed.

Of course, that'd been before his partner in the best sex of his life treated him like he was a damn leper.

All week, he'd been trying to see Willow, but it just hadn't worked out. He, Drew, and Nola had had too much on the docket to allow for much downtime, especially now that they were dealing with bullshit regulations that somehow hadn't been an issue until Dick had arrived back in town. But they were jumping through the hoops, adjusting the bar top height—twice, because, apparently, the first number they'd given had been a *mistake*—and adding more sprinkler heads for the fire suppression system— despite those being inspected and approved already—to name a few.

Busywork. All of it. It was a pain in their asses, but they'd managed to get through it all. There wasn't a doubt in Finn's mind Dick was doing this to try to get them to give up and leave. But what the mayor apparently hadn't learned yet was Finn and Drew *specialized* in making their way through difficult and tricky situations.

The only thing this was in the grand scheme of things was inconvenient, especially given the forward progress he'd made with Willow. If Finn had managed to find a pocket of time and slip away, she'd been unavailable, so they'd had to make do with texts and phone calls. While he hadn't been inside her since that night at his place, that didn't mean he hadn't made her come again in their time apart. And, from her enthusiastic response to those instances, she was having a great time.

Dumbass that he was, he'd assumed that meant things between them were fine. Good, even. But today shot that theory straight to hell.

She'd dodged him. All damn day. And not just dodged, as in kept her head down and pretended not to see him, but actually spinning on her heels and scurrying in the opposite direction when she'd spotted him. Or sitting in her office, hiding behind her shut door while her assistant made up some bullshit excuse about what she'd been doing and why she hadn't been able to see him.

Finn knew what she'd been doing, all right. Avoiding. *Him*, specifically.

"Hey," Drew snapped. "Based on the other shit we're having to redo on Dick's whim, we don't exactly have the funds to put up all new drywall. So how about you stop being an asshole and calm the fuck down."

Finn dropped the sledgehammer he'd been using to demo part of an existing wall and blew out a deep breath as he stared at the carnage he'd inflicted. Yeah, so maybe he'd taken the whole demolition thing a bit too far, but when Nash had mentioned taking down one of the side walls to open up the space and provide a perfect spot for a dance floor, Finn had jumped at the opportunity to pound into some shit. Better than what he wanted to do, which was storm back into Willow's office and demand she tell him just what the hell was going on. Right before fucking her over her perfectly impersonal desk. That'd go over about as well as a screen door on a submarine.

"I've got it under control." Finn wiped his brow with his T-shirt and tucked it back into the waistband of his shorts.

Drew barked out a laugh. "The last thing you are is under control. And I'd place bets on the fact that it has a little something to do with the pretty lady leaving town hall even as we speak."

Finn glanced up in time to see Willow start the trek down the front steps, her gaze fixed on the opened door of the bar. There was no way she could see him from her vantage point, but it was obvious she was looking. He couldn't figure her out. If she went out of her way to avoid being around him all day, why was she peering in his direction? Better yet, why was she purposefully walking so she'd have to pass directly in front of their door when he knew she parked on the other side of the square?

Well, Finn had had his fill of unanswered questions today. It was time to set things straight.

He didn't take his eyes off Willow as he spoke to his brother. "Do me a favor—"

"Yeah, yeah. I'm leaving." Drew's footsteps carried him to the back of the space, then up the stairs to the apartment.

The rest of the crew had left about an hour earlier since they'd been starting the days at six a.m., which meant Finn and Willow would be alone. He waited until she was right in front of the door before he reached out, grasped her wrist, and tugged her inside.

She gasped, stumbling a little as her eyes flew to his before darting around, then looking back out at the square. Goddammit. That was exactly what he'd feared her issue was. She didn't want people seeing them together. And, shit, with their history, he couldn't exactly blame her. Didn't mean he liked being shoved in the closet like he was some dirty secret. Like she was ashamed of being with him.

As one of the Thomas boys from the wrong side of the tracks, he'd dealt with that plenty when he'd been younger. Oddly enough, he'd never gotten it from her. Which meant he certainly wasn't going to put up with it now. Not when he wasn't anything to be ashamed of.

"Finn——" She cut off on a gasp as he spun her until her back hit the wall next to the door.

He stepped in close, crowding her up against the wall. So close her lavender scent filled his nose. Made his mouth water and his cock twitch. He was like Pavlov's fucking dog around her. "Oh, so you *do* remember my name. I wasn't so sure with how you'd been acting today."

She dropped her eyes and glanced off to the side. "I'm sorry, I just——"

"Don't want anyone to know what we're doin'." He stared down at her, hoping with every ounce of his being he was wrong. Maybe he'd misread her. Maybe she *had* just been busy.

But instead of reassuring him, she bit her lip and finally met his gaze, her eyes wide and pleading. *Fuck*. He couldn't say that didn't hurt. Though he also couldn't say he didn't deserve it. He'd been the one to leave, and she'd had to hang around and deal with the aftermath. He didn't blame her for not wanting to go through it again.

Didn't mean it hurt any less.

"Can't say I'm happy about this, Willowtree. Not happy about it at all." He reached up and tugged her lip from between her teeth. "But I understand."

Her mouth dropped open as she stared up at him. "You…you do?"

He nodded then stepped into her until there wasn't an inch separating them. Until she could feel exactly what she did to him merely by breathing. He'd managed to go a decade without her touch, and now that he'd had it again, he couldn't even go a week without burning up for it. He needed her. But more than that, he needed to prove to her she needed him too.

"I didn't make it easy on you back then, and you had to live with the consequences of my choices. But things are different now. I hope you know that."

She glanced away, the apprehension written on her face giving a one-two punch to his stomach. Yeah, he'd have to work on that with her, because he wasn't about to let her worry he'd run away again. Though, really, what did he think was going to happen? The plans were still to stick around just until the bar was well on its way so Nola would be able to quit her job and work full time there. It'd been taking a bit more time than usual—especially with Dick's interference, as well as a lot more details to iron out than any of them had anticipated—but the final goal was still the same.

Eventually, he and Drew would go back to California. And Willow? Willow would stay in Havenbrook.

The thought churned his stomach, but he pushed down the feeling. Didn't have time to worry about that now. What he needed to do was make sure she knew he wouldn't abandon her like before. He might be going, but he'd make damn sure she wasn't in the dark about it. And he'd make damn sure she'd have a hell of a good time while he was still there.

"Okay, we'll work on that," Finn said. "That's on me, and I'm going to prove things to you this time around. While I do, this…us…can stay quiet if that's what you want."

She blew out a deep sigh. "Thank you."

"Not so fast." He gripped her hip and tugged her into him, letting her feel how hard he was for her. "Out there, to everyone else, you can be perfect Willow Haven who doesn't get around with the likes of one of the Thomas boys." He reached up and brushed his thumb over her bottom lip, aching to feel those wrapped around his cock. "But away from prying eyes? You're mine. And you're going to give me everything when we're together."

She didn't say a word, just panted as she stared up at him, equal parts apprehension and arousal written all over her face. He knew her well enough to know she was probably worried about being played for a fool. Again. But one glance at the front of her shirt told him whatever worries she had were fighting hard with her desire. He could work with that. As long as he still had her attraction, he'd prove everything else to her in time.

He'd just have to work extra hard in the little amount they had.

Finn cupped one of her breasts and flicked his thumb over the hardened peak. Then he leaned down, dragging his lip across her jaw until he pressed his mouth to her ear. "I'll be giving you everything too, Willowtree. Don't you worry about that."

No longer satisfied with the feel of her through layers of clothes, he slipped his hand under her shirt, pulled down the cup of her bra, and brushed his fingers over her nipple. Christ, he needed to feel her wrapped around him. Needed to take her right there against the damn wall, surrounded by dirt and dust and God knew what else. He couldn't wait another minute.

"Finn—" She let out a moan and tilted her head back as he kissed and sucked and nipped along her neck, all the while he gripped every bit of her he could reach. "The door..."

Blindly, he reached out and swatted at the main door, finally connecting with it and slamming it shut to keep out any passersby. Couldn't do a thing about the bare windows, but from where they were, tucked a bit to the side, someone would have to walk up and cup their hands around their face to see inside. It'd have to do.

"Any more excuses for me, sweetness?" he asked against her neck, licking up one side and nipping at her jaw.

She panted against the side of his face, her grip on his forearms so tight, her nails left crescent marks on his skin. "None."

Like music to his goddamn ears. "Good."

He thanked the Lord she was in another one of those skirts she seemed to love. He loved them too. Loved seeing her ass showcased in her trim skirts, her long, shapely legs on display. Loved even more that it took hardly anything until he had full access to her pussy. And he was going to take advantage of it.

"You know how many times I've fantasized about this? Dreamed about fucking you against a wall?" He cupped both her breasts as he rained kisses all over her neck and collarbone. "Used to be all I thought about when we were teenagers. Taking you out to the alley after a shift at the shelter, pressing you up against the brick wall, and making you moan my name. Dirtying up all that perfect Willowness. Jesus, the things I wanted to do to you back then would've had your daddy hauling me off to jail. You were always too good for me, weren't you? Still are. Because you deserve to be made love to on a nice soft bed piled high with pillows, but I'm gonna fuck you against this wall like a goddamn animal instead."

"Here?" She moaned low in his ear when he tweaked her nipples, her hips restless against him.

"Right here." He dropped his hands to the outside of her thighs and slid them up, pulling her skirt as he went, until he cupped her ass. Until only a tiny piece of lace covered her from his questing fingers. Her panties were just the right size to hide the sparrow on her hip, and he'd bet one of his balls she bought that style specifically for that feature. She didn't want to see it. Didn't want to be reminded of what they'd had and lost. No, not lost—what he'd ripped from them both.

But he wanted to. *Needed* to.

Finn plucked his T-shirt from the waistband of his shorts and tossed it off to the side, then dropped to his knees in front of her. Gripping her hips, he leaned forward. Placed a kiss directly over her pussy barely hidden behind purple lace. He thumbed down the side of those cock-tease panties until he could see his mark on her. Jesus, what that ink did to him. Made him hard as fucking stone. Reassured him in a way nothing else could. Reminded him what they'd had was real, despite what everyone else had said.

And he'd thrown it all away.

He closed his eyes and leaned forward, scraped his teeth against the black shape before caressing it with his lips, then his tongue. As he focused his attention there, he slid her panties down her legs until she stepped out of them, steadying herself on his bare shoulders.

What a goddamn sight she made. She leaned against the wall, sexy as hell red heels on her feet, black skirt pushed up around her hips, legs spread just enough to let him glimpse at all that delicious pink between her thighs.

Her fingers were restless on his shoulders. "What about Drew?"

"Stop talking about my brother when I'm about to eat

your pussy." With his tongue, he traced a path where her leg met her body, earning himself a shudder from her.

"Finn——"

"That's right. Just my name when I'm licking all this sweet heaven. Don't worry about anything else but how many times you can come on my tongue, all right?"

He didn't give her a chance to voice any other concerns before he lifted one of her legs, tossed it over his shoulder, and fixed his mouth over her pussy. Their groans filled the empty space around them, the tone of hers making his cock twitch. Jesus, had it really been less than a week since he'd tasted her? Since he'd felt her hands in his hair, trying to guide him where she wanted him to go? Since those beautiful thighs had quivered against his face as she'd come?

He hooked an arm over her thigh, sliding his fingers down her stomach and between her legs to hold her open for his tongue. He'd just gotten his mouth on her, but she was already close. He could tell by the way she gripped his hair. How her moans grew more frequent but softer in volume. How she rocked her hips against his face, trying to ride his tongue to her peak.

With his other hand, he gripped her hip and encouraged her movements, guiding her forward and back as he pleasured her with his mouth. She might not be his anywhere but right there, but that was okay. It had to be for now. As long as she gave him every bit of herself when they were together like this, he'd make do. And, while he did that, he'd make damn sure he wrung every ounce of pleasure from her before he ever let her leave his company.

Needing to get inside her before he combusted, he

sucked her clit into his mouth and fluttered his tongue against it at the same time he pumped his fingers inside her to push her over the edge. She gripped his head in her hands as she moaned low through her release, trying to stifle the sound while biting her lip. Christ, what he wouldn't give to hear her scream his name again.

Soon.

He was so worked up, so hungry for her, he couldn't even wait to bring her down. With a final kiss to her pussy, he gently set her leg back on the ground and stood. Goddamn, did he love how proper she looked from the waist up, suit jacket and blouse perfectly pressed, not a strand of hair out of place. But the bottom half told another story. Quivering legs, no panties, a rucked-up skirt, and thighs red from beard burn.

"Not quite sure how, but you get sweeter every damn time." He grabbed a condom from his wallet, thankful he'd had the foresight to add a couple just in case, and pushed down his shorts enough to free his cock. Rolled the latex down his length, giving it a quick tug. "Your legs tired, sweetness? Why don't you come on up here and let me do all the work?" He settled in front of her, cupped her ass, and hauled her up against him, moaning when her wet heat met his aching hardness.

"How do you get me to do this?" she asked, her voice breathless and questioning, even as she hooked her ankles at the small of his back. Even as she groaned in his ear when he ran the head of his cock over her clit. "You make me forget everything."

He pressed his forehead to her neck and notched his

cock at her entrance. Hearing those words, feeling her heat and desire for him, was nearly his undoing. Lips pressed to her collarbone, he clutched her hips and pulled her down on him. Inch by excruciatingly blissful inch. "Then we're even, because you make me lose my mind, Willowtree. Every goddamn time."

Unable to hold back a second longer, he gripped her hips, making sure to keep his hands between the wall and her skin, and thrust hard. Slammed into her over and over again until he didn't know where he ended and she began. Didn't *want* to.

"Missed you," he mumbled into her neck, kissing every inch he could reach. "Missed you so fucking much. You feel how perfect we fit together? You feel that?" He slid deep and rotated his hips against her. "Tell me."

"Yes," she breathed, her lips brushing his ear. Her fingernails dug into his neck, her legs tight around his thrusting hips, like she was holding on for dear life. "Yes, Finn. I've always felt it."

And that was the real kicker. They'd both felt this thing between them, had since day one. The difference ten years brought, though, was he'd been around enough to know how rare what they had was. The kind of connection they shared didn't come around but once in a lifetime. And he'd thrown it away.

Not again.

"Finn...*Finn*," she whispered, her pussy fluttering around his cock as she pulled him to her. Pulled him as close as he could get and fixed her mouth against his.

He fucked her deeper as he brushed his tongue against

hers, thrust into her harder as he worked them both toward their peaks. And when she crested, pulling him right along with her, he knew he couldn't leave again.

He didn't know what he'd have to do. Didn't know how the hell he'd make it happen, didn't even know if she'd welcome him back, but one thing was certain—he was staying. Even if he had to sell his soul to the devil himself, he wasn't leaving again. Not Havenbrook, and certainly not Willow.

chapter sixteen

Willow's plan had gone straight to hell. Though, really, that wasn't necessarily true. She hadn't intended to stop seeing Finn entirely, but she definitely also hadn't intended she'd be sneaking off to all sorts of illicit locations just so they could slip in some kisses and mild groping. It was like they were teenagers all over again. Next thing she knew, they'd be driving out to Old Mill Road and fogging up the windows of his truck like they'd done dozens of times before.

Though she couldn't say she'd mind. Fogging up the windows with Finn had always been worth it back then, and it sure as hell would be worth it now. The man had definitely learned a thing or two while he'd been gone, and Willow was basking in the near-constant glow from being on the receiving end of it.

She wasn't going to think about that now, though, as she sat at her desk in the middle of the day waiting for her family to show up for their weekly lunch date. She could go her whole life without having to explain her flushed complexion to her momma or gran, so thinking about Finn was strictly off-limits.

Her office door swung open, making her startle as if she'd been...well, as if she'd been thinking wholly inappropriate thoughts in a work setting.

Mac popped her head in. "Hey. Nat call yet?"

Willow cleared her throat and willed her red cheeks to recede. At least it'd been Mac who'd happened on her first. Her sister knew every steamy detail of her encounters with Finn—and had ripped Willow a new one for not telling her about them immediately—so Willow's train of thought would come as no surprise.

"No, not yet." As soon as the words left Willow's mouth, a trill came from the computer, indicating an incoming Skype call.

"Perfect timing." Mac tossed her purse on one of the chairs before scooting around next to Willow and perching on top of the desk.

Willow clicked to answer the call and waited for their youngest sister's face to fill the screen. Ever since Natalie had moved away—which had been *the day* she'd graduated high school—they'd done these weekly chats. The Haven women —her gran, momma, and sisters—had always gotten together for weekly luncheons, and had done so for as long as Willow could remember. Seemed it was the one tradition Nat didn't hate.

Of course you'd never catch her actually *at* one of those luncheons, and she always timed the calls so she could avoid talking to the whole group. Willow was pretty sure it wasn't their momma or gran Nat had an aversion to, though. If

Willow had to bet money on it, she'd guess Nat called at those particular times to avoid Rory—those two mixed about as well as oil and water.

"Hey, bitches. What's up?" Nat said before Willow could greet her.

"Blue this time?" Mac asked, leaning down and squinting at their sister's mass of hair. "Shit, Nat, if you keep this up, you're not going to have any hair left to color."

Through a smile, Nat said, "Bite me." She pulled her long hair back and did some sort of magic so it settled into a perfectly mussed up-do. "Sorry I missed our call last week. I had skydiving lessons every day."

Willow just closed her eyes and shook her head. She'd learned long ago there was no talking Nat out of anything she had her mind set on. And apparently this month she was set on death-defying activities.

"How was it?" Mac asked, her voice laced with barely concealed interest. "I've always wanted to try it."

"*Amazing.* 'Course, it helped that the dude I was strapped to was a tall, built, hunk of delicious man meat. Let me tell y'all, you've never had sex until you've had it after falling thirteen thousand feet through the air. My *God*, the orgasms he gave me. Yes, *plural*."

While Willow certainly wasn't a prude like Rory, she also wasn't quite the loose-lipped, free spirit Natalie was. She *loved* talking about what she was getting up to and who she was getting up to it with, and couldn't go a call without giving her sisters a play-by-play.

"Yeah?" Mac grabbed a handful of the candy-coated

chocolates Willow kept on her desk and popped a couple in her mouth. "Whose place did you go to?"

"Why the hell would we wait until we got to one of our places? We were in a field in the middle of nowhere. Rode that man right there like he was a damn horse." Nat leaned closer to the screen and waggled her eyebrows. "He was definitely built like one, if you know what I mean."

That tugged a smile to Willow's lips as Mac barked out a laugh.

"You still seeing him?" Mac asked, but Willow couldn't concentrate on Nat's answer.

Not when a certain someone stood in the outer office speaking with Avery and snagging her attention. A certain someone who'd just happened to have his hand tucked in her panties the night before.

"Well, well, well," Mac said. "Things are about to get interesting."

"What?" Nat asked. "What's happening?"

"Shut up and listen."

Willow wanted to tell them both to shut the hell up and maybe get out. But instead, she just sat there and stared at Finn like she was a starry-eyed teenager all over again. He wore a tight-fitting T-shirt—the same gray one he'd worn on his first day in town if she wasn't mistaken—with thread-bare jeans and work boots. In his arms, he carried a bright pink square box.

He smiled at Avery, then stepped around her and right into Willow's office. "Afternoon, ladies."

"Who is that?" Natalie hissed from the screen.

"Hope I'm not interruptin' anything, but I wanted to pick up that paper you needed me to sign, Willow."

Well, that was a bold-faced lie she hoped no one else saw through. They'd been done with the signatures for a long time. Never mind that she hadn't asked him to stop by at all.

"Swung by The Sweet Spot on the way and grabbed some cupcakes. To thank y'all for your help gettin' everything up and runnin' with the bar." He glanced away to nod toward Avery before locking his eyes back on Willow.

Lord, why did her sisters have to be there right then? She wanted to pull him into her office, lock the door, and kiss the living daylights out of him.

"Oh my God." Natalie again, the loudmouth.

Willow realized she was just staring when Avery cleared her throat at the same time Mac nudged her shoulder. "Um, anytime. It's my job to help."

He stared at her for a moment, his gaze so heated she felt it from her head all the way to her toes and every erogenous zone in between. Then his lips tipped up on one side, and he gave a quick nod before sliding the cupcake box onto her desk. "All right then. I'll catch y'all later. Have a good day."

And out he strode, waving to Avery as he went. Willow barely caught sight of the smirk her best friend shot her since she was too busy watching Finn's ass as he walked away.

"Would someone tell me who the hell that was already?" Nat asked, her voice sharp and exasperated.

"Funny how he never did pick up that mysterious paper." Mac glanced down at Willow with a smirk and plucked the cupcake box from the desk. "Let's see what he brought. Ooh…*gingerbread*! Pretty sure The Sweet Spot only has that in—"

"November," Willow said, her mouth watering. Gingerbread was her absolute favorite, but it was a specialty cupcake the bakery only carried once a year. Which meant—

"Swung by my ass," Mac said. "Finn had to have placed a special order for these. That man is sweet on you, Willow Grace."

"*Finn?*" Natalie asked. "As in Griffin Thomas, one of the trouble twins, the guy who broke our dear sister's heart and made our daddy nearly lose his ever-lovin' mind? *That* Finn?"

Mac inclined her head in acknowledgment. "The one and only."

It was a good thing Mac was speaking for Willow, because she was still stuck on the fact that this wasn't a last-minute thing like Finn had made it out to be. He'd planned to get these for her. Had made a special effort to do so. On top of that, he'd had to have figured out they were her favorite in the first place.

Damn. She was trying really hard not to swoon her pants off for her soon-to-bail-again ex-boyfriend, but it was getting harder and harder when he did things like this. Since their encounter at his bar, he'd done exactly what he'd promised her he would—he'd worked on showing her it was different this time. It'd started with a lunch of her favorite sandwiches magically appearing on her desk the following day when she hadn't had time to run home for a break. And then he'd taken it upon himself to make sure those heavy as hell tables at the cafe stayed where they were supposed to, even though it'd been a constant fight up until then. Now, this. If she wasn't careful, she'd be halfway to falling for him all over again just in time for him to leave.

"Ho. Lee. *Shit*," Natalie said. "I was gonna ask y'all about the rumor the Thomas boys bought the old soda fountain to renovate it, but I guess I don't have to anymore."

"Who'd you hear that from?" Willow asked, finally finding her voice. She was pretty sure she already knew the answer, but it was an easy question to ask and one her sister would answer. Nat and Nash—the person currently helping Finn and Drew renovate—had been thick as thieves growing up. From what Willow knew, they'd stayed pretty close even as Natalie had traipsed all over the world the past several years. There was little doubt he'd been the one to fill in her sister, but Willow was desperate to keep the conversation from her and Finn.

"Nash, obviously, and quit tryin' to change the subject. My biggest concern when I called was finding out if Daddy was losing his shit over those two being back, but I think we have more important things to talk about. Like the fact that one of those boys just brought you cupcakes."

"Oh, he's bringing her a helluva lot more than just cupcakes if you know what I mean," Mac said, taking a huge bite of one of the caramel buttercream-topped beauties.

"Is that right?" Nat narrowed her eyes at Willow. "Somethin' you wanna tell me?"

"Not particularly."

"Maybe it'd help if you were more specific in your questions, Nat," Mac offered. The traitor. "Maybe askin' if she's been havin' any secret sleepovers with a certain someone would get you further."

"I hate you," Willow mumbled under her breath, elbowing Mac's thigh.

"*No!*" Nat's eyes widened, and she shot forward, her face crowding the screen. "Oh my dear sweet sparkling baby Jesus in heaven, tell me *everything!*"

Before Willow could even register they had company, Rory stepped into her office, followed by their momma and gran. "Tell you everything about what? And why don't I ever get Skype calls? I never even get *phone* calls."

Willow snapped her head up and slammed her laptop shut, effectively cutting off Natalie's call. There was absolutely no way she was going to let Nat stay on the line while her momma, gran, and the person set on this earth specifically for the task of making Willow look bad were in the room. Her youngest sister would shout out the details because she gave zero shits about that kind of thing, despite the fact that it wasn't her story to tell.

Willow would have to text her later and apologize, though she knew that wouldn't suffice for long. Natalie would blow up Willow's phone until she finally gave in and answered. And then the pestering wouldn't stop until Willow spilled every dirty detail of what was happening, had happened, and what would happen between her and Finn.

"Nothing. No one." Willow pushed back her chair and stood, smoothing out her skirt. "Y'all ready to go?"

Mac snorted quietly. Out of the side of her mouth, she whispered, "Smooth."

Willow elbowed her in the side and slipped around to the front of her desk, greeting her momma with a kiss on the cheek.

Momma sighed. "I wish Nat would try to time her calls a little better so she could catch all of us. Honestly, that girl doesn't think sometimes. If we hadn't stopped over to see your daddy first, we could've chatted with her."

"Next time." Willow grabbed her purse and shuffled in behind as her momma and sisters filtered out of her office, offering her elbow to her grandmother. "Hey, Gran," she said, bending to press a kiss on her cheek.

"Afternoon, honey." Her grandmother wore a bedazzled track suit—she must've owned a dozen, each one more hideous than the last—her short, dark hair perfectly coiffed from the salon she went to every Monday, Wednesday, and Friday to get styled. As she looped her hand through Willow's elbow, she pursed her lips. "Talked to Maxine earlier today."

Maxine, the owner of said salon, and her grandmother had been best friends for going on seventy years now. And Lord, were they trouble when they got together.

"Oh, yeah? What'd she have to say?"

She hummed low in her throat and slid a look at Willow out of the corner of her eye. "Apparently, one of the Thomas boys placed a special order for some of her grand-daughter's specialty cupcakes."

"Is that so?"

"Mm-hmm. Say, wasn't that a box of The Sweet Shop's cupcakes on your desk?"

Willow nearly swallowed her tongue, her heart speeding into a gallop. She'd been worried this whole time about Finn giving them away, but in the end, it'd come down to Willow turning as red as a tomato in front of her gran and spilling every single sordid detail.

Gran tsked. "Need to give you some lessons on being discreet. For shit's sake, girl, you might as well be wearing a billboard that says *I've been up to no good*."

Willow's eyes grew wide, and she stumbled a bit as they made their way down the hallway toward the front door. The others led the way and were, thankfully, oblivious to their conversation. She opened and closed her mouth half a dozen times, but nothing came out. What the hell could she say, really?

"See? That's what I mean." Gran shook her head. "Worst poker face I've ever seen in my life. And I've lived a long damn time, Willow Grace."

Willow swallowed. "I know you have, Gran."

"Yes, well. About time you got up to some nonsense. Last time was right about ten years ago if I remember right." She shot Willow a side-eyed glance, even as Willow attempted to pretend this was fine. Totally fine. Completely, one hundred percent *fine*. "Oh, relax. I won't tell your daddy. That son of mine could stand to get the two-by-four removed from his ass and have a little fun." She patted Willow's arm and gave her a wink. "Just stick with me, honey, and I'll teach you a thing or two."

Of that Willow had no doubt.

196

WILLOW DIDN'T COME out to Old Mill Road very often—or ever, really. Hadn't had much of a reason to since Finn left. For one thing, it held a lot of memories she wasn't sure she'd wanted to face. And for another, she was a grown woman, and if she wanted to see someone, she didn't need to sneak out to the middle of nowhere to do so.

Except that wasn't exactly true now, was it?

Because despite being a grown woman, she was still sneaking around with a Thomas boy while they got up to no good. Which was how she found herself leaning against the side of her car, watching the breathtaking rainbow of colors as the sun set. The comfort of it, even being out here in the middle of nowhere, was like a blanket wrapping around her.

As soon as she'd slipped back into her office after lunch with her family, she'd sent a text to Finn, thanking him for his delivery and asking if he'd meet her later that night. She hadn't heard back from him. For all she knew, he hadn't even gotten her text or had no intention of—

The rumbling of Finn's borrowed truck on the deserted road cut off her thoughts. He brought it to a stop next to her car, the wheels kicking up a cloud of dust behind it. She couldn't deny how relieved she was to see that beat-up truck. To see Finn slide out of the cab and stride straight toward her, his eyes dark and hungry.

He stopped mere inches from her, his fresh scent invading her lungs as she inhaled deeply. His wet hair confirmed her suspicion that he'd just showered—a fact that, for some reason, just made her want to mess him all up.

This was new territory for them—her making the first move. Asking him to come to her. And Finn proved that by standing there, so close to her but not touching, waiting for Willow.

"Hi." Groundbreaking conversationalist, she was.

His lips quirked up at the side before he glanced around, taking in their remote location. "Been a long time since I've been out here," he said.

She looked around at the clearing, a quiet little spot they'd stumbled upon one night after a shift at the shelter. A small pond—one they'd swum in too many times to count— and an old, long-forgotten barn were the only interruptions in an otherwise giant swath of fields as far as the eye could see.

"Me too." It'd always been their special place, which was why she'd never shared its existence with another soul. Mac didn't even know about it.

Finn's eyes darkened and dropped to her lips as he licked his. "And what made you want to come all the way out here tonight?"

She lifted a shoulder. She couldn't explain it, really. She'd just been feeling the urge to...*be* with him. Not sex—though that always crossed her mind—but be in his presence. Talk to him, learn the things she didn't know, fill in the huge gap of time for which she had no reference. Not knowing how to put that into words, she said, "Just wanted to say thank you. For the cupcakes."

"Swinging into the bakery and grabbing them for you hardly constitutes all this fuss."

"Finn…"

He mocked her tone. "Willow…"

"C'mon now, don't do that." She reached out and wrapped her fingers around his wrist. "I know it was a bigger deal than you're makin' it out to be."

For a long moment, he stared at her thumb rubbing tiny circles along his inner wrist. Finally, he asked, "Are they your favorite?"

"You know they are."

"Then it's no big deal at all." He stepped closer and wrapped an arm around her, bracing his hand at the small of her back. Lord, she got tingles every time he touched her. Tingles that zipped all through her body, pinging this way and that, before settling low in her belly. Building. Growing.

"Why'd you ask me out here, Willowtree?"

"I…I already told you. To thank you."

With his other hand, he cupped her neck, his thumb brushing maddeningly along the underside of her jaw. "Coulda done that in the text you sent tellin' me to come here. Or you coulda stopped by the bar after work. You coulda done it a dozen different ways, but you didn't."

She couldn't very well tell him that besides wanting to be in his presence, she'd also hoped they could take advantage of the secluded location to sate the lust that'd overtaken her. While they'd gotten in some heavy making out and had rounded a few bases during all their sneaking around, the last time he'd been inside her had been that day in his bar. When he'd made her lose her mind right up against the wall. Made her lose her mind and crave him tenfold. The bastard.

"I just… I—" She snapped her mouth closed, swallowing back the words. Saying all that was too much, made her feel too vulnerable when that was the last thing she wanted to feel around him. If this was going to work between them, she needed to stay one hundred percent in control.

Something about her body language must've tipped him off, because instead of pressing, he simply dropped a soft, sweet kiss on her lips, then wrapped his arm around her shoulders and guided her toward the truck. "Sweet as this invitation was, I didn't figure you planned to do much in that tiny toy car of yours."

"Hey, I like that tiny toy car." She elbowed him in the side then glanced at her little Prius. It was perfect for tooling around town and getting her where she needed to go, but it wouldn't serve Mr. Six-Foot-Two very well. And, truth be told, she hadn't thought much past getting him out here so they could be alone. Some planner she was. "Though I guess you're right…"

"Good thing I thought ahead." He dropped his arm from her shoulders and pulled down the tailgate. The bed of the truck was piled high with blankets and half a dozen pillows, a perfect, cozy nest. "What'd you say, Willowtree? Wanna look at some stars with me?"

The words made her pause, made her heart skip a beat. They'd been the exact ones he'd said to her, in this exact location, more than a decade earlier. It'd been their first date, and she'd been such a mix of nerves and excitement, she'd been worried she'd throw up her lunch.

Finn hadn't had much money, and Willow hadn't cared if they'd gone out to eat or to a movie like all her friends tended to do on their dates. Instead, he'd driven them around in his beat-up truck—one so decrepit, she'd prayed it would run long enough to get them back home safely—until they'd found this place. That decrepit truck had lasted dozens of times, taking them from town out to their little pocket of paradise and back again.

Damn. This was bad. *So* bad. She could actually feel her walls crumbling. Cracks and fissures on every surface she'd erected around her heart. Trouble was, even though she knew it was bad, knew it was happening, she had no desire to stop it. She'd spent years feeling nothing more than a mere blip of attraction to a small handful of men. With Finn, it was different, a single star compared to the whole galaxy. It was intoxicating to feel this mix of desire and chemistry again.

As long as she kept things on track, it'd be fine. As long as she kept reminding herself this was temporary, that Finn wasn't there to stay—that their affair would end, again—she'd be fine.

So she smiled up at him, dipping her chin in answer.

"Attagirl." He lifted her straight up into the truck bed before jumping in after her.

"Awful cozy up here, Griffin Reilly." She settled back against the pillows stacked along the cab of the truck, her legs stretched out in front of her. "What, exactly, were you plannin' on gettin' up to back here?"

He lay next to her, the arm closest to her folded behind his head, as if offering his chest for her to snuggle into. Not that she was going to do that. Snuggling was something couples did, and that was one thing they definitely weren't.

"I'm not sure what you're insinuatin', Miss Haven. *I'd* only planned to look at the stars." He pointed to the sky and twirled his finger in an unknown pattern. "Thought we might try to make some dirty pictures out of what we see."

She laughed and followed where he pointed. "That sounds more in line with what I know of you."

He gasped, dropping his hand to his chest as if he were affronted by her words. "*Me?* You're the one who came out here with plans to…what? No blankets in your car, no pillows, no picnic basket, or iPod to listen to." He leaned close, dipping his head down to whisper into her ear. "Were you hoping I'd fuck you up against that tree, or that I'd send you to your knees in the field and take you from behind?"

Sweet Lord in heaven, his words did nothing to abate the burning low in her belly, the ache that'd settled permanently between her legs. She tried not to let her reaction show when she said, "Actually, I thought we might go for a swim."

Finn hummed, not moving his mouth from her ear, and the sound sent ripples of need down her spine. "Pity. I didn't bring a swimsuit."

Funny. Neither did she. They never did—hadn't since the first time they'd done it.

She turned her head so they were nose-to-nose, his warm breath whispering across her lips. "Since when has that stopped you?"

He reached up and brushed her hair away from her face, then trailed a single finger from her temple to her jaw. Leaning in, he nuzzled her neck. "You know what's funny? Everyone thinks you're so innocent, but really you're a terrible influence on me."

She laughed, and he joined along, his puffs of breath tickling her collarbone. When he didn't respond to her original request, she pulled back so he'd lift his head, their noses once again brushing. "So? You gonna let me be a terrible influence on you and drag you skinny-dippin' with me?"

The look he pinned her with said if they did this, they'd be doing a whole lot more than skinny-dipping when they got in that water.

Which was exactly what she'd been hoping for.

———

It was almost midnight before Willow got home, so late the thought that she needed to sneak in to the guesthouse didn't even enter her mind. She slipped out of her car, shut the door, and stepped onto the front walk, head down as she smiled to herself, remembering the feel of Finn's arms around her, his whispered words as he'd taken her in the water under the moonlight.

"Awful late night, honey."

Willow jolted, her head snapping up. Her grandmother sat in one of the beat-up rockers she and Mac had purchased for their tiny excuse for a porch, wearing her housecoat and a pair of scuffed slippers.

"Gran! You scared the livin' daylights out of me."

"Mm-hmm, and I'm sure you bein' jumpy has nothin' to do with you bein' up to no good tonight, isn't that right?"

Willow's face heated, not only from the thoughts that'd just been running through her mind, but from what she'd gotten up to in those thoughts. "What? I wasn't—"

"There a storm somewhere in the county I didn't hear about?" Gran scanned Willow from head to toe, making her feel like she was standing there naked instead of fully clothed. "Better question, if there was, how are your clothes dry, but every other part of you is soaked to the bone? Your hair is positively dripping."

Willow reached up and patted the wet strands. Soaked, indeed. That was because, as prepared as Finn had been, he hadn't thought to bring towels. And as they'd already established, Willow hadn't thought to bring anything but herself. She was a mess. A completely sated, blissed-out mess. "Umm…"

"Mr. Thomas must give out some excellent cupcakes to deal with all this nonsense."

Willow choked on a laugh, her eyes bulging as she stared at her grandmother. There was little doubt *cupcakes* was a euphemism for Finn's dick—something she definitely didn't want to discuss with her grandmother, for heaven's sake.

"Oh, honey, I'm old, not dead. And that's one fine-lookin' man you've got there." She pushed to stand and shuffled her way to Willow, patting her arm as she passed.

The path between here and her parents' house was well lit, so she wasn't worried about Gran finding her way. Still, she said, "You want me to walk you over?"

But Gran just waved a dismissive hand over her shoulder. "Don't worry about me. Go on in, now, before your daddy comes out lookin' for me. And dry that hair before you catch a cold."

Willow stood rooted in place, staring after her grandmother until she slipped into her parents' house, and Willow was out there all by herself. Even though Mac and Avery—and, shit, now Nat—knew about this thing she had going with Finn, she couldn't deny it felt kind of...nice...to have someone else in on it. Especially when that someone else encouraged the madness.

What was it her gran had said earlier? It was about time Willow had gotten up to some nonsense? She couldn't agree more.

chapter seventeen

The long days were starting to wear on Finn. Not to mention the bullshit they continued to put up with thanks to the bastard of a mayor. They'd failed the inspections more times than he could count. So much even Nash, Mr. Easygoing himself, was starting to get pissed.

To make up for the missed time, they'd been busting their asses. Up and working by six a.m., if not earlier, and if he was lucky, he dragged his ass up to the apartment around eight in the evening. Fourteen-hour-plus days of manual labor really sucked the life out of a person. And he was cranky as hell about it.

He and Nash had cut out early since they'd be back later that evening for a quick meeting with Rory. It'd been divine intervention that he and Nola had run into her those weeks ago at the hardware store, because she'd taken it upon herself to help them out of the goodness of her heart. Bossy thing that she was, she'd turned out to be a godsend for them—not only did she know what she was doing, but she was helping them out for free. Which, in Finn's book, made

her damn near an angel, despite the fact that she was definitely a devil to work with.

An incoming text buzzed on Finn's phone. Rory. *Got the
samples in. 8 still work for y'all?*

Finn typed out a quick reply in the affirmative as he
walked out of his bedroom. Drew sat on the couch, typing
away on his laptop.

"Rory's comin' by at eight to show us materials or whatever." Finn bypassed him and headed straight for the
kitchen to throw together a sandwich. "If we still plan to
have the soft opening right around the Fourth of July
parade, we need to get our asses in gear pickin' out
this shit."

Drew grunted. "We'd be a helluva lot further if Dick
would stop with all the damn roadblocks."

He wasn't wrong. Every single one of them had about
had it with the mayor. "Luckily, we've got Nash on our side.
That guy can find his way out of any bit of trouble."

"Trouble in the form of an asshole mayor with a grudge.
If Dick had it his way, we'd have been long gone by now."

Finn didn't have to look up to know Drew was staring
in his direction; he could feel it. There'd been an
unspoken agreement to leave the whole *when are we leaving*
conversation alone. And while Finn had made the decision
that it'd take an act of God to get him to leave again, he
hadn't exactly filled his twin in on it. Though, with the
connection they shared, Finn would be surprised if Drew
didn't already know, or at least have an idea of what was
coming.

"Luckily Dick doesn't always get his way." He finished

off his sandwich in four bites. "I'm gonna call Willow—see if she wants to come over."

Drew narrowed his eyes as Finn strolled back toward his bedroom. "Tell me one thing."

"Yeah."

"Do I need to start figuring out how to get Momma and all our shit back here?"

Finn could lie to his brother, pretend he hadn't already made up his mind. But what was the point? Drew would see through it in a heartbeat. Besides, they'd made it a point their whole lives to cut the bullshit and just go with the truth. "Probably."

Drew hummed low in his throat, as if he wasn't at all surprised. "Good thing I already got started, then, huh?"

"Knew I kept you around for a reason." Finn smiled at the back of Drew's head, then continued on to his room. A weight had been lifted off his chest now that his brother knew his plans. And though they'd never been more than ten miles apart their whole lives, he couldn't deny how relieved he was to know Drew would move back to Haven-brook simply on Finn's desire to do so. His brother could be a real pain in his ass some days, but the truth was Finn would be lost without him.

Once in his room, Finn dropped onto his bed, crooking his arm beneath his head as he dialed Willow's number.

After three rings, she finally picked up. "This is Willow."

He dropped his voice, letting it come out as a low rumble. "What're you wearing?"

She gasped then covered it with a cough. "What can I help you with, Miss Mable?"

"Miss Mable, huh? Last time I checked, my dick was still attached."

"I…I'm certain that's true."

He smiled at her overly formal tone, something she definitely never used with him. "You got someone with you right now?"

"That's right."

"Hmmm…" Finn's smile grew. "This could be fun."

"I'm not so sure about that."

"No? Is it your daddy right there next to you?"

"Yes, ma'am."

He chuckled low. She'd be pissed as hell at him for this, but the opportunity was too good to pass up. "Hey, sweetness. You remember the other night when you rode me in the cab of my pickup because you couldn't wait to get to my place? Just straddled me right there and slid me nice and deep…"

Her breath hitched, loud enough that he caught it through the phone. "I…may recall that."

He reached down and cupped himself through his jeans, rubbing his hand over his hardening cock. "Mmm…then you probably remember how you came all over me too, huh? Shuddered and shook and groaned right into my mouth while your pussy squeezed the life outta my cock."

Her breaths panted into the phone before she cleared her throat. "I'm sorry, Miss Mable, but I'm going to have to get back to you on that."

"Get back to me about it tonight. Come over."

"I'll try."

"Good, I wanna get your opinion on the stain samples for the floor."

A short pause. "Oh, I see."

His lips crooked up on the side. She loved his words as much as she hated them. "And, hey."

"Yes, ma'am?"

"I want a replay of the other night. Need you again, Willowtree."

The smile in her tone carried through the phone line. "I...I'll see what I can do."

Then the line went dead, and all Finn could do was hope she'd show a little mercy to him and sneak by his place for some fun.

HOURS LATER, Finn didn't even let Willow get through the door to his apartment before he pounced. Thankfully, Drew had made a quick run to the store so he could be spared their show, but Finn wouldn't have stopped even if his brother had been sitting right in front of them. It didn't matter if it'd been days or hours since he'd last had Willow in his arms; the urge to be with her again, to feel her under his hands, was too strong to do anything but take.

Willow dropped her purse on the floor just inside the door and looped her hands around his neck as he rained kisses along hers. "This isn't exactly what I came over here for. Thought you needed my opinion on stain for the floors downstairs?"

He walked her backward to his bedroom, stumbling only

a little along the way. Once inside, he kicked the door shut, then reached back to tug off his shirt. "I do. Later." He peeled off her dress in one fluid motion and tossed it to the side, his eyes hungrily taking in every inch of her. Jesus, he could look at her every single day and never get tired of the view.

After shucking the rest of his clothing, he dropped to his bed. Lying on his back, he patted his chest. "Right now, I want you to come on up here and sit on my face."

"Finn!" Her shocked declaration screamed offense, but it didn't stop her from shimmying out of those barely there panties or slipping off her bra. Also didn't stop her from climbing up the bed, her hands running up the length of his thighs as she went, her breath hot on his already aching cock.

He swallowed, the sight of her lips so close to his erection making it twitch. "Thought you were gonna work that pussy over on my tongue."

"I never said that." She wrapped her fingers around his shaft. Flicked her tongue along the underside of his cock, making his whole body jolt with need. "Maybe I wanna have a little fun with you first."

She went straight in for the kill, engulfing his cock without any lead-in. He groaned, long and low, when she sucked him deep into her hot little mouth, swirling her tongue around the head in some kind of mind-blowing move designed to make him damn near lose consciousness.

He swept his fingers into her hair, pulling it back from her face so he could watch himself disappear between those ruby red lips. Her and that heaven-sent mouth drove him out of his ever-loving mind. Forgetting himself for a moment, he thrust up off the bed, his cock going deeper into her mouth as she locked her eyes with his. *Christ*, the sight alone was enough to get him off, but combined with the way she gripped the base of his erection, how she caressed his balls with her other hand, he'd be lucky if he lasted three minutes before shooting off down her throat.

He needed a distraction. He needed *her*.

"C'mon, Willowtree." Finn reached out, like he could extend his arm far enough to touch her thighs. Guide her straight up to straddle his face. "Why don't you come on up here and let me have a taste."

She hummed low in her throat, the sound vibrating along his length and nearly making him see stars.

"Jesus, sweetness, don't do shit like that. Gonna make me come before I give you yours."

Willow sucked up the length of him before releasing his cock with a pop, replacing her mouth with her hands, and giving him the sexiest devil-smile he'd ever seen. "Maybe that's exactly what I want."

He breathed out a laugh, pressing his head back into the pillow and squeezing his eyes shut when she swept her thumb along the underside of his cock and over the head. "C'mon now, you know that's not how it works here. You get yours first, always." His voice was low, gritty. Barely in control. Well, if he had to fight dirty, he would. He wanted her to come on his tongue, and he wanted it immediately. "Don't think I haven't seen you squirming. I know your pussy's wet. Aching. You're just dying to slide your hand between your legs and finger that little clit, aren't you? Come on up here and let me take care of it for you."

His words had the desired effect on her. Her lips parted, her eyes going glassy, and that tight ass of hers wriggled and swayed like she was trying to relieve the pressure between her legs. And then…thank the sweet Lord…she climbed up the length of his body, twisted around, and straddled his face. Lowering that dripping pussy right over his mouth.

"Christ, did sucking me off get you this wet?" He gripped her hips and lifted his head to take a swipe through her slit, licking up all that delicious sweetness.

She moaned, her hand stalling on his cock as she focused on her own pleasure. "That, and a certain phone call may have started me on this path."

"Mmm…then I'm gonna have to call you more often."

"Don't—" She gasped as he sucked her clit between his lips and pumped a finger into her. "Don't…don't stop…"

He smiled around her, certain that wasn't what she'd been planning to say, but he couldn't say he minded. Having her so lost to her pleasure she couldn't throw up future road-blocks was just fine with him. Once again, she engulfed his cock in her mouth, deep suction interspersed with throaty moans.

From somewhere in the distance, he thought he heard his phone going off with an incoming call, but it was hard to tell with Willow's hips rocking over his face and her thighs pressed so tightly to his ears.

Even if it was, he sure as hell wasn't going to answer.

He doubled down on his efforts, sucking her harder, faster, pumping his fingers into her deeper. Driving her further and further toward the edge he knew she was close to falling over.

On a strong pull of her clit between his lips, she gasped, tossing her head back and pumping his cock with her hand instead of her mouth. "Finn...*Finn*."

What he wouldn't give to hear that every night for the rest of his life. She sucked him deep again, moaning around his length...and this time, he was certain it'd been his phone before, as a couple beeps sounded, indicating a missed message.

Attempting to ignore it, he focused all his efforts on her, but it wasn't two minutes before his fucking phone went off again with another text. He wouldn't have cared, but every time that damn sound rang through the room, Willow's once strung-tight body relaxed, like she'd been nearly to the top of that mountain and had slid back down halfway, only to have to climb again. On the fourth trill—and subsequently, the fourth time Willow's body lost the tension of her near-release—he growled and rolled her off him before flipping around and planting himself between her thighs.

"Finn, what— Oh Lord, keep doing that. *Yes...*" She spread her legs wide and reached down, sliding her fingers into his hair and holding on for dear life.

Slipping his fingers inside her, he pumped and curled them, searching for the spot he knew would make her scream. On a soft stroke, she gasped, her hips arching off the bed, and he knew he had it. So he exploited the hell out of it as he flicked his tongue against her clit. None of this slow buildup anymore. His goal was to get her to come before his damn phone went off again.

And she did.

When he sucked her clit between his lips and stroked that spot inside her, she held him close, her moans a high crescendo as she nearly pulled out his hair and pulsed against his tongue. Jesus, was there anything better than making his girl come?

Well, possibly having said girl acknowledge that she was, in fact, his. But other than that, he wasn't so sure anything could beat it.

With a final brush of his lips against her pussy, he climbed up the length of her body, leaving kisses everywhere he could reach, stopping to spend a few solid minutes with her breasts because it'd been at least a day since he'd seen them and that was entirely too long in his book.

"How do you always do that?" she asked, still breathless from her release.

"Do what?" He brushed his lips against one of her hard-ened nipples while she squirmed.

"Turn things around. I wanted to drive *you* crazy for once, and yet I'm still the one who ended up on her back, blissed out of my mind."

Finn could only stare at her for a moment, shocked into silence. Didn't she realize? She drove him crazy every minute—every *second*—of the day, and she was worried he never was?

"Don't you know by now you—" His phone trilled again, three beeps, one right after another. He growled, irri-tation getting the best of him as he snatched his phone from the makeshift nightstand—okay, TV tray. "Should've turned this goddamn thing off."

"Must be somethin' important. Missing out on a hot date?"

He raised an eyebrow as he slid his hand up her leg, tickling his fingers on the underside of her knee. "Not unless we were supposed to be on one and you didn't tell me."

She smiled then, a soft one meant just for him, and relaxed back against the bed. The sooner he dealt with whatever issue this was, the sooner he could be inside her.

He checked his notifications, finding a missed call and voice mail from Rory, followed by five texts. Swearing under his breath, he unlocked his screen and pulled up the messages.

Hey, I left you a voice mail as well, but I need to move up the meet time because the school's putting together a last-minute bake sale fundraiser to help cover the Crawleys' medical expenses from that horrible car accident. Poor family just can't catch a break. I'd like to whip up as many things as I can to help. Can y'all do 6:30 instead?

Finn glanced at the clock. Shit, that was in fifteen minutes. He quickly scrolled through the other messages.

Can you confirm, please?

Hello?

Honestly, I hope your building isn't on fire or anything. I don't want to leave y'all in a lurch, but this fundraiser's important. I need to know if 6:30 works, or I have to cancel completely.

That'll throw off your construction timeline completely, btw, but it's up to y'all.

"Shit." Finn ran his hands through his hair then grabbed his discarded clothes from the varying corners of his room.

"You're leaving?" Willow propped herself up on her elbows, her face a mask of disbelief. And, sweet Jesus in heaven, the sight of her spread out like that, her breasts bouncing with every subtle movement, nearly did him in. He had half a mind to text Rory and tell her to fuck off—nicely, of course—and spend the rest of the evening with his cock buried inside Willow.

But he had to go be an adult. An adult with a raging case of blue balls.

"Your sister's kind of a tyrant." He pulled up his jeans, letting them hang on his hips, before slipping on his T-shirt. "If her interior skills weren't so good, I'd never continue working with her."

"My sis—what?"

"I mean, I know she's always been bossy, but she's taking this bar design thing to a whole new level."

"She does what now?"

Finn glanced up at her as he buttoned his fly. "She's been helping with the design of the bar since our dumb asses didn't think to hire someone. Honestly, she's been sort of a godsend, the tyrant bit notwithstanding. She didn't tell you?"

Willow barked out a laugh and grabbed her proffered

dress from Finn. "No. And she wouldn't. Wouldn't want anything to taint her perfect Rory image."

It took him a minute to figure out why working on a design would taint anything, but when the answer came, it was like a punch to the chest. "Ahh, and workin' with the Thomas boys will do just that. Got it." One would think after all this time, after making something of themselves and using what they now had to the betterment of the town, they wouldn't still be reduced to the damn *Thomas boys*, said with such derision. That they wouldn't be reduced simply to the trouble twins.

"Hey..." Willow must've heard the frustration in his voice, because she stopped the hunt for her panties and came over to him, sliding her hands up his chest and locking her fingers behind his neck. "In the eyes of Daddy? Yes. And you remember how Rory was back then, don't you? A daddy-pleaser to a fault. She hasn't changed—if anything, she's gotten worse."

Finn didn't know if Willow was just placating him, or if she spoke the truth, but he let her words soothe him as he gripped her hips, his cock twitching when he didn't come across any panty lines. "Aren't you always telling me she's constantly lookin' to catch you doing something wrong?"

"Yeah. I swear I think it's her life's mission some days."

"Well..." He leaned down and pressed a kiss to her lips. "Now's your chance to return the favor."

"How do you mean?"

"Since she didn't tell you she was helpin' out, I'm guessing it's because she doesn't want you to know. And she'll be here in ten minutes..."

Willow's eyes widened, then a knowing grin spread across her face. "You're a genius."

When she let go of him and strode toward her panties, he caught her hand to stop her. "Leave 'em off."

She breathed out a laugh, glancing back at him over her shoulder. "You can't possibly be serious."

He tugged her back until she stood in front of him. Placed her hand over his aching cock. "I'm still hard for you, Willowtree. Won't you give me this one tiny thing?"

Finn knew the moment he had her. Her shoulders relaxed, and she melted into him a little, her hand gently stroking against the fly of his jeans.

"*You*, sir, are definitely the bad influence, not me."

"You love it."

For the first time in way too damn long, the look she gave him said she might not just yet, but maybe…maybe someday she could.

And for now, someday was enough.

chapter eighteen

Willow stood in the corner of the open space as Nola, Drew, and Finn all conferred about deadlines and schedules and shipments and everything that still needed to happen before the soft opening around the Fourth of July. She stood off to the side because, for one thing, it wasn't her venture. For another, she didn't know a single thing about what they were talking about. But mostly it was because she wasn't wearing panties under her dress, and that somehow made her feel naked, even though she was perfectly covered. Never mind the fact that her body still tingled from Finn's ministrations, and even though she'd already come, she still ached with need for him. She'd never felt like this before, had never had this unquenchable thirst with any of her past lovers. But, then again, nothing was ever quite like it'd been with Finn.

And that had always been the problem.

"Honestly, I can handle everything just fine, thank you very much." The voice of a snooty princess dialed up to eleven echoed through the space as the back door swung open. Apparently, Rory had arrived.

She stepped into the room, followed closely by Nash, who seemed to ignore her completely and take most of the oversized samples from her arms.

"Didn't you listen to a word I said?"

"Sure did."

Rory huffed. "Oh, really? Then why did you——"

"Y'all about ready to get this started?" Nash called to the trio of owners by the newly completed bar top.

"That was *rude*, Nash King." Rory swept past him, shoulder checking him in the chest as she went. "And I won't forget it."

"Don't imagine you will." He swept out his hand in a gesture that said the floor was all hers. "If you're ready, princess."

From Willow's place off to the side, she could just make out her sister's narrowed eyes and stifled a laugh. Rory didn't take well to people talking back to her, and Willow loved Nash all the more that he couldn't seem to care less.

"There a problem, y'all?" Nola asked.

Rory plastered on a smile. "No, no problem at all." She strode to where Finn, Drew, and Nola all stood, seeming to ignore Nash completely as he hung back, his arms folded over his chest. "All right, now I know y'all are on a tight timeline, so I only focused on products that aren't special order to speed up delivery times." She grabbed a few pieces from the stack Nash had dropped off and arranged them on the bar top. "It's a shame because doing so cut our choices down quite a bit, but I think—" Rory broke off when her eyes finally landed on Willow. "Will, what—"

Four heads swiveled in her direction, Nash being the only other one who didn't already know she was there. She pushed off from the wall and strolled over to the bar, surveying the products on display. Dammit, Rory *was* good at design, if her thoughtful choices were any indication. Couldn't she be bad at *anything*?

"Well, hey, Rory. Fancy meetin' you here."

"What—" Rory cleared her throat, ran a hand down the wrinkle-free silk of her camisole, and darted her eyes to their audience before snapping them back to Willow. "Could I speak with you for a moment, please?"

Without waiting for Willow's answer, Rory grabbed her by the elbow and tugged her into a corner out of earshot from the others as they all looked on with amused expressions. Finn shot her a wink and a smile before turning around and responding to something Drew had said.

"This isn't what it looks like," Rory said, hand smoothing over her perfect chignon.

Willow raised a brow. "No? So it's not you helping out the owners of Havenbrook's very first bar, somethin' Daddy would absolutely despise?"

"What? No, never. I'm here…" She trailed off then leaned closer, her voice dropping low. "Well, I'm here keepin' an eye on things for him, actually. He asked me to—"

"Cut the shit, Rory. Finn already told me."

She froze and blinked, either from Willow's choice of language or what she'd revealed. Finally, Rory huffed and crossed her arms. "All right then, you caught me. But that doesn't answer the question of what, exactly, you're doing here."

"You're right, it doesn't. But you've always been the smart one, so I'm sure you can figure it out."

Rory glanced over Willow's shoulder toward Finn, a single, perfectly shaped brow lifting in question. "Have to say I'm surprised you're okay with me knowing about that. You don't exactly share things freely with me."

Willow would have to be oblivious not to hear the hurt in her sister's voice, but she'd played this game too many times before to fall for it. She snorted and rolled her eyes. "And I wonder why that is, Miss Perfect. Sisterly bonds never meant much to you so long as whatever dirt you had on us got you in Daddy's good graces. I can't count the number of times you tattled on the three of us. And it looks like that's comin' back to bite you in the ass."

Rory's back went ramrod straight. "Wait just a second, now. You don't have to go tellin' Daddy."

"I suppose I don't. But in that same breath, neither do you. Mutually assured destruction is so *sisterly*, don't you think?"

"You can't ask me to lie to Daddy."

"No? Great, then I'm sure he'll be very happy to learn his eldest and most perfect daughter's been helping his nemesis and the rest of the people he thinks will ruin his fine town. Can't wait to tell him all about it!" Willow spun around, her sights on the door, though she hoped with everything she had Rory would stop her. Tattling on her sisters wasn't her style, but if she had to use it for leverage to get Rory to agree not to do the same, then so be it.

She wasn't quite ready for her daddy to find out what she'd been getting up to with Finn again. Not when they were so close to the Fourth of July parade and her big yearly event. Not when he'd finally given her praise. Not when he was close to finally recognizing her worth around town, seeing that she brought something of value to their namesake. In her daddy's eyes, being tangled up with Finn would only damage that, despite the fact that she'd been doing her job just fine.

Rory didn't let her get three steps before she wrapped her fingers around Willow's arm and tugged her back. "*Fine*. But if I'm gonna be lyin' to Daddy, then I better get somethin' else outta this."

It was probably too much to ask that her sister just do it out of the goodness of her heart. She'd participate in every fundraiser under the sun, be the first to pass around a get-well card or send a casserole over to a new momma, but she didn't have quite the same generosity toward her sisters. Baby steps, and all that.

"Bonding with your sister isn't enough?"

Rory rolled her eyes. "You know what I mean. Just...we can help each other, all right? Cover for each other, maybe, if we need to."

Willow tried and failed to keep her mouth from dropping open. "You, Aurora Jane, first daughter of Mayor Richard Haven of Havenbrook, want to strike up...a *lying* bargain?"

"Well, you don't have to make it sound so scandalous. I

just thought—"

"Deal." Willow grabbed Rory's hand and shook it before she could offer any stipulations. "Fair warning: I'm telling Mac."

"That's not fair!"

"Why not? You're going to tell Sean. I don't have a husband, so Mac it is."

Rory's body language went cold as she snapped her mouth shut and averted her eyes.

Odd. "Hey, is everything—"

"Fine, you can tell Mac. But absolutely not Nat. I have to draw the line somewhere. Girl's got a mouth bigger than an eighteen-wheeler, and she doesn't care who knows her business—or *ours*."

"Agreed."

With a clipped nod, Rory stalked back toward the group waiting by the bar, immediately diving into a spiel about stone samples for the front of the bar surround and matching it with an accent wall to give it a nice pop.

Well, that was easier than she'd thought it'd be. Half of her expected Rory to recant on their agreement and run off midsentence, straight to their parents' house, and spill everything that'd make Willow's life a living hell. But she was going on a bit of blind faith here. This was a chance for her and Rory to grow closer, and she got the distinct feeling her sister needed it even more than she did.

As Rory spoke, Willow sidled up next to Finn, no longer able to deny the relief she felt whenever another person found out about the two of them. It made her giddy…and a little foolish. Reaching out, she hooked her finger around his pinkie. He slid her a look, his lips tipping up at the corners at what could be considered the subtlest touch by anyone's definition. But to Willow, her pinkie hooked in his felt like a proclamation from a mountaintop.

She wasn't quite ready for that. Wasn't sure she'd ever be. Not when Finn was still leaving and heading back to California. But maybe it was okay in this small circle of people—people Finn trusted. And if Willow couldn't trust her sister to have her back, she had more problems than the fury her daddy would rain down on her if he ever found out she was tangled up with one of the Thomas boys again.

Rory glanced over then, cutting off midsentence as her eyes dipped to where Willow's finger was hooked in Finn's. For the briefest moment, Willow swore she saw longing cross her sister's face. A second later, the perfect Rory mask was back in place, and all was right in the world.

WILLOW SAT ON HER PARENTS' back porch swing, her sisters flanking her. They'd gotten a bit of a reprieve from the heat wave, and a nice breeze—warm as it was—made the evening June air almost tolerable, especially with the chorus of cicadas singing and frogs croaking, the sounds of her childhood making her feel at home. Their weekly family dinners were as carved in stone as the girls' lunches, and the four of them—three, now that Nat had left—had always sat outside after supper and cleanup. It'd been the one time they felt close, even if they weren't.

After a few moments, Mac finally broke the silence.

"Can't quite figure it out, Rory."

Rory stiffened but kept on her calm-as-a-cucumber mask. "What's that?"

Mac leaned forward so she could see Rory around Willow. "Why you're helpin' the Thomas boys. And don't worry—I'm not gonna rat you out." Mac rolled her eyes as though the idea were ridiculous. Which it was, especially from Mac—she was the most loyal person Willow had ever known.

Rory was quiet for a minute, just the creaking of the porch swing filling the silence. "I'm... I've been thinkin' about maybe using my degree."

Willow snapped her head to stare at her sister in shock. Yes, Rory had gone off to college to get a degree, but Willow had always assumed it had just been for show. That her sister had no real desire to do anything but be the perfect wife and mother—something she was exceptionally good at. "You have? Since when?"

Rory shrugged, keeping her gaze straight ahead. "Couple years."

"*Years?*" Mac asked, astonishment ringing in her voice.

"Since Ella started school and I didn't need to be around as much. But I—" Rory snapped her mouth shut and shook her head.

Willow glanced back at Mac and gave her a *what the hell* look because you could about knock her over with a feather. She'd never in a million years dreamed her sister would actually be *longing* for something. Just went to show not everything was always as it seemed. Mac just shrugged and shook her head in response.

Willow turned back to her older sister. "Well, I think it's…"

"Dumb," Rory said. "It's dumb."

Willow reached out and placed her hand on her sister's arm. "No, Rory. I don't think it's dumb at all. I think it's great."

Rory twisted her head in Willow's direction, her mouth dropped open. "You do?"

"I really do. From what I've seen at Finn's, you're good at it—*really* good at it. And it's about time you did something just for yourself." Willow'd always thought Rory had felt completely fulfilled being a wife and mother, but maybe that hadn't been it at all. Maybe her sister longed for things she didn't think she could have…just like everyone else.

Mac leaned forward to peek around Willow. "Have you talked to Sean about it?"

Rory straightened, her lips pressing into a tight line. "No. Which is why I'd appreciate it if this could stay between the three of us."

Willow and Mac exchanged another look—they'd definitely be talking about this once they got home. But for now, Mac answered for them both. "As long as you've got Willow's back, we've got yours."

That look of longing Willow swore she'd seen on Rory's face at the bar swept over her features once again. "You two always were the closest, weren't you? I know you think I'm impossible most of the time, but it was tough growin' up as the oldest. Tryin' so hard to please Daddy when he wanted somethin' I could never be. No matter how many tests I aced or how many trophies I brought home, he'd never get his boy." She kept her gaze on her leg as it pushed off the porch, gently rocking them back and forth. "Sometimes I wonder if I went from one overbearing, insensitive know-it-all to another."

Without trying to give away how shocked she was, Willow slid Mac a look out of the corner of her eye. Her younger sister shrugged, clearly at a loss, same as Willow. She'd always assumed her sister and brother-in-law's marriage was perfect, just like everything else in Rory's life. But maybe Willow had been so busy *wanting* to see that perfection so she could hold a grudge that she hadn't really paid attention to what was there.

"Is everything okay between you and Sean?"

Just as fast as the conversation started, it ended. "What? Of course. Everything's just fine. You know who you should be worryin' about is Trish Parkins. Poor girl's workin' three jobs just to keep a roof over their heads while her deadbeat husband drinks all day. Honestly—"

Willow tuned out as Rory expertly shifted the focus from herself to others who seemingly had more problems weighing them down. And now that Willow really thought about it, her older sister did that an awful lot. Maybe she wasn't the annoying gossip Willow assumed she was. Maybe she was just as confused and lost as the rest of them but was desperate not to show it to anyone.

Honestly, Willow was…relieved. For the first time in as long as she could remember, she finally felt a connection with her older sister. Rory didn't have it all together? Welcome to the club. Willow might as well be president.

chapter nineteen

W illow sat in her office the following week, sorting
through the mess of papers her daddy had piled
on her head. Like she didn't have enough to do, now that
they were mere days away from the Fourth of July parade.
But, like always, Willow took the extra load with a smile and
shuffled everything else around so she could make it work.
She always, *always* made it work.

A knock sounded at the outer office door, then the
quiet rumbling of voices between Avery and whoever had
come in, but Willow was too lost in her spreadsheet to pay
much attention. She had a tight budget to work with for
any and all events, and the parade was no exception. No
matter how she crunched these numbers, she was still
coming out in the red. Which meant she'd have to dip into
her own money to foot the bill for some of the items.
Again.

"Looks like someone has a secret admirer." Avery
strolled into Willow's office, a gorgeous arrangement of
Stargazer lilies hiding her face. She set the vase on the

corner of Willow's desk and raised her eyebrow. "You decide to go public?"

Willow's heart skipped a beat before tumbling into a gallop, her stomach bottoming out over the prospect of her and Finn's pseudo-relationship getting out. "What? No. No, we—" She shook her head and snatched the card from the arrangement.

It didn't say anything—it was simply a rough sketch of a willow tree. And while there weren't any words written on the white notecard to give away who the sender was, it might as well have been an ad in the newspaper for as loud as it screamed to her.

"Finn?" Avery asked, slipping around the side of Willow's desk to peek at the card.

"Ohh...what a pretty arrangement!" Edna, their mail carrier, stepped into Willow's office and handed Avery the stack of envelopes. "I didn't know you were seein' anyone, Miss Willow."

"What? Oh, I'm not. It's just—"

"Oh my heavens, that's even better! A secret admirer. How lovely!" She braced her hand on Willow's desk and leaned forward, her eyes sparkling with interest. "Do you know who it might be?"

If Rory was a gossip princess, then Edna was the queen. The woman spread it around their town like bees spread pollen. There was no way in hell Willow was giving her even an ounce of information. Thankfully, her best friend was well aware of the gossip title Edna held. She was also a master at diversion.

"That sounds like that Hallmark movie you were telling

me about last week." Avery stepped around the desk and placed her hands on Edna's shoulders, turning her around and directing her out of the office. "What was the title of that one again? Maybe I'll watch it tonight."

Willow breathed out a sigh of relief as Avery diverted Edna's attention. The gossip queen and Avery chatted for several minutes about some romantic comedy while Willow just sat and stared at the drawing on the card, her fingertip running over the slight indentation from the pen.

She'd thought she and Finn had a good thing going. While it wasn't ideal, it worked for them. And it worked for *her*, which, to be honest, was her top priority after how their first relationship had ended. She didn't think Finn had minded the sneaking around, but if this was anything to go by, he did. Or, worse, he just didn't care that *she* cared. She'd told him point-blank they needed to be discreet if they were going to start something, and he'd readily agreed. So much for that promise.

The more she thought about it, the more hurt she got. It was like he was playing with her all over again. By the time Avery stepped back into Willow's office, she was good and frustrated.

"I can't believe he did this."

Avery snorted. "Yeah, what an ass. Sending you flowers. You want me to key his car?"

Normally, Avery's sense of humor could defuse even the tensest situations, but Willow didn't want to hear it now. "You know that's not what this is about. He's not supposed to be spreadin' it all around town."

"I hardly think sending you flowers is spreading it all around town."

"No? How do you think he got those flowers?" She held up the card with the sketched willow tree. "He drew this, Avery, which means he had to walk into the shop and order them. Give them my name for the delivery. And now Edna of all people knows about it. I'll be lucky if I don't have a line out my office by the end of the day, people wantin' to know my business."

"Honestly, Will, I think you're overreacting just a bit."

Before Willow could tell Avery exactly how much she *wasn't* overreacting, her cell phone rang. Rory's name and photo flashed on the screen. Willow wanted to believe it was about the bar reno, or maybe about their dinner they had scheduled for later in the week—something they'd never done before, but something Willow was actually kind of excited about. Since their talk on their parents' back porch, things had shifted between the three of them—shifted for the better.

But even with all those possibilities, the *probabilities* weighed on her as she swiped to answer. "Hello?"

"You'll never guess what I just heard."

Willow swallowed, closing her eyes and saying a quick prayer it wasn't what she feared. "What's that?"

"Apparently you've got a secret admirer."

She let out a gusty sigh. Dammit. She didn't want to be right, just this once. "Who told you that?"

"Edna. Honestly, I don't know how that woman gets any mail delivered. I swear she just speed-walks to the nearest warm body whenever she gets her hands on some juicy gossip. Mrs. Thompson stopped by while Edna was tellin' the story, and now they're talking about a pool as to who the possible suitor could be."

"Oh my Lord."

"Anyway, I just wanted to warn you about what they're sayin'. In case you didn't already know."

"Thanks, Rory."

"I thought y'all decided to keep this quiet?"

"I thought so too. Apparently Finn needs a reminder."

Willow hung up with her sister and lifted her brow in Avery's direction. "Still think I'm overreacting?" Without waiting for Avery to answer, Willow pressed Finn's number on her phone and hit send.

He picked up after the second ring, a smile in his voice. "Hey, Willowtree. You get my delivery?"

She clamped her teeth together. He couldn't even *sound* remorseful? She wasn't sure which hurt worse—the fact that he'd ignored her wishes or that he didn't seem to care that he did. She took a deep breath, attempting to keep the emotion from her voice. "Yes, I got it, and half the town already knows about it. There's a bet going on about who my *secret admirer* is. You agreed we'd keep this quiet. You *promised*."

Clanging came through the line, the far-off noise of a saw, before it quieted, like he'd walked to another room. "Wait…are you *upset?*"

So much for tamping down that emotion. "*Yes*, Finn, I'm upset. How did you think I was gonna react to you goin' back on a promise, not to mention half the damn town discussing my love life?"

"I didn't—shit, Willow, it wasn't my intent to break the promise. I wanted to send you somethin' nice, and I just thought—"

"I'm pretty sure you *didn't* think. And that's the issue. We had a deal. Keep this quiet, period. And you agreed to that."

"Feels pretty damn quiet to me with you sneaking in and out of my apartment at all hours of the night."

"Yeah? Well, it doesn't feel so quiet to me when half the town's placing bets on who I'm seeing. They're going to find out."

A noise of frustration came across the line. "And, apparently, that'd be the worst thing in the world. For the good people of Havenbrook to know Willow Haven is sullying herself with one of the Thomas boys. Again."

"Don't turn this back around on me, Finn. That's not fair."

"Seems pretty clear to me that's exactly what it's about. Doesn't matter that I've made something of myself. Doesn't matter that we're takin' a building no one else wanted and finishin' the revitalization of your precious downtown. None of it means shit, isn't that right? Not when I've got Thomas tacked on the end of my name."

Willow's ire died a little more with each word coming out of Finn's mouth, reminding her of what he'd said in his apartment the other day. She'd mentioned it was just her daddy and sister who'd thought that, but was she really any better? Her once-heated temper cooled until it was nothing but steam, and she felt each of Finn's accusations like a spear through the heart. While she was worrying about her daddy finding out about her and Finn, he was dealing with years of shit that'd been heaped on him because of his teenage rebellion, or worse, simply the stigma of being born with his last name.

"Finn, I'm—"

"I gotta go. I'll talk to you later."

"Wait—" But the line was already dead, so all Willow could do was stare at her phone, her stomach somehow churning more now at the thought of hurting Finn than it had when she'd thought the whole town would know her business.

"I take it that didn't go over well?" Avery asked.

Willow stared at the phone and blew out a sigh. "I don't know what to do. He wants something I'm not ready to give. Not after—" She swallowed, not quite ready to say the words aloud. *Not after he left me all those years ago. Not when he's going to leave me again.*

"Look, I'm not going to pretend I understand what you went through back then. Your relationship with Finn is hella complicated, and your worries and concerns are completely valid."

"Why do I feel a but coming on?"

"But…" Avery reached forward, tapping her nail on the drawing of the willow tree. "He's sweet on you. I feel like you're carrying too much baggage from the past to see it for what it is. And, really, who cares if people know you're together? You're a grown-ass woman and can make your own decisions. Even if your dad doesn't want you to realize that."

Willow finally gave life to the one thing that'd been

weighing her down since she dove headfirst into this thing with Finn. "He's leaving, Avery."

"Yeah." The main phone rang, and Avery stood and strolled to the edge of the office, glancing back before she stepped out. "But wouldn't you rather have something real while he's here than spend the next ten years wondering what could've been?"

Willow stared down at the card again, replaying Finn's words in her head. Hearing the tinge of hurt lacing them. They were at an impasse—both of them wanting something the other couldn't give. And Willow could admit that now—that she wanted Finn as much as she'd wanted him when they'd been teenagers. What she felt for him had never truly faded over time. With him being back, with them spending time together, those feelings had only blossomed and grown.

And now there she was, almost exactly where she'd been back then: in love with a Thomas boy who had no intention of staying in Havenbrook.

WHY COULDN'T THERE BE any demo left to do? The one day Finn could really use it and there was nothing. Not even a fucking nail to pound in. Instead, he grabbed a paint roller and went to town. Wasn't quite the same as breaking shit with a sledgehammer, but it'd have to do.

He certainly couldn't do what he wanted, which was go over to town hall and give Willow a piece of his mind before kissing the ever-loving shit out of her. If her phone call was anything to go by, him actually showing up would give her a coronary.

He'd been trying damn hard to prove to her this time was different. Ever since their talk a couple weeks ago, he'd made an effort. Except it hadn't really felt like an effort at all because what he was doing made her happy. Or so he thought.

This morning shot that theory straight to hell.

He'd woken up and decided to send her flowers on a whim—her favorite and something he'd never been able to afford to get her when they were teenagers. Nola was friends with the owner of Bloom, so he'd asked her to do him a favor. *Technically*, Willow's secret admirer everyone was going on about was Nola. She'd brought him the card which he'd drawn on, and he'd given her the money to pay for them, but the order and delivery instructions had come from her.

Which Willow would know if she'd given him a damn second to explain.

"*Dude*. What the fuck is wrong with you?" Drew asked. "You've been stomping and huffing since you got off the phone."

Finn had half a mind to tell his brother to fuck off, ignore him altogether, or blow smoke up his ass, but none of it would be any use. Drew would bother Finn until he came clean—might as well get it over with.

"Willow is what's wrong with me. She's fucking with my head." He tossed the roller into the paint tray and linked his hands behind his head. Jaw ticking, he paced back and forth next to the bar top. "She doesn't want people to know we're together again, but with the way this town is? Do you know how fucking difficult that is? I get it and I'm tryin' to respect it, but I'm walkin' on eggshells around her—around *everyone*—when all I wanna do is grab her and kiss the hell out of her in front of the whole damn town."

He blew out a deep breath and dropped his hands. "When it's just us, it's amazing. Better than it was back then, even. But whenever other people are thrown in, she's colder than a walk-in freezer. And forget about doing something nice for her! Bites my damn head off. Jesus, I love the girl—you know that—but it feels a helluva lot like this whole thing is one-sided."

The sounds of saws and power drills filled the space as Drew stared at him. Then his shit of a brother let out a booming laugh. "You're such an ass."

"What the fuck."

"Man. Seriously." He shook his head and clapped a hand on Finn's shoulder. "Good job, you did a few nice things for the girl you're in love with. Someone get this guy a cookie," he called over his shoulder.

"Why are you being a dick right now?"

"Because I'm the only one who's gonna give this to you straight. Yeah, you're doing nice shit for her, and that's great. But *you left her*," he said, enunciating every word. "I think you forget how much you broke her. You're lucky she can even be around you without kicking you in the nuts. And she took your ass back!

"Now just imagine for two fucking seconds what it'd feel like if she picked up and left you. Right now. Just packed her shit and bailed without a word. No goodbye, no reason, not even a fucking note to tell you why she'd gone or where she went off to. You with me?"

Drew didn't wait for Finn to respond before he continued. "Now imagine being an eighteen-year-old girl who'd just slept with a guy for the first time, and then he bailed shortly after. Man, you should thank your lucky stars she can even *look* at you. So, yeah, you've got some shit to deal with. I don't care if you give her the whole fucking galaxy every day for the rest of your life—she still doesn't owe you any favors, and she certainly doesn't owe you a free pass. You wanted her back, and now you're bitching about having to earn it? C'mon now. Don't be a dick."

Drew shook his head. "If you ask me, I think you did a shit thing back then—you know how I felt about it."

Finn narrowed his eyes, curling his hands into fists. That was a shitty move to play, and he didn't appreciate it. It wasn't like he'd run off into the sunset. Between what Dick had forced upon him and their sick momma, he hadn't had much of a choice. "I did it for Momma."

Drew nodded. "I know you did. And even if I could, I wouldn't want to go back and do it differently, because it allowed her to be with us now. But it also doesn't change the fact that it was a shitty thing to do. You could've handled it a hundred different ways, but you didn't. And now, comin' back here? You fucked with her head again. Have you even told her we're plannin' on stayin'?"

Finn crossed his arms over his chest, his jaw ticking. His silence was answer enough for his brother.

"Yeah, thought so. Look, man. I'm glad you two are back at it—you deserve someone who makes you happy, and

Lord knows she does. But here's the thing: you're gonna have to keep climbing those fucking mountains every day to win her over. To *continue* to win her over, just to prove you're not that same nineteen-year-old jackass who left her without a word. Every damn day, for as long as she'll let you. That's all I'm sayin'."

Power tools continued to whir in the background as Finn stared at his brother, letting his words sink in. *Dammit*, he hated when Drew was right.

"Wow."

Finn and Drew both turned to find the source of the voice. Nash stood several feet away, drill in hand, his attention locked on them.

"What?" Finn and Drew said at the same time.

Nash shook his head. "Damn, that was some straight-up Lifetime channel shit. You been spendin' your time watchin' talk shows, Drew?"

"Fuck off. You're supposed to be workin'. Go fix shit."

Nash's laugh boomed over the sound of his drill whirring, and he turned his back on them.

Before Finn could thank his brother for being a dick, for giving him the kick in his pants he needed, his phone buzzed in his pocket. He pulled it out, expecting to see a message from Nola or maybe Momma. Instead, it was from Willow.

I'm sorry. Can you get free tonight? Tree house at 9?

Finn's pulse pounded in his ears. He hadn't been in the tree house since the night he'd slept with Willow for the first time. Walking home from there had been when everything had started on the downhill slide into a pile of shit. Her daddy'd seen him sneaking back to his car late that night, his shirt on backward and inside out, hair a disheveled mess, leaving very little question as to what he'd been getting up to with the mayor's baby girl. Dick had taken it about as well as could be expected. He'd promised Finn his time with Willow was coming up, but, with the untouchable air of a cocky nineteen-year-old, Finn hadn't believed him.

He should've.

Drew stepped close and glanced down at the screen, his brows lifting once he'd read the text. He clapped a hand on Finn's shoulder. "She's meetin' you halfway, man. Don't fuck this up."

No way in hell did he plan to. Looked like he had some work to do.

chapter twenty

I t'd been a long time since Willow had made the trek to
her childhood tree house. Truth be told, she had no idea
what kind of shape it was even in. It'd been years since she'd
been back. It'd just been too difficult, climbing up there and
being immersed in the kind of memories she and Finn had
made there once upon a time.

But she also knew she needed to extend an olive branch,
and she figured this was the best way to do it. She'd screwed
up with him that afternoon. He was trying, attempting to
prove himself to her all over again, and she needed to give
him credit for it instead of biting his head off for doing
something nice for her.

She'd *really* felt like an ass when Avery had done some
sleuthing and found out it hadn't even been Finn who'd
placed the flower order, but Nola. If any of the Havenbrook
busybodies found out that tidbit, it'd be easy enough to
brush off as a thank-you gift for all of Willow's help in
dealing with the red tape surrounding the bar renovation.
So Finn *had* taken her reservations into account and had

found a way to work around them. And Willow had spat all over his gift. A gift that, as she'd had time to gain some perspective on the situation, meant the world to her. He'd thought enough of her to let her know she was on his mind, and he did so with her favorite flowers. Which she knew for a fact she hadn't mentioned since he'd been back. He was trying to prove himself to her every day, and it was time she got out of her own way.

Besides that, Avery had been right—Willow was a grown-ass woman, and it was about damn time she started caring less about what her daddy thought and more about what she actually wanted.

Dusk had settled in fast, and while there wasn't much to be scared of in good old Havenbrook, and even less on her family's acreage, she still walked a little faster as she hurried toward her destination, her phone's flashlight guiding her path. Their daddy'd had the tree house built when Willow had been only three—too young to go in it then. It perched in a thicket of trees, far enough away from the main house that she and her sisters had always felt a sense of independence whenever they'd played there.

Although considering what she and Finn had gotten up to in there, perhaps building it such a distance from the house hadn't been her daddy's brightest idea. Even before she and Finn had slept together, they'd done *everything-but* enough times to lose count, all in that hidden-away place in the trees. But that night… Willow smiled to herself, the memory sitting bittersweet in her chest. She'd been scared and nervous, but he'd been so gentle. So giving. So loving.

He'd made her come twice before he'd even slid inside her, just to make sure it was good for her.

At the time, she'd thought they had the world at their feet—that they'd go off to college in Nashville, start a life together.

Days later, he'd been gone.

She shook away the memory as she tucked her phone into her pocket and climbed the ladder into the tree house. Finn had only sent her a short *I'll be there* response, so she couldn't even begin to guess what his reaction to her apology was going to be. For all she knew, he was going to tell her to take a hike. That this, as fun as it'd been, was over. That it was too big of a hassle to continue with anyway, given he was leaving soon.

The thought pierced her chest, leaving a hollow ache in her heart.

But she wasn't going to think about that now. Finn leaving had been a foregone conclusion. Their relationship would end the same as before. The only difference was, this time, she'd gone into it with her eyes wide open. When her heart broke open again, she'd have no one to blame but herself.

As soon as her head crested the tree house floor, she looked up and gasped. Inside was a fairy wonderland. Hundreds of white twinkling lights draped down from the peaked ceiling before flowing down the walls and bordering the windows. Lush pillows and blankets covered every square inch of the floor. In the center of the space sat a picnic basket with a bottle of wine and two glasses.

And in the corner stood Finn. "Hey."

Willow climbed the rest of the way, not able to stop gawking at what he'd done. There was no way this space had been in any semblance of decency as of this afternoon. As far as Willow knew, no one used it anymore—she and her sisters were too old, and Rory's kids were too busy with their twelve-thousand extracurricular activities to ever take advantage of it.

"What—when…" She shook her head then locked her eyes with Finn. "Why did you do this?"

His long legs ate up the space between them, and then he stood in front of her, his body heat seeping into her bones. He reached out and linked their fingers together, resting his other hand on the curve of her neck. "I was an ass."

"You—*what*? No, *I* was the ass. You did something lovely, and I threw it back in your face. I'm sorry."

Finn was shaking his head before she'd even finished speaking. "Don't steal my thunder, Willowtree. It'll screw with my seduction plan."

She laughed, her head tipped back as warmth filled her chest. She felt…content. For the first time in so long, she was happy. As much as the lead-up to the Fourth of July parade depleted her energy, she loved this part of her job. Like the entire town was her canvas—a living, breathing creation. On top of that, her daddy had finally started to see her worth, she was getting along with all her sisters, and her love life wasn't a pile of ash like it'd been for so long.

"You're so fucking beautiful." Finn brushed his thumb down the column of her neck, his breath warm on her lips. And then he dipped lower, bringing their mouths together.

She sighed into his mouth, loving how seamlessly they fit. How he knew exactly where to touch her, exactly the speed to go, exactly the words to whisper to make her melt into a boneless puddle of need at his feet. That wasn't something you could teach, something that developed after years of intimacy—it just was. Pure, raw chemistry.

And they had it in spades.

"You hungry?" His words rumbled against her neck as he rained kisses there, punctuating them with licks and nips with his teeth.

"Not for food."

He groaned, the vibration sending a shiver down Willow's neck and shooting straight to her nipples. They hardened beneath her tank top, ached for his hands or his mouth or both.

"You're making it damn difficult to give you the romantic replay of that night—the one you deserved that I couldn't give you then."

She pulled back and cupped his face, the couple days' worth of scruff scratchy against her fingertips. "You can romance the hell out of me. After."

He placed his hand on the small of her back, pulling her in until their bodies were flush. Pressing her against the hard ridge of his cock. "Last chance, Willowtree. You gonna let me be a gentleman, or what?"

Finn and gentleman didn't belong in the same sentence, especially in regards to the bedroom—or tree house, as it were. And that was one of the many reasons she loved him. He took what he wanted without apology, doled out pleasure like candy, and she was ready for every bit of it.

Stepping back, she gripped the hem of her tank and pulled it up and off, leaving her bare under his gaze. One of the benefits of having small breasts—no need for a bra. Something Finn definitely approved of, if his heated gaze and low growl of appreciation were any indication.

For two breaths, neither of them moved, both frozen, and then it was like something snapped in each of them. They crashed together, hands grappling with clothing, peeling layers off until they were both finally bare. Tripping over the picnic basket, they tumbled into a pile of pillows in the corner, their mouths never breaking.

Finn swept his tongue against hers, his hands roaming her body, exploiting all the places that made her weep with pleasure. When he grazed her clit, she tipped her head back, a moan lodged in her throat. Once he slid his fingers deep inside her and rocked his palm against her, that moan broke free, her hips lifting to meet his hand.

"Ahh, you are hungry for it, aren't you? My greedy girl."

Willow groaned, her head tipped back as he sucked her nipple deep into his mouth, his fingers still working their magic inside her. She was already close, though she shouldn't have been surprised. Finn had a way of wringing every ounce of pleasure from her body—pleasure she didn't even realize she was capable of reaching.

"You're gonna come all over my fingers, aren't you? Christ, can't wait to feel that pussy squeezing my cock. C'mon, sweetness. Give it to me so I can slide nice and deep." He pumped his fingers into her harder, faster, his palm a constant pressure on her clit.

Three more thrusts and she peaked, her body going

taut, her breasts jutting out to meet his tongue as she pulsed through her release. Struggling to catch her breath, she managed to get out, "Finn…" But he knew what she wanted. What she needed.

Sometime while she was lost in her bliss, he'd sheathed himself with a condom, and then settled his weight between her thighs, his cock nudging her entrance before he slid inside. The girth of him stretching her, just this side of painful.

"Sweet fucking Jesus, how does this pussy get better every time you let me inside?" He pulled out, soft and slow, letting her feel every generous inch of him before he snapped his hips forward and drove deep. "Anyone who says heaven isn't on earth's never been inside you, have they?"

Willow couldn't answer—how could he expect her to? Especially when he sat back and propped her ankle on his shoulder, his hips rolling forward, sliding him even farther inside with each thrust.

"Look at you, taking me so deep. That sweet, pretty pussy spreading wide around my cock." He turned, pressed his lips to her ankle. "Tell me how much you love it."

"So, so much," she managed to get out through panting breaths.

He stared at where they were joined, his thumb brushing in a mindless pattern against her hip. Except when she glanced down, he wasn't tracing something random on her skin. And he wasn't watching where he disappeared inside her. Instead, his thumb traced the sparrow at her hip, his eyes locked on it, lips parted.

She reached out, brushing her fingers down the wispy

leaves of the willow tree on his side. Caressing each winding path of the roots. Her heart swelled as she split her gaze between those black marks on his skin and his focused stare on her tattoo, the reverent way he traced the mark, the soft words of adoration spilling from his lips.

And hell. She'd known this would happen. There hadn't been a doubt in her mind when he'd come back, when he'd focused his attention on her, that they'd end up here. That *she'd* end up here. In love with a Thomas boy who wasn't going to stick around.

She was so screwed.

FINN ROCKED INTO WILLOW, a slow roll of his hips, wanting to do everything in his power to prolong the pleasure of being inside her. She traced his tattoo with her fingertips and shot sparks off under his skin, hardening his cock even more.

For years, he'd imagined this—had hoped he might one day be with her again, but he'd never actually thought it'd happen. He couldn't believe he was lucky enough to be experiencing this with her again. That she'd not only let him inside, but welcomed him. Time and time again.

It was, quite literally, his dream come true.

On a sharp thrust, Willow curled her fingers against his side, her nails digging in as her eyelids fluttered closed and a moan slipped from her lips. He couldn't help how his cock swelled at the proof of how much pleasure he brought her. That he was the one wringing those moans from her, the one she squeezed with that tight as hell pussy.

"Is it good, sweetness?"

"Oh *Lord*. So good." She dug her nails into his side, trying to pull him closer.

He bent forward, pushing her leg toward her chest and opening her up to take him even deeper, eliciting a gasp from her. "You okay, Willowtree?" He pulled nearly all the way out before sliding inside, a slow glide of skin on skin, the tight fist of her pussy nearly driving him out of his goddamn mind.

"Don't stop."

"Never," he promised, meaning it more than she could know. He was never, ever going to stop with her. Not again. He'd made that mistake once, and it would haunt him for the rest of his life, even if she did take him back for good. And, just like his brother had pointed out to him, he'd spend every day for as long as he was breathing trying to make it up to her. Proving his love. Because it was real and true, and he wanted her to feel it. To know it. To never, ever doubt it.

"Finn—" She cut off on a moan, her eyelids fluttering closed as she pulsed an erratic beat around his cock. "I'm gonna…"

"Come all over me, I know." He hummed low in his throat and kept up his rhythm, making sure he grazed her clit with every deep thrust. Making sure to keep her on edge, push her right where she needed to go. "You're gonna strangle my cock, aren't you?"

She gasped and opened her eyes just as her pussy tightened around him, staring straight at him while she started to come. Dropping her leg from his shoulder to hook over his elbow, she pulled him closer, fusing their mouths together as she reached her climax.

It didn't take but three more thrusts into her pulsing heat before he pushed deep and spilled inside her, her name moaned between them as they kissed through it all. His heart full to bursting.

Later, they faced each other, Finn in his jeans and Willow wearing nothing but his shirt. Doing a damn good job of driving him crazy. She sat with her legs crisscrossed, which meant if he looked—which he was trying hard not to —he'd see all that gorgeous pink heaven between her legs. But if he went down that path, he'd be fucking her on the floor of the tree house again, and he'd be no better than his nineteen-year-old self.

He was desperately trying to be better than his nineteen-year-old self.

"I'm going to start to think this is the only thing you can make." Willow bit into the peanut butter and banana sandwich he'd brought. It didn't exactly pair with her favorite red or the candy bar—also her favorite—that was waiting for dessert, but this wasn't about an exquisite culinary experience. It was about showing Willow he knew her—then and now. He listened when she spoke, and he remembered everything about her.

He smiled over the rim of his wine glass. "I better rectify that soon, then. Name the day, Willowtree, and I'll cook you a three-course meal."

"Will one of those courses be these sandwiches?" She held up the sandwich in question, her brow cocked.

"I see the skepticism written all over your beautiful face, sweetness. You wound me."

She laughed, a tinkling sound that filled up the intimate space. "Sorry, I don't mean to tease. It's just hard."

He raised a brow, because, yeah, he was definitely hard. Had been even though it'd been less than half an hour since he'd come inside her.

She pursed her lips and rolled her eyes. "I have no doubt *you're* hard. Honestly, are you ever not?"

"When you're around? No."

"What I *meant* was it's hard picturing you, wearing an apron and flittin' around the kitchen."

"I do not *flit*. I stomp around like a manly man." Finn finished off his sandwich as Willow laughed. "And if you want to know about the apron, you'll just have to accept my invitation."

The statement was innocent enough, but it hung between them, weighted. By the look on Willow's face, she realized exactly what he was asking. Her inviting him here was an olive branch. That she'd share this with him again after what'd happened last time meant more than he could articulate. He just hoped it was a step toward what he wanted with her: permanence and public declarations.

"I..." Willow averted her eyes as she took a sip of wine, and his heart dropped. She wasn't going to accept, and Finn would have to decide if he was okay with that. If he could live with taking whatever small bit she could give, whenever she could give it.

The answer, of course, was an unequivocal yes. Without doubt, he'd take whatever she was willing to give him.

"Okay." Her soft voice filtered into the space between them, and Finn jerked his head up, snapping his eyes to hers. She was already staring at him, looking gorgeous as hell, even more stunning now that she'd basically said yes. Yes, to him. Yes, to them.

Unable to hold back anymore, he shoved everything between them aside, slid his hand around her neck, and brought her face to his, claiming her mouth in a kiss.

"I won't let you down," he said when they finally pulled apart. He meant more than just the meal—he only hoped she realized it.

She trailed her hand down from his neck to his chest, tracing the rough sketch of a map and the coordinates that just happened to be this exact location. "Will you tell me about these?"

"What do you want to know?"

"Everything?" She dropped her fingers to the willow tree on his side. "It's weird, feeling like I still know you so well but having this gaping hole in time where I know nothing."

His chest ached, regret over costing them so much time nearly consuming him. "I know what you mean."

"Question for a question?" she asked, reminding him of a time long ago when she'd sat in his beat-up truck and said the same thing.

"You first." He shifted to lean back against a stack of pillows and lifted his arm, hoping she'd settle in to his side.

She didn't disappoint. Once she'd snuggled in, she traced one of the twisted roots over his hip bone. "There are more roots here than when you left. So many more."

He'd been waiting for this, had wondered how long it'd

take her to ask about it. He pressed his lips to the crown of her head. "That's not a question."

She pinched his side and tilted her head back to meet his gaze. "Tell me about it?"

Reaching up, he brushed the hair back from her face, stroked his fingertip down the slope of her nose, around the outline of her lips. "That first year..." He swallowed, averted his gaze, and guided her head to rest on his chest again. Thinking it'd be easier if she wasn't staring at him with those beseeching eyes. "On your nineteenth birthday, I was in a bad place. I fuckin' *missed* you. Every day, but especially that day. I passed a tattoo parlor on my way home, and I didn't even think—just pulled in. Hoped like hell they had an opening. I got the first root added that night. The others happened every year on your birthday."

She was quiet for a moment, then she whispered, "Why?"

Would it be too much to tell her it was the only thing he'd had of her when he'd been gone? That he'd craved that connection, even when he'd been the one to sever it? Probably.

"Uh, uh. My turn, sweetness."

She huffed, pinching his side again. "Well, come on, then."

There was really no question what he wanted to ask. The same thing he'd been desperate to know since he'd found out she'd moved back to Havenbrook after college. "Why're you back here, Willowtree? Why didn't you go to Nashville and do what we planned? Are you as happy here as you would've been there?"

255

"You think if you shove three questions together real fast it'll only count as one?"

"Umm...I was sorta hopin' it'd work like that, yeah."

"Cheater." She didn't put any heat into the insult, though. "I'm here because it's my home, and leavin'—much as I yearned for it then—felt...wrong. And, yes, I'm happy. For the most part. I have good days and bad days, same as anyone, I suppose. But I really do love what I do—or I do when I'm not doin' the work of three people. Revitalizing the square..." She shook her head against his chest, her deep breath brushing across his skin. "Seeing it come to life because of what I did? It's like a living, breathing canvas."

He waited for her to answer why she'd hadn't gone to Nashville like they'd planned, but when she didn't, he nudged her. "And?"

"And...it's your turn for a question." She turned on her side and propped herself up on her elbow, using her other hand to trace the numbers over his heart. "Coordinates?"

He swallowed, watching her as she stared at his skin. True, he'd only added to her tree on her birthday, but every other tattoo he had on him was a tribute to her in some way. The map and coordinates reminding him where his home was. The compass because she was his true north. "Yeah."

"Of what?" She looked up at him then, her lip caught between her teeth.

Reaching out, he tugged her lip free, brushed his thumb across it. "This. Here."

"Here?" She furrowed her brow. "The *tree house*?"

"The one and only."

Her mouth dropped open, her eyes full of something he couldn't quite name. "Finn—"

"My turn. Tell me about Nashville."

She looked like she wanted to argue, wanted to press, but then she shrugged, dropping her gaze. "Nothing to tell. You left. I withdrew my admission and went to MSU instead."

"Because?"

"Because…what I thought I wanted wasn't the same without you there too."

Damn, this hurt. Getting all this out in the open was good for them, but he couldn't deny the way his stomach clenched over all the time they'd lost. All because of the decisions he'd made—decisions he hadn't been given much choice over, but his all the same.

"I'm sorry, Willowtree." He cupped her neck, needing to feel her any way he could. "Even though it won't give us back the time we lost, I want you to know I'm sorry. And not a day went by when I didn't think about you. About coming back to you."

She stared at him for a moment then opened her mouth, no doubt to ask why the hell he didn't. Before she could do so, he pulled her toward him. Pressed his lips to hers and waited for her to melt into him. Hoping with everything he had that her doing so meant maybe, just maybe, forgiveness would come eventually.

chapter twenty-one

After round two where Finn had taken Willow nice and slow, trying to show her in every kiss, every roll of his hips how much he still loved her, he walked her to her house, their fingers linked between them. It'd been a long damn time since he'd done something as simple as holding hands—in fact, the last time had probably been with Willow.

Considering how much they'd shared in the tree house, it was no wonder they walked the path in silence until they got to her front porch, the soft glow of the outside light illuminating her face.

"Thank you," she said, her finger hooked in his belt loop. "For tonight."

"Anytime." He curled his fingers around her nape, brushing his thumb along her jaw as he pulled her in for a kiss. Their lips met with a spark, that always-evident chemistry between them coming to life as he slid his tongue along hers, pulled her body tight against him.

Jesus, how could he be ready to go again? This girl drove him absolutely fucking crazy in the best possible ways.

Panting, she broke away and dropped her forehead to his chest, her hands resting on either side, his shirt clutched in her fists. Well, one thing was for certain—she was just as affected as he was.

"You should go inside before I take you right here on the porch for anyone to see." He ran his hands down the length of her back as her laugh puffed against his T-shirt.

"I know I should be scandalized by that, but is it bad that I'm actually considering it?"

He groaned, fisting her tank top at the small of her back and tugging her against him. Letting her feel how hard he was for her. "That's just cruel, woman. Don't tease a man in this state."

She laughed, a tinkling sound, and looked up at him just as the front door swung open. Mac stood on the other side, mouth hanging open, eyes pinging back and forth between her sister and him.

"What the hell?"

Finn's lips quirked up at the corner. "Hey, Mac. Havin' a good night?"

"I... Um..." She narrowed her eyes before settling them on Willow and giving her what could only be interpreted as a "we'll talk later" look. Then she walked away, leaving the door wide open.

So much for the whole against-the-house scenario.

"Seems y'all have some talkin' to do, so I'll leave you to it." He pulled Willow close, pressing a soft, chaste kiss on her lips. Against them, he whispered, "'Night, Willowtree. I'll see you tomorrow."

He walked backward, their fingers clasped between them until he couldn't hold on any longer, and then he turned and strolled toward his truck near the front of the property. Leaving was the last thing he wanted to do. Hell, if he had it his way, she'd invite him into her home, into her room, into her bed. He'd spend the night with her, wake her up in the middle of the night with his lips on her, spend an hour inside her, then wake for the day with her in his arms. Pure heaven. Something they'd never had the luxury of doing, but something he wanted to experience almost as much as he wanted his next breath.

Someday. Someday, she'd trust him with that. Maybe. Hopefully. Especially after what they'd talked about tonight. Someday—maybe even sooner rather than later— they'd get to be a couple like that. He could stay at her place, or she could stay at his. They'd wake up, head down to the square, and grab breakfast at the diner. Everyone would look, of course. But she and Finn wouldn't care. Hell, he'd be damn glad for all the gawking, because it'd mean Willow was his girl for the entire town to see.

So lost in his thoughts, he didn't realize he wasn't alone until he nearly tripped over Willow's daddy. Dick stood off to the side, rage written all over his face. And, shit, wasn't this just history repeating itself? The last time Finn had made this trek, Dick had stopped him then too. Face as pissed as it was now, spitting fire and threats.

Difference was, Finn was no longer that scared, nineteen-year-old kid with a sick momma and not a whole lot of hope for the future. Now? Now, he had that hope in spades.

"Evenin', Dick. What can I do for you?"

"What can you *do* for me? You can tell me what the hell you're doin' on my property before I call the sheriff to haul your ass off for trespassin'."

Finn cocked his head. A voice whispered that he shouldn't taunt the man, shouldn't rub what he'd been doing in his face. But pride was a bitch sometimes, and the satisfaction of pissing him off was too good to pass up. "Been a while, but I think you'll probably remember if you try hard enough."

Dick delivered the reaction Finn had wanted, his face reddening, hands curled into fists at his sides. Finn could practically see the smoke emanating from the older man's ears, and he couldn't say he was even a bit sorry about it. While Finn wouldn't go back and change the events that'd led to him leaving—because without them, his momma may not...probably wouldn't...have been with them now—but he couldn't help hating Dick for tearing him and Willow apart. For not even allowing him to tell her goodbye.

"I don't know what you're up to here," Dick said, "but you best finish what you came for and leave. Before I make you. You remember how that goes, don't you, boy?"

Boy? Finn hadn't been a boy in a long damn time— since well before he'd left in the first place. He laughed, a loud booming sound in the otherwise quiet night. "Guess you haven't heard the news."

"What news?"

Oh, this was going to make his whole year. Watching

Dick's face as Finn delivered the information that would ruin his precious little town—at least, in his eyes. "We're stayin'."

"You're *what*?"

"C'mon now, Dick, I know you heard me. Despite you trying your damnedest to run us out with all that red tape nonsense and bullshit regulations, we're not goin' anywhere. We're making Havenbrook home again."

"You...you can't do that."

"Can and will. Drew and I are making one last trip to California to get packed up and bring Momma back with us."

"No one here wants your kind in Havenbrook." He spat the words like they were weapons.

Finn stared at the older man, waiting for the shame to come. But it never did. He knew his worth now, knew it didn't rest solely on where he lived or what part of town he was from, or whether or not his daddy was in the picture. Knew it stemmed only from the kind of man he was. "Once upon a time, that might've hurt me, but I'm not a kid anymore, and preying on what you perceive as weaknesses isn't going to do jack shit. I'm not quite as easy to get rid of as I was back then."

"You think giving you fifty-thousand dollars to get the hell out was *easy*? How much'll it take this time? Seventy-five? A hundred?"

Anger mixed with regret swirled in his gut. Dick knew damn well the money hadn't been why Finn had left—it'd been the threat of what would've happened if he'd stayed. If he'd gotten hauled off to jail, there would've been no way

Drew could've taken care of things with their momma. And Dick had known it, had used it to his advantage, like the prick he was.

Finn had no idea why he'd tried to protect Willow from this man, tried to salvage their relationship. The man was an asshole, and it was about damn time his daughter realized that.

Finn stepped up until he was toe-to-toe with him, getting some pleasure in the fact that Dick had to tilt his head back to look Finn in the eyes. "You could promise me a million— hell, a *billion*—and it still wouldn't do jack. Try to come up with some more bullshit charges for me. See what black-mailing me does. It would make my fucking year to go down that path with you. I'm stayin', Dick. And there's nothin' you can do to stop me."

With that, he turned and walked away, his head held higher than it had been so many years ago. But just like all those years ago, his stomach churned. Dick wouldn't give up. Wouldn't stop until he'd gotten his way, or he had some-thing else to focus his efforts on. Seeing as how Havenbrook was about as hopping as Mayberry, there wasn't much else for him to focus on. And seeing as Finn wasn't going anywhere... Well, it was going to be a long rest of his life.

But one that was worth it a thousand times over if it meant he got to spend that life with Willow.

BY THE TIME Finn got home, his anger had dissipated some. Not much, but some. Instead of focusing on what a piece of shit human being Dick was, Finn'd thought about what his next steps needed to be.

The money, for one thing. The money Dick had paid him off with to "ensure he didn't have any reason to float back to Havenbrook" needed to be given back. Despite the circumstances surrounding it, Finn couldn't deny what a life-line the money had been, a tiny bit of light at the end of a very long, very dark tunnel.

It'd been just the three of them for as long as he could remember, their daddy having never been in the picture at all. And Momma had been sick. Fucking cancer. Working four part-time jobs—the only things that'd been available in a small town like Havenbrook—meant no health insurance. No relief from the mounds of bills sure to pile up—the prescriptions and the treatments and the office visits. At nineteen, he and Drew had had to discuss things with their momma a child never should, debating between bankruptcy or her death.

The shadows on his momma's face, the resignation in her voice when she'd told them she hadn't wanted her sick-ness to follow them even after she was gone still haunted him to this day. He'd hated that that'd been the hand they'd been dealt, that they'd never been able to get a leg up, no matter what they'd done. Even knowing how desperately they needed they money, he'd turned Dick down flat when he'd approached Finn in the first place. Back then, he'd thought that would be that.

But, of course, Dick always got what he wanted. And he'd wanted Finn gone.

Finn walked through the empty bar, the workers long

since gone for the day. Pride swelled in his chest over what he, Drew, and Nola had accomplished—three trouble-makers from the wrong side of the tracks. The opening was close now. Real close.

The bar top shone, the stone they'd picked out for the front a perfect contrast to the corrugated steel and barn wood throughout the space. Accent walls in that same stone were interspersed throughout the bar—a strategy Rory had come up with and he'd just nodded along to. Industrial lighting hung from the open rafters of the ceiling, a few lantern sconces—and yeah, he now knew what those were—on the walls. It was everything he'd imagined when he hadn't even known what to dream up. There was no denying Rory knew what the hell she was doing, and she was damn good at it.

He climbed the stairs to the apartment before unlocking the door. Drew sat on the couch, TV on and beer in his hand. He lifted the bottle in a wave without turning around.

"We need to talk." Finn tossed his keys on the beat-up card table posing as a dining table and strode into the living area.

Drew furrowed his brow as he looked at his brother. "What the hell happened tonight? It didn't go well?"

"With Willow? Nah, it went great. Perfect."

"Then what's all this?" He gestured in Finn's general vicinity.

Finn didn't take time to wonder how Drew already knew something was up. Par for the course with the two of them. "History repeated itself tonight."

Drew's brows shot up. "No shit? Dick?"

"The one and only."

He leaned forward, resting his elbows on his spread knees. "What'd he say?"

"The usual. How much money'll it take to make you leave, get out before I make you, that sort of thing."

"I see his originality is still horseshit."

Finn hummed as he collapsed onto the couch next to his brother. Originality Dick didn't have, but he *did* have something he could hold over Finn's head, and Finn wanted it gone. It'd always be there, of course. He could never take back what he'd accepted, but he wanted to wash his hands of it as best he could. "We still have that fifty-thousand set aside?"

Drew took a slow sip of his beer, then nodded. "Yeah."

"I need it."

"All right."

No hesitation. No questioning. No inquisition.

"That's it?"

Drew glanced at him. "Should there be somethin' else?"

"You're not gonna ask what I need it for?"

He tapped his temple. "Twins. Besides, it doesn't take a rocket scientist to figure out you're lookin' to pay back that slimy asshole so it's not hangin' over your head anymore. Been wonderin' what was takin' you so damn long, to be honest."

Finn blew out a harsh breath, head resting on the back of the couch. "You remember after we left, how I'd fantasize about comin' back here and all the ways I'd throw that money in his face?" He didn't wait for a response because, of course, his brother remembered. "But when I finally got the chance, it just...wasn't as important. I had other things on my mind."

"Willow."

"Yeah, Willow. And the bar. And talkin' you into movin' back here."

"Didn't have to do much coercin' on that."

"Don't usually with you."

Drew shrugged. "Nothin' holdin' me back in California. And where you go, I go. You know that."

"I do." Same as Drew knew it. Their bond was unbreakable.

Finn pushed to stand and strolled toward his bedroom. "When can you get the money?"

"It'll take a couple days. Our bank doesn't have a location 'round here, so I'll have to make some calls. By the end of the week, I'd say."

"All right. And we'll still be doing okay once that's gone?" Finn leaned against the doorjamb, arms crossed. "We still have enough assets to pay all of Nash's people for the bar and get Momma moved out here? I know we've run into some added expenses with this venture."

Drew barked out a laugh then downed the rest of his beer before standing. On his way to the kitchen, he stopped and clapped a hand on Finn's shoulder. "I know you don't pay much attention to the statements I send you, but trust me when I say we're doin' just fine. That 50K was nice to get us started, but we haven't needed it in a long damn time."

Because Drew had made sure of it. Fifty-thousand was a lot of money, especially to two kids like them, but it wouldn't have even put a dent in cancer treatment bills. They'd had to make more money and make it fast. Fortunately, his brother was a goddamn genius with the stock market. All they'd needed had been the starting capital, and pretty soon, they'd had a nice little nest egg, even after paying for their momma's ungodly high treatment bills.

If it hadn't been for Drew, they'd have ended up no better than they'd left Havenbrook. And Finn couldn't lie that it was a damn nice feeling to know how much they'd changed since leaving, how much they'd flourished, despite what half the people in their hometown thought of them.

That was the one and only thing he'd thank Dick for. And he would too. At the same time he threw all that money back in his face.

chapter twenty-two

I t'd been a busy week, and despite what Willow and Finn
had said the evening at the tree house, they hadn't had
much time to spend together. They were back to stolen
kisses here and there, but it seemed to work for them, especially because she wasn't trying to hide anything from
anyone. Not anymore. While she wasn't screaming it from
the rooftops, she also wasn't going to lie if asked.

Of course, that hadn't been put to the test as of yet,
because all anyone wanted to talk to her about was information on the Fourth of July parade. And now that the parade
was in full swing, Willow's love life was the last thing on
anyone's mind.

She stood under an awning against the brick exterior of
a building in the square, a brief reprieve from the battering
sun, just taking a moment to absorb it all. Havenbrook had
events to mark every major holiday—and even some non-
major ones—but this was the largest and most grueling. And
while she hated the prep for it, swore at how much time it
took and all the hoops she had to jump through to make

sure everything was in order, she couldn't deny the swell of happiness at seeing her work come to fruition. Willow Haven put on a damn good parade, if she did say so herself.

The small details probably went unnoticed by most of the attendees, but Willow was aware of every single one. The red, blue, and white flowers she'd spent hours planting that dotted the parade route. The colored lights she'd strung between the lampposts along the square. The flag bunting on all the balconies and porches of the homes and businesses in the historic district. Uncle Sam doing balloon animals for the kids. The sight of it all coming together made her happy...content. The same feeling she got when she finished a painting. The proof of a job well done—a job well done with her own two hands.

"Nice parade, Will!" someone called out to her, owner of the voice unknown. Willow just smiled and waved at the praise, thankful she was getting it at all.

It'd probably been too much to hope she'd get it from her daddy.

"Hey." Mac sidled up next to her, Rory on Willow's other side.

"What's up?" she asked, dividing a look between her sisters.

"You ready for the game?" Rory asked.

Willow groaned internally—and, okay, a little externally as well. The annual softball game wasn't something she could skip out on, though she desperately wanted to. She'd been up since five a.m., and she was dead on her feet. But her job wasn't anywhere near done. The parade might have been winding down, the fire truck with firemen atop it tossing out candy to the passersby signaling the end of that particular event, but she still had so much to do.

First the game, then the soft opening of *the bar*—which was what Finn, Drew, and Nola were still calling it, not having settled on a name yet—then cleanup. She'd be lucky if she saw her bed before two in the morning.

"Do I have to?" Willow whined, though she didn't actually mean it. Of course she had to. If she didn't, who else would?

Mac and Rory exchanged a look, then Rory said, "I take it you haven't heard yet."

"Heard what? Oh Lord, did those kids mess up the baseball diamond? Dammit, I told them last week to stop four-wheelin' all over it."

"The diamond's fine, and the kids are the last thing you need to worry about."

"Well, someone better tell me what I *should* be worrying about, because I'm findin' I don't have a lot of patience for y'all right this second."

"We've got a new opposing team this year."

Willow's brow furrowed. Every year it'd been the firefighters against the Havens, which consisted of their family and a handful of town hall workers. Not even close to an fair match, considering most of the firefighters were a bunch of athletes in peak physical condition and the Havens' team consisted of a slightly overweight man nearing sixty, a handful of people who'd played some kind of sport way back in high school but not much since, and the rest of them who were mostly artistic types without an athletic bone in their bodies. Their saving grace every year was Mac, who'd played softball all through high school and even some college. Despite the uneven playing field, somehow they won. Every year. Imagine that.

"Somethin' come up with the firefighters?" she asked.

"Rumor has it someone sweet-talked them into sittin' out," Rory said.

"Really? Who? We got a shot?"

Mac snorted. "A shot at trouble."

Willow did *not* have the patience for her sisters today. "Would someone just spit it out already?"

"We're up against Drew, Finn, and their old crew." Mac smiled. "And by the looks of it, they're out to win. Maybe I'll finally get some competition out there."

Willow's mouth dropped open. "But——" Lord, she didn't even want to think of the tantrum her daddy would throw if he lost the game for the first time in…well, she wasn't sure she wanted to make such a broad sweeping statement as to say *ever*, but…ever.

As if reading Willow's mind, Mac said, "Yep. Daddy's gonna get his ass handed to him." She hooked her arm through Willow's and tugged her toward the baseball field, pure glee written over every inch of her body. "I feel like we're gonna need popcorn for this show."

———

FINN STOOD IN THE DUGOUT, Drew, Nola, Nash, and Ty BSing with each other. They were still waiting for a handful of people to arrive, and then they could get this show on the road. He wasn't sure he'd ever anticipated something more, with the exception of seeing Willow again.

All week they'd been putting the finishing touches on the bar, and he and Drew had been closing out details of their life in California while looking for a place for their momma to live in Havenbrook. But during that time, he'd also sat and stewed, really contemplated how he was going to give that money back to Dick.

He hadn't waited ten years just to mail a check back to him.

Finally, as he'd been walking home one night, a town flyer about the parade had caught his eye, and he'd remembered the annual softball game—how the Havens' opposing team had always, without exception, thrown the game. What he wouldn't give to see the look on Dick's face if someone actually challenged him.

And in that moment, he'd known that was it.

He'd made a few calls, sweet-talked some people, and then they were in. He and his misfit crew of friends were taking on the mayor. And they certainly wouldn't be throwing the game. Then, after, the cash. Shoving the money down the mayor's throat, along with a bit of humility, would make Finn's whole year.

"You really sure you wanna go through with this?" Ty asked.

There wasn't a doubt in Finn's mind everyone else was thinking the same thing—with the exception of Drew. But of course, Drew wouldn't question it at all because he'd been there. Through every up and down, every decision made between a rock and a hard place, every day of the past ten years. No, Drew wasn't thinking it because he knew how badly Finn wanted this. How it wasn't about beating the mayor, though that was definitely the icing on the cake. This wasn't even about a stupid game, but about so much more.

As if he'd conjured her up in his mind, Willow came strolling onto the field, slipping into the dugout on the opposite side of the baseball diamond. She stood in a tank top and shorts that left very little to the imagination, her smiling face hitting him straight in the gut.

Goddamn, did he love her.

To Ty, he said, "Abso-fucking-lutely. I'm playing for more than the game."

He never took his eyes off Willow, and eventually, she glanced his way. She froze for just a moment, and he held his breath, waiting to see what she'd do. This was the first time they'd be seen in public together since the night at the tree house, and he couldn't deny he was anxious as hell to see how she'd respond to him.

After what felt like a lifetime, she bit her bottom lip then lifted her hand, fluttering her fingers as her sisters looked on. He couldn't stop the smile from spreading across his face at her acknowledgment of him.

"Shit, man," Drew said, clapping a hand on Finn's shoulder. "I sure hope you're ready for what you're starting here."

Ready for it? He had no idea if he was or not. All he knew was he was tired of waiting.

CHRIST, it was hotter than Satan's ballsac out here. Finn's shirt was soaked to his chest, and from the looks of things, none of the others on his team were faring much better. They'd been playing for an hour already, the imbalance of aptitude between theirs and Dick's teams glaringly obvious in the disparaging lengths of time each group was up to bat.

Despite the ravaging heat, it'd been an absolute pleasure watching the mayor's reaction as the game had progressed. When Finn's team had scored the first run, Dick's eyes had narrowed as if warning them with a glance to fall in line. Finn had merely saluted him—not the one-fingered salute he'd wanted to give, which, he thought, was damn kind of himself. At the fourth run, Dick's jaw had been tight, his fists clenching his handkerchief as he'd mopped sweat from his brow. By the eighth, he'd looked ready for murder. Finn would bet the check in his pocket the thought had crossed good ol' Dick's mind a time or twenty.

Regardless of being on the losing team, the other players seemed to be having fun. Especially Mac. She was their main force to be reckoned with, and she put everything she had into the game. Willow, though not as competitive as her younger sister, was smiling more often than not, her and Finn's gazes locking more times than he could count.

Christ, he couldn't wait until this stupid game was over. He'd corner Dick, give him back the money, and then he needed to find Willow. No more tiptoeing around the facts. He'd been afraid of damaging her and her daddy's relationship, but he was more concerned about *their* relationship. That was his top priority. And now, after having seen father and daughter in action, seeing how the man belittled her, made her constantly feel less than, he wasn't sure what he'd been trying to protect in the first place.

After Finn came clean about why he'd left and about the money, he'd tell her of their plans to stay. That everything was already in line, and they only had to make a quick trip back to finalize some things and then they'd be home. Back in Havenbrook for good.

"Finn, you're up!" Ty called.

Time for their team's last play. Finn slipped on a helmet and took a few practice swings. It'd been a long time since he'd played, but it was like riding a bike. He, Drew, and the rest of their friends had spent hours down here when they'd been younger. Trying like hell to stay out of trouble. Hadn't always worked.

"Go easy, will you?" Nola said as she passed him, having just scored another run.

He smiled at her. "Now where's the fun in that?"

With narrowed eyes, she said, "Dammit, Finn, I mean it. Knowing him, he'll find a way to fuck up the opening."

He couldn't argue with that based on what Dick had tried already, but he also couldn't say he gave a damn. Irresponsible when the bar hung on the line? Maybe. Probably. But this was about so much more than just a game. This was about Finn showing Mayor Haven that he wasn't going to roll over for him anymore. That the older man didn't get to push people around, didn't get to have his way simply because he ruled the town that was his namesake.

The bases were loaded, and Dick stood in the outfield, looking as pissed as ever. Since the Havens were considered the home team, they still had another inning, but unless

Babe Ruth materialized to play for their team, they were going down. There was no way they could come back from an eight-run lead.

First pitch was a swing and a strike. He shook it off and looked over at Willow, who guarded first base. The side of her lips quirked up, and that was all he needed.

On the second pitch, his bat connected with the ball, sending it flying in Dick's direction. Finn took off, sailing past Willow and straight to second, but not before brushing her hand with his as he went.

One thing he hadn't counted on was Mac's dedication to covering her father's shortcomings—at least, when it came to sports. She scrabbled for the ball as Finn rounded third and headed for home, and the crowd went wild. Finn pumped his legs harder, hoping she'd send it to the pitcher and buy him enough time to get home. Except the catcher stood right behind home plate, watching the sky as if awaiting a throw, and Finn did the only thing he could. He slid home, closing his eyes and praying he'd get there a millisecond before the ball.

He came to a stop as the mitt connected with his foot.

"*Safe!*" the umpire yelled.

Finn didn't even have time to enjoy the call before Dick was shuffling into the infield, his voice loud enough to be heard over the crowd.

"That's a bullshit call, Vern, and you know it!" he shouted, his hands gesturing wildly toward where Finn stood, wiping sand from his pants.

"The only call I could make, Mayor. He was safe."

"Bunch of horseshit. I saw it with my own eyes, and he was clearly out!"

"Saw it all the way back in left field, did ya?" Finn asked.

As if Finn hadn't even spoken, Dick continued, "I thought you were on our side."

"Can't be on anyone's side, I'm afraid. That'd be a conflict of interest as an ump."

Dick's belly-aching had drawn a crowd, many of the onlookers shifting closer to be able to hear exactly what was going on. The rest of Dick's team looked embarrassed, especially Willow. She'd taken a couple steps closer, but she still stood near first base, biting on one of her nails as she looked on.

"Conflict of interest?" Dick shouted. "I'll tell you what a conflict of interest is. It's *him*"—he shoved a meaty finger in Finn's direction—"playin' this game like he's part of Havenbrook. He's not even a real member of this community. What's he done anyway? You forget about the half-dozen times he egged your place, Vern? Or when he took out all those mailboxes on Main Street? Or when he got hauled in for spray-paintin' the road signs?"

The ump shrugged. "Don't really see how that's got anything to do with baseball. Besides, he was just a kid then. You need to let the past lie. Lighten up, Richard."

That settled it. Vern was getting a year's worth of beer on Finn's dime.

Vern's casual dismissal of the mayor only seemed to enrage Dick more. His face reddened even further—which, to be honest, Finn hadn't thought possible. His fists were clenched at his sides, and he kept darting his gaze to the bystanders, all of whom were now gawking at their mayor.

He gestured wildly in Finn's direction, his voice a barked command. "He's not even a real member of this community. He might be bringin' a business to the square, but y'all'd do well to remember exactly what that business is. There'll be drinkin' and partyin' goin' on till all hours of the night, all thanks to him. Exactly what we fought for years to keep out of our quiet little town. Shouldn't be a surprise, though, given where he came from. Where they all came from." He glared at Finn and his team, who now stood behind him, supportive even in their silence. Dick looked him up and down, a sneer marring his face. "Just 'cause you were born here doesn't mean you belong."

Willow gasped, drawing Finn's attention to her. In the time her daddy'd been throwing his tantrum, she'd walked closer and now stood just on the other side of her father. "Daddy!" she snapped. "I can't believe you just said that."

"I don't have time for this nonsense from you, Will."

Willow's eyes narrowed the smallest bit. It was a tiny tell, really. One only Finn probably noticed, but he knew what it meant. He'd been on the receiving end of it enough times to know she'd reached her breaking point, and her daddy'd just shoved her over it.

She squared her shoulders and stepped up to her father, something Finn hadn't ever see her do before. "Considering *you're* the one who interrupted the game for this *nonsense*, I believe you do have the time."

Dick's eyebrows shot up, his mouth dropping open. "Excuse me, young lady? I'll not have you talkin' to me—"

"And I'm not gonna stand by and listen to you disparage one of our own. Finn grew up here, same as me. Same as you."

"He's nothin' like us! He's—"

"Opening a business that'll help Havenbrook thrive. A business you might not be fond of, but one this town desperately needs. We are bleeding residents, and any new businesses that'll help prevent that are a benefit to Havenbrook. He has as much right to be here as any one of us." Willow crossed her arms and stared at her father. "Stop being such a sore loser about it all."

Murmurs of agreement spread through the crowd as a hurricane of emotions flooded Finn. His chest swelled with pride over Willow finally standing up to her father. And doing so for *him*? Well, he didn't want to pour gasoline on an already raging fire, but he desperately wanted to stride over to her, take her in his arms, and kiss the living daylights out of her. Right there, in front of everyone.

Except it turned out he didn't need to walk to her at all. Instead, she took cautious steps toward him, her eyes full of a thousand questions. He hoped he answered them all as he watched her step up to him. She hooked her finger through his, her lips quirking up at the side a moment before she pressed up on tiptoes to brush her lips across his.

As the whole town watched on.

A few gasps went off, but he stopped hearing them after a moment. How could he pay attention to anything else when Willow's mouth was on his? He reached up and wrapped his fingers around her nape, bringing them closer.

She might've started this kiss, but he sure as hell was going to finish it.

With his friends at his back, Willow in his arms, and the entire town paying witness to her very public declaration, Dick's check burned a hole in his pocket. Where earlier Finn had been dead set on shoveling a heaping pile of humility into the mayor's lap, now he just wanted to be with Willow. And as much as he loved this bit of PDA, what he really wanted to do to her wasn't fit for public consumption. He wanted to spend an hour kissing every freckle and birthmark on her body. Wanted to spend all night between her thighs, showing her over and over again how much he loved her. Wanted to tell her everything so they could finally start the rest of their lives together.

Tonight couldn't get here fast enough.

chapter twenty-three

At the start of the day, Willow certainly hadn't intended to make her feelings for Finn quite so… known. Or make them known quite so loudly or so publicly. Yes, she'd made the decision to stop hiding her relationship with Finn. It was childish and stupid, and she was done with that. But she'd assumed it'd get around like everything did in Havenbrook: someone would see them together, laughing or talking or walking a little too close for friendly acquaintances, and so-and-so would tell someone else, and pretty soon it'd spread like wildfire.

Hadn't happened exactly like that.

But, hell, she'd been so damn mad at her daddy, she hadn't stopped to think. A fact which her sisters hadn't let her forget since they'd dragged their asses away from the baseball diamond—losers for the first time ever.

Willow, her sisters, and their gran had escaped to Rory's house since it was closest to the square, their momma staying behind to try to calm down their father. Like that'd ever happen.

"Tell me somethin', Will," Rory said, pouring four glasses of lemonade. "Did you wake up this mornin' and think, 'What can I do to royally piss off Daddy?'"

Willow rolled her eyes as Gran snorted.

"Lay off her, Rory," Mac said.

"I'm serious. What in heaven's name coerced you into behavin' that way?"

Because, *of course*, her older sister would think Willow had been the one out of line. While she and Rory had had fun the couple of times they'd gone out since their understanding, their shared secrets tying them together in a way they hadn't been before, apparently it was too much to ask for an entire personality transplant for her sister.

"He was acting like a spoiled child," Willow said, struggling to keep her voice level. "I simply spoke up about it."

"I wish I'd had my phone with me." Mac smiled, her eyes sparkling. "Nat would've *loved* to see video of that. She hasn't responded to my text yet, but I hope you're prepared for her."

"As prepared as I'll ever be," Willow mumbled before taking a sip of her drink.

"I just..." Rory shook her head, perfectly manicured nails—despite the afternoon playing softball—tapping the side of her glass. "Don't you think there were better ways to handle that? Instead of tellin' Daddy off in front of the whole town, embarrassing him and our whole family, then makin' a spectacle of yourself with Finn?"

"The only one in the family who needed to be embarrassed was Daddy," Mac said, her temper showing in the reddening of her cheeks.

"Oh, I see." Willow straightened, her shoulders nearly up to her ears at how rigid she stood. "Speaking up when Daddy's saying disparaging things about our residents—who were *standin' right there*—and then kissin' my—" Well. She'd been about to say *boyfriend*, but they hadn't exactly had that conversation. And could someone who was leaving in a few days' or weeks' time even *be* someone's boyfriend? Forcing that thought away, she swallowed and set down her glass. "Look. It already happened. Can't do anythin' to change it, and to tell you the truth, I wouldn't want to. Daddy had every bit of that talking-to comin' to him after how he spoke."

"Well, I don't know about—"

"She's right, Rory," Gran said, lifting a brow when all three girls turned to stare at her, mouths agape. "What? 'Bout time one of you stood up to my jackass son and put him in his place. Was startin' to think I might not live to see the day, especially after Nat left. And to be honest, I'm a little surprised it came from Will first, but I'm damn glad about it." She placed her hand over Willow's on the counter and winked. "Didn't I tell you gettin' up to no good would be fun?"

There was a brief bout of silence between the four women, then Mac raised her glass and tapped it against their grandmother's. "Amen, Gran."

For a moment, Willow stared at her grandmother, mischief sparkling in her eyes. She thought back to all the times her gran had told her things like that, encouraging her to be a little wild. To have a little fun. Let loose just a tiny bit and see what happened. Had she been encouraging it the whole time? Had she also been doing the same thing to Willow's sisters? Of that, she wasn't sure, but one thing was for certain: she was glad she'd finally listened. Standing up to her Daddy had given her a high she'd never before experienced.

Of course, she knew, sure as she knew the sun would set, that her daddy wouldn't allow her to have the last word. And that conversation, when it came, would be hell on earth.

———

AFTER WILLOW, her sisters, and Gran had finished their lemonade and impromptu chat, they'd headed back toward the square since the fireworks would be going off soon.

When they arrived in the center of town, everyone scattered, Gran going off to find their momma, Rory to wrangle her kids, and Mac to get some free beer. Willow followed her sister's trail as she strode toward the far side of the square where Finn, Nola, and Drew had set up a little stand outside. The inside space wasn't quite ready for customers yet, but they'd agreed to host this when Willow had approached them about it. When she'd had the idea, she'd figured it'd be a win-win for them and the town—bringing customers to Finn's bar while enticing the residents to stay in the square a little longer, maybe spend some money at neighboring businesses.

She'd been right. The line to their counter stretched halfway across the square. Her heart slowed, warmth sweeping through her body as she stood back and just watched. Finn chatted with a few residents as he served beer, a smile spreading across his face as he nodded to someone. Lord, he was handsome. And kind. And giving. And he was hers. For as long as he was in town, he was hers. It wasn't what she wanted—because what she wanted was everything with him: the white picket fence and two-point-five kids and happily ever after—but it was what she'd been given.

And she was going to take every little bit of it she could.

"See nothing's changed with you." Her daddy stood next to her, his gaze fixed where hers had just been.

Looked like the fireworks were starting early.

Willow snapped her spine straight and tightened her jaw. Gave herself a minute to calm down before she did something horrible like tell her daddy to go to hell.

Ignoring the underlying dig her daddy sent her way, she tipped her chin in Finn's direction. "They got us a good turnout. The parade's always busy, but once it's done, half the crowd leaves the square. We got lucky Finn, Drew, and Nola agreed to open up their business to entice the residents to hang around. I've spoken with some of the other business owners, and their sales are up thirty percent from last year. That's—"

Her daddy tsked, shaking his head. "Just as blind as ever."

Biting her tongue was getting harder than ever, especially after she'd had a taste of letting loose. "I'm not sure what that's supposed to mean. I haven't been blind to what they could bring to Havenbrook. *You* have."

So much for diplomacy and tact. But, *hell*, he just got her so damn mad. And she was done. She was finally, *finally* done. Especially today—a day she worked her ass off on for the majority of the year, not to even get a *good* damn *job* from the mayor? She'd had just about enough of that, of giving herself to people and things that didn't give a damn about her. That just took and took and took—

"You ever ask him why he ran off so fast in the first place?"

The question was so out of the blue, Willow could only stare at her father for a moment. It'd crossed her mind, of course. Had been the single most frequent question that'd arisen while Finn had been gone. She'd been close to asking him that night in the tree house, then he'd kissed her, and, well, she'd lost her nerve.

"No," she said. "I don't really see how it has any bearing on the present."

Her father chuckled under his breath and shook his head. Even though the residents of Havenbrook surrounded them, no one paid them any mind. They were off to the side, tucked against a building, while everyone else gathered around the center of the square, the majority of the people clustered over by Finn's bar.

"Well, can't say I didn't try to stop this from happening. Tried not to let you get played for a fool, but you just kept goin' straight for it, didn't you?"

She blew out an exasperated sigh, wanting desperately for her daddy to just get to the point so she could go over and congratulate Finn on his win—both on the baseball diamond and with their soft opening. "What are you talkin' about?"

Her daddy twisted toward her, his lips turned down like he was concerned. "The money."

"What money?" Honestly, if he didn't get to the point, she was going to walk away. Just turn and walk straight over to Finn and ignore her daddy—

"The money I gave him to leave town. Now, I know it wasn't my best move, honey, and I'm sorry about that. I truly am. But that boy...well, he wasn't ever good enough for you. Wasn't ever good enough to be attached to a Haven. Since you were too blind to see it back then, I had to take matters into my own hands. Had to get that boy out of town before y'all did somethin' you'd come to regret. And you *would* regret it. Of that I have no doubt." He reached out and gripped her shoulder. "I did it for your own good, you see."

Her father's lips were still moving, words coming out of them, his expression proclaiming *concerned parent*, but she couldn't pay attention to what he was saying. Her pulse thrummed too loud in her ears, years' worth of memories flipping through her mind.

The day she'd woken up and Finn had been gone.

Running to the tree house, hoping to find a note, a message, *something* that'd tell her why he'd had to leave. Why he couldn't say goodbye.

Falling asleep with her cell phone in her hand, just hoping and praying he'd call her or text her. If not to tell her why he left, then at least to tell her he was okay.

Lying in her bed weeks later, the night she'd finally accepted he wasn't coming back. That he'd left her, despite their plans, and Havenbrook was no longer his home.

Then months later, withdrawing her admission to Tennessee State University. Because she wasn't the girl she'd been with Finn. He'd stripped that from her, had taken every ounce of fire she'd had and blown it out as he'd flown from town.

Her father squeezed her shoulder again, pulling her from the fog. "Sorry to have to tell you like this, Will. But I couldn't watch you go down that path again. Just wouldn't be right for me to sit by and say nothin'."

She nodded as if she understood. As if everything she'd put back together wasn't cracking at the foundation. After her daddy's show earlier at the baseball diamond, she certainly couldn't trust what he said as gospel. But the seeds of doubt he'd planted were enough of a push to get her to finally have that conversation with Finn. Much as she'd worried about the answer, it was time to find out once and for all why he left all those years ago.

chapter twenty-four

F inn wasn't sure it'd have been possible to have a better day than today. By the time he, Drew, and Nola had finished up serving in the square and closing up, they'd been sure of one thing: this business of theirs was actually going to succeed.

And wasn't that a fine revelation to come to when only hours before the town's mayor had disparaged them in front of everyone, claiming they weren't worth the dirt beneath his feet?

Just went to show Dick didn't know shit. Not about Finn, and not about Havenbrook. And he certainly hadn't had the majority of his town's interests at heart when he'd thrown up all the roadblocks for them to start the business. Havenbrook was thirsty—pun intended—for a gathering space. Somewhere they could kick back with friends and hang out without having to drive thirty minutes to do so.

Finn was damn glad they were the ones providing that to the people who'd once looked down upon him and his brother, but now saw them as equals.

His main focus all day had been finding Dick and taking care of the little matter of that cashier's check still in his pocket, but by the time they'd gotten cleaned up long after the last firework had gone off, the square had been empty. Besides, he didn't want to waste his time with Dick right then.

He wanted to see Willow.

While they hadn't made plans, Finn figured her show on the baseball diamond was invitation enough for him to knock on her door. Even if it was after midnight.

He pulled up to her and Mac's place, thankful to see lights still burning behind the drapes. Maybe, if he were lucky, she'd make his fantasies come true and let him stay the night. Wake up with her in his arms. He didn't figure Mac would mind too much. When it came to Willow's younger sister, she didn't seem to mind too much at all.

At his knock, the door flew open, doesn't-mind-much-Mac's face as red as a fire hydrant, her glare aimed directly at him. "What the fuck do you want?"

"I—what?" Finn furrowed his brow as he scratched his jaw and looked over Mac's head, trying to puzzle out why she'd answer like that. A joke?

"I *said*, what the fuck do you want, Griffin?" She crossed her arms, foot tapping on the hardwood floor.

Shit, maybe Mac was pissed about how the game had gone down earlier. He'd thought she'd had a good time despite losing, but maybe she wasn't as easygoing as he'd assumed.

"Hey, I'm sorry about the game. You played great, and—"

"You think this is about the goddamn *game*? Shit, you're an asshole *and* an idiot."

"Mac, what the hell's—" But his words caught in his throat because over Mac's shoulder, he caught sight of Willow standing on the staircase, her face passive and emotionless as she stared at him. No smile. No twinkle in her eye. Nothing. His stomach twisted, the urge to go to her too strong to resist. "Willowtree? What—"

"I know you said you wanted to chat with him, Will, but I could knee him in the balls for you instead," Mac called over her shoulder, blocking the doorway so Finn couldn't get through. "Just say the word. It'd be my absolute pleasure."

He stared at Willow, her questioning eyes connecting with his. She stood silent for an eternity. Finally, she said, "Maybe after we have that chat."

Thank Christ. A chat would do Finn some good. He could find out what the hell had happened to Willow between when he'd last seen her in the square, looking beautiful as hell and smiling at him like he hung the damn moon, to now when she looked ready to murder him.

Mac shoved her finger into his chest, pressing deep as she leaned close. "She might be willing to give you the benefit of the doubt, but I'm not finding myself quite so gracious given your history. Just remember I'm a fifth-degree black belt. And I'm pretty sure no one would fault me for shooting you in the ass with a BB gun when it's after midnight, so you better be damn careful with your words. Never can be too sure who's breaking and entering, now can you?" She spun around and headed for the steps, squeezing

Willow's arm as she passed. "I'll be upstairs if you need me."

After aiming one more glare in Finn's direction, Mac shot up the stairs, and then it was just him and Willow.

He stepped inside, closing the door behind him, before striding over to her. Needing to touch her, to feel her, reassure himself she was all right. "Tell me what's goin' on. Mac said you wanted to chat? And why is she ready to shoot me with a damn BB gun? Is it about the game? I'm sorry 'bout that. I should've talked it over with y'all first, but I—"

"You think this is about *baseball*, Finn?" She crossed her arms, her eyes narrowed as she stared at him.

"I have no idea what this is about, but I'm hopin' like hell you'll tell me and tell me quick so I can fix it." He reached out, intent on smoothing his hands over her shoulders, but she jerked back, out of his reach.

She stepped around him, farther away. Out of touching range. "Is it true?" Her voice was quiet. Calm. Like the eye of the storm.

"Is what true?"

She stared at him for long moments, her eyes seemingly doing their best to read him. "You know, every time we've been together I've wanted to ask why you left the way you did. Why you never called or wrote. Why you never, ever came back, but something always stopped me. Fear, I guess." She glanced down and shook her head, a new fire in her eyes when she met his gaze again. "But I'm done living in fear. And I want to know. If you don't tell me, I'll have to assume the story my daddy fed me was the truth."

Finn's stomach bottomed out, his face draining.

Dammit, he wasn't ready for this conversation. He might've had ten years to prepare himself, but he wasn't even close. Not when the outcome could so easily go out of his favor. Not when what he gambled was something as precious as Willow.

He stared at her, trying to find the words to tell her why he'd done the things he had, how it'd ripped his heart out to go, and how every mile away from her had felt like the worst kind of torture.

Her eyes crumbled in his gaze, her stoic expression melting into devastation. "It's true, isn't it? What he said."

"Willowtree, I—"

"Do *not* call me that. You don't get that privilege. Not when all it took to get you to leave me behind without a word was a little cash."

Finn's body turned to ice as a boulder settled in his stomach. He hadn't been fast enough. He should've found Dick and gotten it taken care of earlier in the day. No, what he should've done was figure out a way to tell her well before today, to hell with her relationship with her daddy. Because now…now everything he'd ever wanted was getting snatched away in front of his eyes. He could see it in her face when she looked at him. The disappointment. The anger. The hurt.

It killed him to know he caused it.

"Can't believe I let you play me for a fool. Again," she whispered, shaking her head as a tear slipped free and rolled down her cheek. She swallowed, licked her lips. Took a deep, ragged breath. "I've spent the whole night hoping with everything in me what my daddy said wasn't true. It couldn't possibly be. You'd tell me it was a lie, that it never happened. That my daddy made it all up just to turn me against you." She huffed and shook her head. "I thought that naïve part of me was dead and gone, buried alive after you left. The part that was stupid enough to believe everything you said. To believe we had somethin' special. To believe in an *us*."

"We *do* have somethin' special. You're the most important person in the world to me." He reached for her again, desperate to feel her under his fingers. Desperate to wipe away her tears and comfort her. Even though he didn't deserve such a privilege. "Willow—"

"Don't touch me." She slapped his hands away, her face growing redder by the second. "I can't believe I let this happen again. I knew it would. I knew, somehow, you'd make me out to be the idiot Haven girl just like I was back then."

It didn't make sense. Didn't add up. Her daddy never would've told her the circumstances surrounding Finn's departure. Not when the mayor had blackmailed Finn, forcing his hand. Even without a sick momma, he hadn't had a choice. It was get the hell out with fifty grand or stay and be indicted for a crime he never committed—underage alcohol consumption and distributing to minors in a dry county. Apparently, that was one of the benefits of having the sheriff for a best friend.

Unless... Unless Dick didn't tell her the whole story. Only the part that made Finn look like a money-hungry coward. Not the part where Dick was close to the devil himself.

He stopped himself from reaching for her again, just

barely. But he stepped closer. Displayed as much sincerity in his voice as he could. "Please, sweetness, will you let me explain?"

She breathed out a laugh. "I waited ten years for an explanation. Ten *years*, not to mention all these weeks we've spent together. And now you want to give it?" She shook her head and strode to the front door, not an ounce of hesitation in her movements when she opened it for him as a clear sign to get the hell out. "After all the chances I gave you, I find I'm not much interested in listenin' anymore. Goodbye, Finn."

FINN WOKE to an incessant pounding in his head. Though, that was no surprise. For the past—shit, how long had it been?—however many days, he'd woken up the same way. Except as he opened his eyes, becoming more aware of his surroundings, he realized the pounding wasn't a headache, but rather came in the form of his brother.

"'Bout damn time you woke up." Drew stopped thumping Finn's forehead and yanked the pillow out from under his head.

He groaned, clutching his aching skull. "The hell, man?"

Since the pillows were gone, Drew moved on to Finn's feet, hauling them off the couch and letting them drop to the ground.

"Seriously, I'm not in the mood for this, Drew." Finn's head was killing him, and his mouth felt like he'd swallowed an entire bag of cotton balls. Soaked in roadkill. And then left to marinate for a week in the Mississippi sun.

"No?" Drew said. "Let me tell you what I'm not in the mood for. I'm not in the mood for my shit-for-brains brother to start demanding things when he's done fuck all the past three days while moping like a teenager who just got his phone taken away." Drew kicked Finn's foot. "Time to get your ass up. Get your shit together and join the land of the living. I've covered for your sorry ass, but my patience is gone."

Finn was way too hungover for this conversation. Or, actually, maybe he was still a little drunk. He groaned and sat up, propping his elbows on his knees and cradling his pounding head in his hands. "Look, I'm sorry about the bar—"

"You think this is about the bar?" Drew snorted out a laugh. "We've got it handled. This is about me watching you for the past ten years, you finally gettin' what you want, only to let one little fight end everything."

Finn breathed out a humorless laugh, the image of Willow's face from that night blinking in his mind. It was all he'd been able to see every time he closed his eyes. The pain and betrayal so vivid on her features. While nothing he did erased it, the alcohol numbed it a little.

Hence why his mouth tasted like ass and gnomes were using ice picks to pound away at his skull.

"It was more than 'one little fight,'" he grumbled.

"I don't care if it was fucking World War III. Absolutely nothin' is gonna come from you locking your mopey ass away in the apartment, drinkin' your weight in bourbon."

Finn glared up at his brother. "No? What the hell else am I supposed to do? The woman I love just told me to get out of her life. *Permanently*. I don't think some flowers and a dozen cupcakes is gonna cut it this time."

"You're an idiot."

Finn rubbed his eyes, trying to will away the headache raging behind them. "Tell me something I don't know," he muttered.

"When you two eventually get married, I hope you know I'm using this story in your toast."

Marriage? Willow wouldn't speak to him—he'd tried that, calling her a dozen times before giving up. Then he'd resorted to texting her—none of which she'd answered. She also probably couldn't even look at him, though he hadn't tested that theory since, instead, he'd chosen to stay home and get drunk off his ass. And his jackass brother was talking about marriage? Not fucking likely. Not after Finn had fucked everything up. "Now who's the idiot?"

"Still you." Drew took a seat on the battered coffee table directly in front of Finn. "Here's what you're gonna do, dumbass. First, you're gonna take a damn shower because you smell like a homeless man who just went on a bender. Then you're gonna do what you'd already planned to—bring that check back to our illustrious mayor."

"It won't matter." Finn shook his head, pressing his palm hard against his forehead. "None of it'll matter now."

"Maybe not. But it might." Drew paused, long enough that Finn finally looked up at him. "Dick doesn't play by the rules, so maybe you shouldn't either." He raised a brow.

Finn snorted. "Yeah, I definitely see the sheriff helpin' me out with this little situation I'm in."

"Who said you needed the sheriff? Way I see it, all you need is a convincing argument on why he should come clean to Willow about all he did back then. You said it yourself—there's no way he'd have told her the whole story...just enough to pit her against you. So make him."

Finn ran a hand through his hair, his mind whirring with possibilities as he finally saw a tiny pinprick of light at the end of a long, dark tunnel. Drew was right. This might not do anything. But maybe, just maybe, it could. And didn't he owe it to himself and Willow to at least try? To try absolutely everything in his power before giving up?

He squinted at his brother, the harsh light coming in from the front window killing his eyes. "Where was this brilliant advice three days ago? I've wasted a lot of time getting...well, wasted. Maybe *too* much time."

"First, you kind of deserved it. A little payback for walking away from her in the first place. Second, you're sucking down all our open stock for the bar, and Nola said I better get your ass under control before she comes over and does it her damn self." Drew pushed to stand and looked down at him, shaking his head. "She's scary-feisty, man."

Finn wasn't arguing that. And he was ashamed it'd taken her getting fed up with him before he came to his senses. Jesus, some pile he was. Not only had he been an absolute worthless excuse for a human being, not helping with the finishing touches at the bar, but he'd been drinking through their stock too. Drew was right. It was time to get shit done.

After a shower to help him feel half human again, he

had some unfinished business with Mayor Haven to attend to.

It was dusk by the time Dick showed up where Finn had instructed. Getting him there had been a miracle in and of itself. But Finn'd had to be strategic about it. He certainly couldn't show up at the mayor's office—not with Willow right down the hall, liable to pop in at any moment. Same went for Dick's home.

Quiet and secluded it was, like some kind of back-alley drug deal. Come to think of it, this location wasn't all that different from where they'd met all those years ago.

"All right, boy," Dick said as he heaved himself out of his car. "Best be tellin' me what this nonsense is about before I make some calls."

Finn slid his hand into his pocket, not moving from where he leaned against the side of his truck, like he didn't have a care in the world. Like his whole future didn't ride on the outcome of this meeting. "Ah, yes. Calls to the sheriff, isn't that right? Must be nice to have such a close, personal friend in law enforcement. Allows you to do all kinds of shady shit."

Dick stepped closer, his eyes narrowed. "You gonna spit it out already?"

Plucking the check from inside his pocket, Finn pulled it out and pinched it between two fingers, holding it in Dick's direction. "Gotcha a little somethin'."

"What's this?" Dick snatched the check from Finn's

fingers and unfolded it. His brows shot up, eyes going wide. "This some kind of joke?"

"'Fraid not, Dick. This is payback." Finn smiled. "Quite literally in this sense."

Dick barked out a laugh. "If you think this'll make everything better with Will, you're even dumber than I gave you credit for."

"This? No. This isn't gonna do anything with Willow. We both know that. This just settles the score between you and me. I'd been plannin' on giving this back to you for some time. Just hadn't gotten around to it. Wanted to wash my hands of your sins."

"*My* sins? I didn't do nothin', boy, except—"

"Except blackmail a nineteen-year-old kid with nothin' but a run-down trailer to his name and a momma who was facing a death sentence." Finn nodded. "Nothin' there but good old-fashioned neighborly advice, isn't that right?"

"Now, you listen here—"

"Nope." Finn pushed off from the truck and took a step in Dick's direction. "I'm done listenin' to you. Time for you to do some of it." He reached out and plucked the check from Dick's fingers, folded it up, then stuffed it in the mayor's shirt pocket. Patted it twice. Possibly slightly harder than necessary. "That might've been years ago, but we've got a long memory in Havenbrook, don't we? You proved that on the baseball diamond. Sure would be a shame for all your constituents to learn what you did back then. Especially now that the boy you did it to turned into a man who's bringin' value back to your precious town. Bringin' jobs and revenue to the people who need it most."

Dick narrowed his eyes so much they were just beady little slits, glaring in Finn's direction. "What're you tryin' to say?"

"I'm not tryin' to say anything. I'm merely suggesting you *might* wanna be honest with your daughter about the circumstances surrounding my departure. Or those circumstances *might* become common knowledge for the lovely folks of Havenbrook."

"How dare you! That's blackmail!"

Finn finally smiled for the first time in three days. "I know. Isn't it great?" He clapped his hand on the mayor's shoulder and directed him toward his car.

"You've got until next week." He opened the door for Dick, pressing hard on his shoulder to guide him inside. With his hands braced on the window frame and hood of the car, Finn leaned into the space of the opened door. "Now, Dick, I don't *want* to ruin your career, but I will. I warned you it wouldn't be so easy to get rid of me this time. Tellin' Willow before I had a chance to didn't make me run away." He stepped back and shut the door. Through the open window, he said, "It's only gonna make me fight harder."

With two hard taps to the roof of Dick's car, Finn turned and strode away, feeling lighter than he had in ten long years, even despite the heaviness of his heart weighing him down.

chapter twenty-five

W illow might've been too old to be curled up on the couch with her head in her momma's lap as they watched a sappy romance on the Hallmark channel, but she didn't care. For the first few days after she'd said goodbye to Finn, she'd tried to keep her stoic mask in place. Which had been easier said than done, especially after the idiotic show she'd put on at the softball game. If she hadn't gone up to Finn and kissed the hell out of him for the entire town to see, no one would've had anything at all to talk about.

But because she had, the whispers had followed her for days, though nothing was said to her face—it never was. It was all pointed stares and not-so-subtle fingers directed her way when they thought she wasn't looking.

Well, she'd had about enough of it. And after putting up with it for that long, who could blame her for partaking in some much-needed Momma time? Especially when Momma time came with chicken and dumplings and warm, freshly baked chocolate chip cookies, her favorite comfort foods.

"How long before Mac gets home, sweetheart?" Momma asked, her fingers trailing through Willow's hair as they both watched the hero of the movie run through a bus depot, frantically searching for the heroine, inevitably to tell her how sorry he was for royally screwing up.

If only things happened like that in real life.

"Dunno," she said. "What time is it?" She had no sense of time today. After toughing it out for too many days, she'd finally decided to take a mental health day and called in sick to work—for the first time. Ever. Avery had been shocked but had told Willow not to worry about a thing. That she'd hold down the fort and then would stop by after work if Willow wanted her to.

In fact, all the people she loved had offered that—her best friend, both her sisters, and now her momma. She was damn lucky was what she was. Even if her heart did feel like it'd been put in a blender. Repeatedly.

"A little after four. Think she'll want some chicken and dumplings? I could get it heatin' up for y'all for supper."

"We'll be fine, Momma. We can heat it up when we're ready."

"All right, if you say so." She continued her soft caresses through Willow's hair, lifting up pieces here and there. "Sweetheart?"

"Hmm."

"I've been here for hours now. I'm tryin' not to push, but…"

Willow sighed. She'd hoped she could escape this conversation, though she had no idea what made her so delusional. "But what?"

"Come on now, talk to me. What's goin' on with you and Finn?"

"What's goin' on, or what *was* goin' on? Because they're two very different things."

"Now I'm sure that's not—"

"Did you know?" This part hurt almost as much as knowing Finn had taken the money in the first place. Willow could see this kind of thing coming from her daddy—actually hadn't been even a bit surprised about it—but from her momma? That'd be a hard pill to swallow.

Her fingers paused in Willow's hair. "Know what?"

"About the money."

"The money? What're you—"

A knock sounded at the front door before it opened, and her daddy poked his head into the space.

"Richard? You can't be hungry already," her momma said, a note of exasperation in her tone. "It's not even five!"

"What?" her father asked as he stepped into the house and shut the door behind him. "Oh no. No, that's not why I'm here. I, uh…" He shifted on his feet, wiping a hand across his forehead.

Willow furrowed her brow, trying to puzzle out what was happening here. Something wasn't quite right. She'd never seen her daddy…well…*nervous*. And that was exactly what he was, shuffling his weight from foot to foot, his gaze darting between her and her momma before flitting off to the side.

"You're here to what, honey?" Momma asked. She tipped her chin in the direction of the TV where the movie still played on, the hero and heroine wrapped in each other's arms. Damn, Willow had missed the best part. "Willow and I are just finishin' this movie, and you interrupted a bit of girl talk. Can it wait?"

He glanced back at the TV before turning to face them once again. "I'm afraid it can't, darlin'. I really need to speak to Will about…about somethin' important."

Willow sat up, glancing at her momma who shrugged in response to Willow's unasked question as she pressed pause on the movie. "What is it, Daddy?"

"Well, see… I…" He cleared his throat, rubbed his hands together. "What happened was…"

Her momma huffed. "Oh, for heaven's sake, Richard, would you just spit it out already?"

"Now just hold on. It's gonna take me a minute to get this out. Just…just bear with me for a bit." He turned to Willow, his expression more sincere than she'd ever seen. "Will, I just want you to know before I tell you this I…well, when I did this, I thought I was doin' the right thing. For you."

Well, now he was just scaring her. She'd never, not once in all her twenty-eight years, seen her daddy behave this way. So nervous and unsure. So…desperate, almost. He'd already told her about the money, and he'd barely blinked at that. If this was worse than paying her boyfriend off to leave her, well, she wasn't sure she even wanted to know.

He cleared his throat. "You, ah, you remember when Finn left all those years ago?"

Her stomach squeezed, clenching in painful memory—both from what had happened back then as well as what had happened just last week. She slid a glance to her momma. It was an unspoken rule in the Haven household that they didn't really speak of that time in her life. An unspoken rule she'd been quite happy to partake in, because it saved her the humility and hurt of reliving it.

Looked like it just wasn't her week.

"Yes."

"Well, he...um, he may have been...*coerced* to leave like he did. Without word or contact to you."

Willow blinked at her daddy for a handful of seconds before she managed, "Excuse me?"

Her momma, however, was much more eloquent. She narrowed her eyes at her husband. "Does this have somethin' to do with the money Willow mentioned?"

"She told you?" he asked, shock evident in his tone.

Momma pointed a finger in his direction, her jaw tight with anger. "You better start talkin' real fast, Richard James Haven, because I am *this close* to losin' my patience with you."

"You have to understand," he said, hands held up like he was trying to calm a rabid animal, "I thought I was doin' what was best."

"Spit. It. Out." Momma stood, arms crossed, toe tapping on the floor, glaring Daddy down.

He looked at them both, inhaled sharply, then said in one breath, "Finn may have been blackmailed to leave town based on a threat of false charges."

Willow sucked in a breath at the same time her momma gasped.

Then, in the scary-calm voice that'd always spelled

trouble during Willow's childhood, her momma asked, "*May* have been blackmailed? By whom, exactly?"

Though he didn't say anything, the look in his eyes spoke volumes, and Willow's heart cracked open. "Now, I didn't send him packin' empty-handed. I wrote him a check. To... to help them get settled. Elsewhere."

"And you somehow think that's *better*?" Her momma stomped over to her father, hissing under her breath at him, but Willow couldn't pay attention.

Her stomach roiled, a hornet's nest kicked over, and her pulse pounded like a racehorse. The mix of emotions was almost too much to bear. There was overwhelming anger at her daddy, though the shocking part was she...wasn't shocked. This was exactly like something he'd do—take it upon himself to set things just so, especially when he wasn't satisfied with the alternative. Especially when his precious Haven reputation was at stake. But more than the anger, there was relief warring with disbelief over the fact that Finn hadn't left because he'd stopped loving her. Hadn't, in fact, wanted to leave at all.

What would've become of them if he'd had the chance to stay?

"Will..." Her daddy sat next to her on the sofa, his features blurring through a sheen of her tears. "If you'll just give me a chance to explain..."

She blinked back the tears, though one slipped out, and tried to swallow down the anger she felt for him. Did it pain him so much for her to be *happy*? Not once, but twice he'd taken it from her. Taken away something so perfect that'd made her the happiest she'd ever been. Had seen to the demise of something wonderful and beautiful, simply because he didn't like it. "I'm not really sure how you can explain this away, Daddy."

"I'm afraid I have to agree with our daughter, Richard. I'm so disappointed in you right now. I can't believe you did this."

"I understand you're both angry with me. And you have every right to be. But I… I know you may find this hard to believe, but I thought I was doin' it for your own good. I just want what's best for you and your sisters."

"Your best might not be ours, Daddy."

"I—" He cleared his throat and seemed to bite his tongue and take a moment to really think about what he was going to say. First time for everything. "I realize that now. I just have so much faith in your potential, and I don't want to see you throw it away."

"But I didn't throw anything away. You did that before I had the chance to." Willow's voice caught as she tried hard to halt the tears threatening to spill like a waterfall. She didn't want to lose it—not in front of her father.

Thankfully, her momma realized this and ushered Daddy to the door. "Time for you to leave, Richard. While I try to fix this mess you made." She pushed him out the door. "And don't you think for a second this conversation is over. When I get home, you and I are going to have words."

Willow had already dissolved into tears by the time her momma wrapped her up in her arms, rocking her back and forth and telling her everything would be okay. Now that they knew the truth, everything would be all right.

Except it wouldn't. Because, truth or not, Finn had left.

The rumor mill was still cranking full time in Havenbrook, and she'd heard just that morning he and Drew had headed back to California.

Once again leaving Willow behind.

WILLOW KNEW she shouldn't take advantage of her daddy's guilt by continuing to call in sick to work, but three days over the course of five years could hardly be considered abuse of sick days. Besides that, she needed time to process what her daddy had done before she saw him again. And she definitely couldn't process that on top of all the whispers in town.

So she'd holed up in her house, her ass making a permanent indent on the couch as she'd watched daytime television and ate her weight in microwave popcorn. She hadn't even had the desire to paint anything, her half-finished canvas sitting and waiting for her. But she'd started it when things had been good with Finn. Though it was just a painting of the sunset over the field on Old Mill Road, it oozed happiness. Contentment.

If she touched it right now, she'd ruin it.

Her front door opened, the smell of Chinese food wafting over to her. She twisted her head to look behind her toward the front door. There stood Mac, Rory, and Avery, one holding dinner, one carrying The Sweet Spot's signature bright pink box, and the other a stack of movies.

"Reinforcements have arrived," Avery said, dumping the movies on the table. She lifted Willow's legs off the couch and sat down, then draped them over her lap. "And we picked up a stray along the way." She tipped her chin toward Rory.

"We're here to smother you with affection." Rory walked past Willow, heading into the kitchen with the box of cupcakes.

"And shitty movies." Avery patted Willow's leg.

"And shittier food." Mac pulled out a white carton and passed it to Willow. "Kung Pao Chicken—or what passes for Kung Pao Chicken in good old Havenbrook." She grabbed another carton and passed it to Avery before pulling a third out. "Sweet and sour for the wild child, Ror—"

Willow glanced up only to find Mac's mouth dropped open as she stared behind Willow. She turned and looked into the kitchen. Rory stood at the counter, biting into what appeared to be her second cupcake, one liner already discarded on top of the box.

"What?" she snapped, her mouth full, chocolate icing rimming her lips. "I'm an adult, and if I want to have my dessert first, I can." Rory made quite a sight, her hair perfectly done, makeup a bit heavier than usual but still subtle, wearing a pretty dress as she inhaled a cupcake. She looked like she was headed for a night out on the town, not a night in with takeout and bad movies.

"How come you're all dressed up?" Willow asked.

"I don't wanna talk about it." Rory grabbed the carton Mac held out, then plucked out a piece of chicken with her fingers and popped it into her mouth.

Willow exchanged a look with Mac. Had their sister been possessed? It was probably nothing, but truth be told,

Willow latched on to any small thing that took her mind off the tragedy that was her love life.

Fortunately, Mac was on the same page. "The girls at home with Sean?" she asked.

"No. The girls are with the sitter I hired so Sean and I could enjoy a lovely dinner out. But he thought working late would be a better use of his time on our anniversary. Never mind that he's worked late every damn day for the past two months. Never mind that whenever I've called on those late nights, his new assistant, *Desiree*, has been there too." She shoved another piece of chicken in her mouth. "Now, can we drop it, please? And will someone put in one of those shitty movies already?"

Willow's eyes grew huge, her shock mirrored on Mac's face. Willow could count on one hand the number of times she'd heard Rory swear. Or talk badly about her husband—come to think of it, Rory had *never* spoken poorly about Sean. And while Willow certainly didn't have a lot of experience in marriage woes, in her inexperienced book, skipping your anniversary dinner with your wife to hang around at the office was epic level of douchiness.

"Hey, Rory?" she asked.

"*What?*"

"You wanna borrow some yoga pants and a shirt?"

Rory's shoulders sagged, and she gave the subtlest dip of her chin in acknowledgment. It probably made Willow a horrible sister, but it was nice to know she wasn't the only one whose love life was imploding. And to see it happening to Perfect Rory? Was there hope for any of them?

chapter twenty-six

It'd only been a week since Finn had left Havenbrook without a goodbye. Though, could Willow really blame him? She'd told him to get out of her life for good. Hadn't answered his calls or his texts when he'd tried getting ahold of her. And by the time she'd found out the truth from her daddy, he'd already been gone.

Only a week, and yet it felt like a lifetime. She'd thought the pain she'd felt when she was younger had been raw and intense, but the truth was it had nothing on what she felt now. Because now, it wasn't just sadness over his absence. It was regret for not listening to him when he'd tried to tell her —and she had no doubt that was exactly what he'd tried to do. And mourning for a lost love so powerful it could've moved mountains.

Despite wanting to hide away in her house, she'd done the adult thing and had gone back to work. The whispers had stopped, surprisingly. She wasn't sure what had their attention that was more intriguing than her and Finn, but she wasn't complaining.

She'd been home for a couple hours already. Had made herself a gourmet dinner of frozen pasta in a cardboard box. She had all the fixings to make her favorite, but those damn sandwiches were so intertwined with Finn now that she couldn't stomach them. It turned itself inside out at the thought. So instead, she was the frozen meal queen, at least when Mac wasn't home to shove something down her throat.

Her half-finished painting still sat displayed on the easel in the living room since she couldn't bring herself to complete it, nor could she bring herself to put it away. So that meant she was in her room, on her bed, reading the same paragraph over and over again because she couldn't concentrate on anything.

The front door opened and closed, murmured voices filtering up the steps followed by feet pounding the stairs. Avery and Mac stood in her doorway, both looking ready for a night on the town.

"Will." Avery looked her up and down, disgust curling her lip. Possibly over the ratty clothes she was wearing. Or possibly over the spilled marinara sauce on said ratty clothes. "What're you doing."

She held up her paperback. "Reading."

"Last I checked, you weren't eighty years old, which means you shouldn't be reading at eight o'clock on a Friday night."

"I don't know what age has to do with it," Willow said. "What's wrong with reading, even on a Friday night?"

"Absolutely nothing, except you're on the same damn

page you were on this morning." Mac raised a brow. "Yes, I checked."

"Well—"

"C'mon. Come out with us. The grand opening's tonight. They're doin' two-for-one drinks till nine."

Willow's stomach clenched as overwhelming sadness swept over her. "I...can't."

Avery plucked Willow's book from her hand, then yanked her up by the arms until she stood next to her bed. "You can and you will. This is the final piece in the square revitalization, and you deserve to see it. *You* did this, Will. We want to celebrate it with you, and everyone in Havenbrook does too."

She looked from her best friend to her sister, both of them imploring her with sincerity in their eyes. They were right, of course. This was what she'd been working on for the past five years. Was what she'd fought with her daddy over—because she believed in what was coming, and in what it could do for the hometown she loved so much.

"Someone find me something to wear, because I obviously can't go in this."

Avery and Mac exchanged a look, then Avery strode to Willow's closet and began shuffling through, mumbling about this color matching that. Mac gave Willow a one-armed hug and pulled her close.

This would hurt. Seeing the business Finn worked so hard on without him there would crack her heart open, no doubt about it. But she wanted to. Wanted to see the outcome of her hard work and determination for the past five years. Wanted, too, to see what he'd been able to accomplish with the odds stacked against him. Especially since he wasn't there to see it himself.

By the time the three of them got to the square, it was packed. Nearly as full as it'd been during the Fourth of July parade. Hundreds of Havenbrook residents convened outside the space as they didn't seem to be letting anyone inside.

Willow allowed herself to take it in, really look at it for the first time since the Fourth. The once-peeling paint of the window casings and rotted front door had been replaced. The cracked pavement in front of the building had been repoured. And since she'd last paid attention, a sign now hung above the front door, a white drop cloth draped over it hiding the name they'd finally settled on.

Mac waved to get someone's attention, but Willow was focused on the building, where everyone else seemed to be looking. Waiting for...what, she didn't know. And then Nola's head popped up over the crowd as she stood on a raised platform directly beneath the covered sign. She brought her fingers to her mouth and let out a loud wolf whistle, quieting the crowd immediately.

"Hey, y'all! Thanks for comin' out tonight to help us celebrate the grand opening of Havenbrook's *very first bar*." A bright smile swept across her face as hoots and whistles burst from the crowd. "Now, I know y'all've been promised somethin', so I won't take up more of your time. I just want to welcome everyone"—she grabbed the white cloth draped over the sign and yanked it down, revealing the logo beneath —"to The Willow Tree."

Claps and hollers sprang up around her, but Willow couldn't pay attention to any of them. Her gaze was fixed on the sign Nola had revealed. Letters spelling out The Willow Tree were punched out of steel, and beside it was a logo with a beer bottle as the trunk of the tree, leaves sprouting from the top and spilling out on either side.

Her heart thrummed in her chest, her eyes filling with tears, her throat clogging with emotions so deep she could hardly breathe. Finn. Finn had done this—one last thing to show her how much he loved her, even after he was gone.

And now, she was going to have to walk by it every day, was going to have to see it outside her window at work, and *ache*. Ache knowing she'd lost the love of a lifetime not once but twice. Knowing she'd never, ever get it—

"Are those good tears or bad?" a voice whispered right in her ear. A voice she'd know anywhere.

She spun around and there stood Finn, in the middle of Havenbrook Square, like it was the most normal thing in the world. "Finn, what—"

"Come over here with me for a sec?" He held out his hand and tilted his head toward the other side of the square where no one lingered.

She looked down at his hand and bit her lip, then looked back to find her sister and Avery. They were already swallowed up by the crowd, but Willow could still make them out. Avery smiled at her, and Mac gave her a thumbs-up. So she did the only thing she could. She slipped her hand into his, exhaling as his fingers closed around hers, his grip steady and firm. Comforting. Easing an ache in her chest that'd been there since she'd told him goodbye.

When they were away from prying ears, he pulled her to a stop in front of him, their hands still connected between them. Then he just stared. Ran his eyes over every inch of her, cataloging each one of her features while she did the same for him. His hair was wild—like it got when she'd been running her fingers through it—his jaw covered with several days' worth of scruff. Light bruises marred the skin beneath his eyes, as if he'd been sleeping about as well as she had. Which was to say, not at all.

She wanted to throw her arms around him, feel his wrap around her. Wanted to kiss him and tell him she loved him and she'd missed him. But she had so many questions, she didn't know where to start. So she blurted out the first thing that came to mind. "You're supposed to be in California."

His lips quirked up at the side, and he reached out tentatively, his hand inching closer to her face. When she didn't flinch or pull away, he swept his fingertips down her face from her temple to her chin. "Why would I be there when the woman I love is right here?"

"But you… Everyone said you'd gone—"

"You listenin' to all that blatherin'?" He shook his head. "Just went back to pack up, sweetness. And to get Momma, but we were comin' back. We were always plannin' to come back." He slipped his fingers around her neck. "I couldn't leave you again, Willowtree. No threat was great enough to get me to go this time."

But last time, it had been. She and her daddy'd had a long talk, where she'd listened as he'd confessed every detail of what he'd done all those years ago. Her momma had sat next to her, anger and disappointment cloaking every bit of her body. He'd told them of what he'd done back then, and what he'd *tried* to do now. She hated her daddy for forcing Finn's hand. For making him choose between jail time for a crime he didn't commit, leaving his brother to fend for their sick momma, or leaving Havenbrook with enough cash to help his momma get better but leaving Willow behind. She couldn't begin to fathom having to make that choice—between the love of your life and the person who *gave* you life. She wasn't sure she could.

She squeezed his hand. "My daddy told me. All of it." She took a deep breath, dropping her eyes before meeting his gaze once again. "I'm sorry I didn't listen before, when you tried to tell me. I'm sorry—"

He tutted, pressing his thumb to her lips to silence her. "Now, you've got nothin' to be sorry about. This was all on me. I made a mistake—a whole damn lot of them, actually —and this lands squarely on my shoulders."

"But Daddy—"

"He had a hand in it, yeah. He was the one who put everything in motion, but I was the one who walked down the path." He removed his thumb from her mouth and slid his hand around so he cupped her face. "I wanna get that right out in the open. I don't want to keep any more secrets from you. If we're gonna make this thing work—and, *Jesus*, I really want to make this thing work—I need you to know everything. Will you let me tell you?"

If that was what they needed to start fresh, she'd do it. The truth was, she'd already forgiven him. But it seemed like he needed to get this off his chest, so she simply nodded.

Blowing out a deep breath, he relaxed his shoulders. "I wish things had gone differently. I wish I hadn't had to leave in the first place, but I can't say I'd go back and change it if I had the chance. It allowed Momma to get the treatment she needed—something I'm not sure we'd have been able to do while stayin' here. And I wouldn't chance that again, even if it meant I had to rip out my own heart and leave you behind."

He stepped closer, bringing their bodies flush. Brushed his thumbs along her jaw as he lowered his head to stare directly in her eyes. "But I want you to know, Willowtree, I'm never, ever leavin' again. If you say yes—if you want to do this thing with me—I want you to know what you're signing up for. This is it. Me by your side for the rest of my life. I love you. So damn much. Have *always* loved you. And this time, it really will take Jesus himself to pull me away."

She'd believed him the last time, and he'd taken her trust in him and ripped it to shreds. But things were different now —she could see that in the way he looked at her. And he'd proven it, hadn't he? He hadn't succumbed to her daddy's threats a second time. Had given back every bit of the money her daddy had paid him off with. Had come back, put everything he had on the line for another chance with her, despite the possible outcome. Because that was what you did when you were in love. Soul-crushing, mind-bending, all-consuming love.

She licked her lips, her gaze dropping to his. She wanted to feel those on hers with an ache she could hardly ignore. "I just have one question."

"Anything. You can ask me anything, and I'll be honest with you. I swear it."

"How'd you get everyone to keep quiet about this? About the name of the bar and about you bein' back in town?"

His entire body must've been coiled tight waiting for her question, because everything in him seemed to relax on an exhale as he smiled. "Bribed every one of those meddlers with a free first round."

She breathed out a laugh and shook her head. "And Mac and Avery?"

"One round wasn't enough for them, so I'm afraid I'm indebted to them both indefinitely."

She tsked. "Tough luck there. I sure hope it was worth it."

"Oh, sweetness. Don't you know by now you're worth absolutely everything to me?"

He leaned down, pressed his lips to hers. And she did know. Knew it was the same for him as it was for her. Knew it'd take a force of nature to tear them apart again. Because as soon as their lips touched, everything inside her shifted into place. Settled and calmed, while at the same time sparking anew and coming to life.

A life she couldn't wait to share with Finn.

epilogue

At nineteen, Finn never could've imagined his life would look like this. Ripped from the only girl he'd ever loved, with a sick momma, a brother just as lost as he was, and a fire burning under his skin to simply survive, he'd had no idea just how far they would manage to come.

And just who'd be by his side once he got where he was going.

He glanced at Willow across the bar. She still took his goddamn breath away every time he caught her eye. Every time she tipped her lips up in his direction, every time she reached for him, every time he woke in the morning with her cradled in his arms.

He figured he was the luckiest bastard on the planet.

They'd had plans tonight—a trip to the tree house to celebrate three months of business ownership. It'd been a rough three months—lots of long hours and stumbles as they'd found their footing with employees and figuring out how to run a business. But Willow had been there with him, had stood by his side through it all. Hadn't complained when he'd had to work sixteen-hour days, when the only time she'd seen him had been for fifteen minutes on her lunch break.

And finally, tonight he was taking an evening off. The three owners had agreed they'd each have a night off this week to decompress and celebrate their success...*away* from the bar.

But fate, it seemed, had different plans for him tonight.

Willow looked up and shot him an apologetic look, but he merely shrugged. He wasn't asshole enough to demand they go out while her sister drowned her sorrows in vodka— who knew Miss Prim and Proper was a hard liquor kind of girl? Sure as hell not him. But he didn't blame her for downing one shot after another.

Hell of a way to find out your husband was fucking his assistant—surprising him at work in a last-ditch effort to save their marriage. That was what he'd overheard her say to Willow anyway. What a scumbag. Rory could be a lot to handle, but she was good people when it came right down to it. And any asshole who didn't see that wasn't welcome in his establishment, plain and simple.

There'd been rumors floating around about Sean and Desiree before now, but given Finn's history with Havenbrook and the busybodies working their mouths overtime, he hadn't put a whole lot of stock in it. At least, not until he'd heard the story directly from the horse's mouth. Well, the horse was now nose-deep in a shit-ton of vodka and well on her way to a nasty hangover come tomorrow.

"Hey, man." Nash took a seat a couple spots down from the sisters and lifted his chin in their direction. "What's doin' over there?"

Finn lifted a brow as he poured Nash a glass of his usual. "You ain't heard already?"

"Heard what?"

Finn rested his elbows on the bar top and leaned forward, dropping his voice to be sure it didn't carry. "Sean's been sleepin' with his assistant. Rory walked in on it tonight. Was headed there to surprise him with a night out, I guess."

Nash glanced over at Rory, still dolled up in a pretty black dress, her hair loose and lips painted bright red, and let a string of curses loose under his breath.

"My thoughts exactly," Finn said. "I'm torn between tellin' her to slow down so she doesn't get a bitch of a hangover tomorrow and giving her the whole damn bottle."

Nash reached into his back pocket and pulled out his wallet, shuffling through his cash. "How much?"

"For what?"

"The bottle of whatever she's drinkin'." He tossed a couple twenties on the counter. "Gimme a shot glass too, would you?"

Shit, was he going to have two drunk asses on his hands before the night was over? Though, if anyone was going to get drunk with Rory, there were worse people than Nash King to be by her side.

Finn grabbed the bottle of Grey Goose he'd been pouring for Rory and passed it, along with a shot glass, to Nash. He slid off his stool and walked toward the sisters,

Finn following behind the bar, eavesdropping as Willow chatted with her sister.

"Shut up, Rory. I'm serious," Willow said firmly. "I'm not gonna leave you alone at the *bar* drinking your night away just because I had plans."

"Not just any plans. Plans to have amazing sex with your hot boyfriend."

Finn choked out a laugh and tried to cover it with a cough. Well, shit. Maybe he'd given her too much to drink already.

Willow didn't even glance his way, too busy staring at her sister, her eyes nearly bugging out of her head. "Oh my word, you've had enough liquor for one night. Hell, I think you've had enough for the whole damn year." She reached for the empty shot glass in front of Rory, but her older sister slapped her hand away.

"Leave it! Listen to me now, I'm the oldest and I know best." Rory sniffed, tilting her head up—and nearly falling off the stool in the process. "And what's best is me getting shit-faced right here in this beautiful bar I helped design in secret. All 'cause I was too worried about what my lyin', cheatin' asshole of a husband would think about me doing somethin' I loved. When that dickface was out doin' *someone* else."

"Oh shit," Finn said under his breath.

"Rory. Honey. Why don't we get you on home? You can stay with me and Mac tonight. I'll have Momma get the kids, and you don't have to worry—"

"Oh Lord, the kids," Rory moaned, looking close to tears.

Willow shot him a panicked look, and Finn could only shrug in response because...yeah, no, he definitely didn't have any idea how to handle that pile of shit.

"Hey, ladies. I'm not interruptin', am I?" Nash slid onto the stool on Rory's other side, setting his glass right next to hers before pouring them each a shot. He lifted her glass and held it out to her, brows raised as he waited for her to take it.

"What's—" Willow started, but Finn placed his hand on her arm.

"Just give it a minute," he murmured.

Rory shifted her gaze from Nash to the glass he held out and back again. Finally, she took it, and he clinked his glass with hers, then they both downed the shot.

"You can go ahead with whatever you had planned, Will," Nash said, pouring them both another. "Been a rough day, and I could use a few more of these."

Finn didn't buy the lie—Nash never had rough days. The man was as easygoing as a golden retriever and never let much get to him.

Fortunately, Rory was too far gone to notice anything. "Yeah, Will, you heard the man. Go make out with your boyfriend. Have the kind of amazing sex I've never experienced. Do it for both of us, all right? I'mma have a few drinks with this hot man who isn't fucking his assistant." She turned to Nash, eyes narrowed and lips pursed. "You're not fucking your assistant, are you?"

"Don't have an assistant, princess, so that'd be a no."

"Perfect. No assistant-fuckers allowed in this part of the bar." She gestured wildly around them, nearly knocking over the bottle of vodka. "This is an assistant-fucker free zone, people!"

"Oh Lord," Willow said. "Rory, let's—"

"C'mon now," Finn said, tilting his head to the side. "Let her be, and come over here with me for a bit."

She looked like she wanted to argue, but she finally slipped off the stool and walked around the bar to meet him at the back. "Okay then, but you just remember I told you so when she's hating herself tomorrow for how she's acting right now. I've never in my *life* heard her drop an f-bomb, and she just dropped four of them in a minute! I'm so worried about her, Finn. I've never seen her like this."

Just then, Rory's laughter rang through the bar, and Willow whipped her head in that direction. Nash was staring at Rory, his lips quirked up at the side as she cackled about something he'd said as if it were the funniest thing she'd ever heard.

"See? She'll be all right. You can take her home and coddle her a bit later. But let her be for just a little while." He glanced around, checking to make sure Drew and Nola had everything out there under control. Nola stood by one of the high-top tables, chatting with a group of people, and Drew stood behind the bar, restocking.

Perfect.

He tugged Willow's hand toward the office and walked backward, hoping like hell she'd follow him. "Come back here with me. I wanna show you somethin'."

She glanced over her shoulder at her sister once more, finally seeming to be reassured when Rory was still laughing.

Turning back to face him, she smirked. "Is this somethin' in your pants by any chance?"

He gasped, bringing his hand to his chest as he opened the office door and guided her through, then shut it behind them. Leaning forward, he whispered, "There you go, bein' a bad influence again. All I wanted to show you was this beer mug penholder Drew bought, and all you're thinkin' about is my cock. Such a dirty girl…"

Willow tipped her head back in laughter, the sound soothing his soul like nothing else ever could. She slipped her arms around his waist, tucking her hands into the back pockets of his jeans. "I've missed you. Sorry I couldn't get away tonight." She shot a worried look toward the door again, so Finn did the only thing he could to distract her.

He cupped her face and brought his lips to hers, starting the kiss slow and sweet. But things never stayed that way for long, not when they had the kind of chemistry they did. Soon enough, she had her legs wrapped around him and he was gripping her ass, grinding her down on his aching cock. Christ, he wanted her. Wanted her with every fiber of his being. But now wasn't the time. She had too much on her mind, and he knew she wouldn't be able to lose herself when her sister was in so much pain.

So he calmed himself down. Loosened his grip on her ass until he was just kneading it gently, a companion to the slow glide of his tongue against hers.

With three small, chaste kisses, he pulled back enough to look her in those eyes that he wanted to see every day for the rest of his life. "That's all right, Willowtree. We've got all the time in the world."

SIGN UP FOR BRIGHTON'S NEWSLETTER and receive a free copy of *The Neighbor*! Being part of the newsletter also unlocks your access to exclusive content and giveaways! brightonwalsh.com/newsletter.

OTHER TITLES BY BRIGHTON WALSH

Reluctant Hearts series

INTERCONNECTED STAND-ALONES

Caged in Winter

Tessa Ever After

Paige in Progress

Our Love Unhinged

Captive series

INTERCONNECTED STAND-ALONES

Captive

Exposed

Stand-alone titles

Dirty Little Secret

Plus One

Season of Second Chances

The Neighbor

ACKNOWLEDGMENTS

This book was more than a year in the making, and it was one of the hardest years of my life (and subsequently books of my career). Recently, The Fresh Prince made me aware of a pretty amazing quote by Rumi: "Set your life on fire, and seek those who fan your flames." Or, in Philly terms, "Don't be hanging with no jank-ass jokers that don't help you shine." No jank-ass jokers in my tribe, and I owe them my eternal gratitude.

To Christina, your suggestion to set this in your little pocket of Mississippi was the best idea you've ever had (and you've had a lot), because it meant fiiiiiiiiiinally meeting in person, which was long overdue. I don't know what I'd do without you, and that's no exaggeration. I'm certain I would spend my days staring blankly at a white screen, because when I hit a snag or a block, you're the first one I go to. And you always, always talk me through, usually while making me laugh. There's no one I'd rather twin with than you.

To Jeanette Grey, my CP, conference wife, SSLP, and

2050 Paris Partner, nine years we've been doing this, and I'm so glad we're going through this wild, ridiculous madness that is publishing together. And that we finally got our shit together and coordinated our schedules enough to mesh so I could put my eyes on your pretty words again and vice versa. No matter how many books you've helped me through, you still manage to teach me something with every single one. You make me and my books better because of your input and guidance, and I love you for it.

To my bitches, who not only fan my flames, but make it like a damn inferno in our group. Ann, Elizabeth, Ellis, Esher, Jen, Helen, Laura, Melly, and Suz, not a day goes by that you don't make me laugh. What started as a one-time retreat with the hope we'd at least get along well enough to share a house for a few days blossomed into lifelong friendships. We've supported each other through triumphs and tragedies, and I'm so very thankful we somehow managed to find each other through some miracle of the universe. You're the craziest, most beautiful, unique, and wonderful bunch of women I've ever known, and my days would be a hell of a lot more boring without you in them. Also, FYI: I call the Hannibal Lecter mask next year.

To Ellis (yes, again), for being by my side over the past year as we traversed this weird, anxiety-inducing new world and decided *fuck it, let's write tropey smut*. I had the most fun writing London books with you, and I honestly don't know where I'd be or if this book even would've been completed if I hadn't gone through that process. Thanks for writing blowies with me in Corner Bakery.

To Mandy Hubbard, for your unwavering support in my career, no matter what path it takes.

To Lisa Hollett, Editor Extraordinaire, thank you for your eagle eyes and suggestions to help make this book shine.

To Nina Grinstead, thank you for your help, input, and guidance, not just on this book, but on my career as a whole.

To the Brigaders, thank you for sticking with me as I took 2017 to be London Hale and set my books on the back burner. Thank you for hanging out in the group, for clamoring for my next release, and for being the best dirty-minded cheerleaders I know.

Last but never least, to my guys. You each push me in your own ways to be and do better, and your support in my career is unfaltering. For that and so many other countless things, I love you. (More.) (The most.) (The supercalifragilisticexpialimostest.)

ABOUT THE AUTHOR

Brighton Walsh spent nearly a decade as a professional photographer before deciding to take her storytelling in a different direction and reconnect with her first love: writing. When she's not pounding away at the keyboard, she's probably either reading or shopping—maybe even both at once. She lives in the Midwest with her husband and two children, and, yes, she considers forty degrees to be hoodie weather. Her home is the setting for frequent dance parties, Lego battles, and more laughter than she thought possible.

www.brightonwalsh.com
brighton@brightonwalsh.com

facebook.com/brightonwalshwrites
twitter.com/WriteAsRain_
instagram.com/WriteAsRain_

CPSIA information can be obtained
at www.ICGtesting.com
Printed in the USA
FFOW03n0145090518
46519005-48486FF